I0802664

MURDER AT THE GRAND ALPINE HOTEL

ALSO BY **LUCY FOLEY**

The Midnight Feast

The Paris Apartment

The Guest List

The Hunting Party

Last Letter from Istanbul

The Invitation

The Book of Lost and Found

LUCY FOLEY

Agatha Christie

MURDER AT THE GRAND ALPINE HOTEL

A MISS MARPLE MYSTERY

WILLIAM MORROW
An Imprint of HarperCollins*Publishers*

AGATHA CHRISTIE, MARPLE, the Agatha Christie Signature and the AC Monogram Logo are registered trademarks of Agatha Christie Limited in the UK and elsewhere. All rights reserved.

www.agathachristie.com

Without limiting the exclusive rights of any author, contributor or the publisher of this publication, any unauthorized use of this publication to train generative artificial intelligence (AI) technologies is expressly prohibited. HarperCollins also exercise their rights under Article 4(3) of the Digital Single Market Directive 2019/790 and expressly reserve this publication from the text and data mining exception.

This is a work of fiction. Names, characters, places, and incidents are products of the author's imagination or are used fictitiously and are not to be construed as real. Any resemblance to actual events, locales, organizations, or person, living or dead, is entirely coincidental.

MURDER AT THE GRAND ALPINE HOTEL. Copyright © 2026 by Agatha Christie Limited. All rights reserved. No part of this book may be used or reproduced in any manner whatsoever without written permission except in the case of brief quotations embodied in critical articles and reviews. For information, address HarperCollins Publishers, 195 Broadway, New York, NY 10007. In Europe, HarperCollins Publishers, Macken House, 39/40 Mayor Street Upper, Dublin 1, D01 C9W8, Ireland.

HarperCollins books may be purchased for educational, business, or sales promotional use. For information, please email the Special Markets Department at SPsales@harpercollins.com.

hc.com

FIRST EDITION

Designed by Liam Allaire

Library of Congress Cataloging-in-Publication Data has been applied for.

ISBN 978-0-06-337669-4

ISBN 978-0-06-356770-2 (international edition)

Printed in the United States of America

26 27 28 29 30 LBC 5 4 3 2 1

To my parents, who listened to my endless stories in the back of the car and who encouraged my love of both books and mountains!

MURDER AT THE GRAND ALPINE HOTEL

PROLOGUE

9:25 a.m.
The top of the Grand Alpine gondola
Swiss Alps, 1950

The gondola rises silently through the bank of clouds into the frozen world at the top of the mountain. It is a wonder of modern engineering, gliding between stanchions drilled into ancient rock, the red lacquer of its body gaudy against the bleak palette of white and gray.

There's someone in the gondola. One of the hotel guests, most likely, eager to make the first tracks of the day. Fresh snow fell last night, leaving a pristine covering of powder over the mountain and softening the glacier that sweeps down one side. In the early morning light, it gives off a nacreous glow. Faint bluish indentations on the surface whisper of hidden, lethal chasms beneath.

In the tiny cabin beside the lift the attendant stamps his feet in his boots, blows on his hands to keep warm. He's looking forward to interacting with another human being, however briefly. It's a lonely existence up here with only the eagles for company, the only sounds the otherworldly groaning and cracking of the glacial ice as it continues its endless creep toward the town. He knows the fears of his ancestors, how they believed in malign mountain spirits and giants living among these peaks, why they shunned them as a place of dark magic. Sometimes—when the *seracs* fall with crashes that seem to echo infinitely among the surrounding rock, or when a winter storm crackles with purple lightning, or when the low growl of an avalanche sounds at a distance—he's not completely sure he doesn't believe in such things himself.

The shadowy figure in the gondola sits with their head thrown back against the rear window; perhaps in awestruck appreciation of the view.

The mechanism grinds to a halt. The doors begin to open. The seated figure does not move.

The attendant peers through the cabin window. Are they asleep? Are they not intending to get out? Perhaps they've come up here for the sights and will simply stay put and travel back the way they've come. More snow is on the way, after all: a great deal of it.

And yet . . . there's something odd. A peculiar stillness about the scene. The attendant feels that he is just as alone as he was before the gondola and its occupant emerged through the clouds.

Should he go and see?

He doesn't want to see.

He's struck by the sudden impulse (odd; he's a good Swiss Protestant) to cross himself.

Just as he steps out of his cabin into the freezing air the gondola gives the mechanical shudder that locks it into the final position. This is when the seated figure falls, stiff and inert as a Dresden doll knocked from a mantelpiece, keeling face-first onto the metal floor of the cabin.

For a moment the attendant watches in horror. Then he springs into action. But he knows, even as he hastens along the ice-slick path, that it is no use. The gondola's passenger is already dead.

PART ONE

Two days earlier

DIANA GLASS

The Help

"Oh, look!" Mrs. Bantry says. "How charming! I can't remember the last time I saw skaters at home. Can you, Jane?"

The Grand Alpine Express is skirting a frozen lake. The skaters are bright points of color and movement against the paleness of the scene as they flit to and fro.

"No, my dear," says Miss Marple. "Yet for those of us who had a Victorian childhood it was such a mainstay of the winter."

"Diana," Mrs. Bantry turns to me. "Did you check the timetable, for the trains? If we should want to come back down the mountain for anything?"

"Yes, Mrs. Bantry," I tell her. "The last one down's at ten p.m., the last one up half an hour later. And in the morning the first one down is at eight, the first up at eight-thirty."

"I wonder why they run so late?" Mrs. Bantry says.

"I suppose so that guests can visit the town for dinner," I say. "And there's a casino—one of the only legal ones in Switzerland."

"Well, we shan't need that, shall we Jane?" Mrs. Bantry says. "But perhaps a nice supper . . ."

"I do enjoy a game of bridge," Miss Marple says, thoughtfully. "But I would never play cards for money. It has never seemed to me something a real lady should do. Perhaps I am very old-fashioned."

Mrs. Bantry's friend is the perfect image of a little old lady—almost too perfect, in fact—with a pile of fleecy wool in her lap and her knitting needles clicking together almost in time with the clackety-clack of the cog railway system. Nothing puts her off her rhythm: not the juddering of the carriage or the jostling of the man's shoulder beside her, nor the sudden change in gradient as the train begins its climb up the mountain.

"The hotel does have its own games room," I say. "Just off the library, according to the brochure."

"Diana," Mrs. Bantry tells her elderly friend, "is frightfully efficient and really makes life so much easier, especially now that I don't seem to be able to hold a fact in my head for longer than a couple of minutes."

I like Mrs. Bantry, even if she does sometimes talk about me as though I'm not there. Now she turns to me: "How many languages is it that you speak, Diana?"

"Three," I say.

"You met one another on a train, I think?" Miss Marple asks.

"Yes," I explain. "I was coming down from London to visit my aunt, in Much Benham. Mrs. Bantry and I began talking and she mentioned she needed someone to help get her affairs in order after—" I pause, not quite sure how to go on.

"After Arthur's death," Mrs. Bantry supplies matter-of-factly.

"Yes," I say, gratefully. "And to help with booking some travel. I was ready to drop my secretarial work at the War Office down to a day a week, so we made a plan there and then."

Mrs. Bantry smiles approvingly. "You have been such a comfort to a lonely old woman these past few months, my dear. Of course, I have my four and they have made sure to visit their old mama, but they're all so busy with their own lives!" She sighs, then seems to rally as she takes in the view. "And it was you who suggested this place, wasn't it, Diana? Or . . ." she frowns, "or did I read about it in the paper? See! I'm becoming so forgetful."

"I think you received a brochure, Mrs. Bantry," I say.

"Yes, I remember it! A glorious full-page color thing. One wonders if they specially target widows looking to fritter away their husbands' estates. And they always make things seem rather better than they really are. Though this may be the exception. Just look at it!" She sweeps a hand at the view through the train windows.

The carpet of fallen snow seems to glow as though lit from within. A tiny, downy black squirrel springs from one laden fir branch to the next, showering snow. And as we round the next bend, I catch a shiver of movement among the dark sentinel firs and three chamois, shaggy in their brown winter coats, spring gracefully away from the red metal monster that has just disturbed their peace.

The little train is really grinding its way up the mountainside now. You can feel the weight of it being tugged effortfully up the slope as the cogs clunk into place with the teeth on the track. There are exclamations as several traveling cases and a couple of bags begin a slow slide down the aisle.

Through the trees on the far side of the train one has glimpses of St. Celeste down below: a toy town now, any signs of life lost to view. We pass through a brief band of cloud and everything disappears for a few moments—then we are above them and I am reminded of the few times I have been in an airplane: that strange sense of disconnection from the world below. A Frenchman points out an eagle soaring in graceful arcs some way beneath us.

Inside the train there's a press of bodies, our fellow hotel guests, a moist fug of breath. Static prickles as fur-clad shoulders rub together. There was a slightly unseemly rush when we boarded for the windows on the side with the better views of the peaks. The British in our group were left huffing crossly about continental sharp elbows.

I look about at our fellow travelers—our fellow guests. The Americans appear slightly healthier and more prosperous than the rest—the lack of rationing. The French have the best furs, the Italians the most elegant luggage. The English, unfortunately, seem rather gray and dull. There are even Germans. Every time they speak the old British army type across the aisle visibly bristles. There are also some five or six groups of nuns, differentiated by slight differences in their robes: navy, black, pale blue.

I look back at the two elderly women and experience a small shock as I realize that Miss Marple is watching me with those china-blue eyes, her head tilted slightly to one side. I smile, politely, wait for her to glance away. She doesn't, apparently entirely unembarrassed to have been caught out in her curiosity.

I can't help wondering what she sees. Is she looking at me with a kind of fellow feeling? Another spare woman. The four or so decades that separate our ages don't signify. We are just as useful (or useless) to society. Neither of us is *productive*—of children or anything else. We are the companions. The left-behind women. Mrs. Bantry, as a married woman—albeit recently widowed—is of a different register. She carries with her an authority that we will never achieve. I like helping Mrs. Bantry, though. It gives me a sense of purpose and also camaraderie—a definite improvement on some of the duller work in the War Office.

"That's a beautiful necklace, dear."

I take a moment to realize that Miss Marple is speaking to me, looking over her knitting needles.

"Thank you."

"May I . . . ?"

"Oh, of course." I lift it out of the neck of my shirt to show her the ring on its chain.

"Silver," she says, almost like a jeweler appraising it, "two hearts and seven garnets. How charming."

"Thank you." She lets go and I sit back, rather relieved when Mrs. Bantry turns to Miss Marple and says, "What would you like to do while we're here, Jane?"

"I think I shall mainly enjoy sitting inside and looking out at the mountains," Miss Marple says. "I feel their freezing majesty can be best appreciated from a position of warmth and comfort. Also, there is my rheumatism. I've brought my bird-watching binoculars, too."

"But Jane," Mrs. Bantry says, "it's wintertime! Surely there won't be any birds worth watching."

"Oh," says Miss Marple, widening her faded blue eyes just a little, "but do you know, I'm sure that I will find there is enough to look at. There usually is. Certainly, that is the case in St. Mary Mead."

"Jane," Mrs. Bantry says, indulgently, "somehow you manage to look the very picture of innocence saying that. And yet I'm sure you are being rather devious."

Miss Marple pats the pile of fleecy wool in her lap as though it were a small patient dog. "But not at all, Dolly. Not at all."

"What is that you're making, dear?"

"This? Oh, it's an Alpine sweater for dear Raymond. I think it will suit him so well, if he can be persuaded to wear it: he does like to dress in such a *modern* way. Do you know, I think this will be one of the first times in recent years when I have been on a little holiday without Raymond's patronage. He is so generous. But at the same time, one can feel somewhat . . . beholden. Oh, perhaps that isn't the right word. But he does like to express—opinions on where I travel, that sort of thing." And then, hurriedly, "Only, you know, because he is so protective."

"Well, I forbid you to feel beholden to me," Mrs. Bantry says. "We have dear old Gossington Hall to thank, really—may its new owners treat it well."

The train lets out a long, mournful howl as it enters the mountain tunnel, the staccato of the cog mechanism sounding now like a gigantic sewing machine, echoing off the rock. I read that they had to bore the track into the rock here because the mountain is completely sheer outside.

The train feels warmer, even a little stifling, as the outside world recedes. And suddenly the window has become a black mirror. My face is reflected back at me: paler, stranger, hollows where the eyes should be. A death's head. I turn away.

And then we are out of the tunnel again. My ears pop from the altitude. The world below us is completely lost to view beneath a swirling layer of cloud. The snowpack is visibly thicker up here, the branches of the trees, too, laden with snow unlike the ones below. We have our first sighting of the hotel between them: like glimpses snatched through a torn white curtain.

Waiting for us—which only adds to the sense of otherworldliness—are several horse-drawn sleighs, the horses tossing their heads with a cascade of sleigh bells, and huffing white steaming breaths into the frigid air. Each one is helmed by a driver in red and gold livery, gold-braided pillboxes atop their heads.

"Jane," Mrs. Bantry cries, in delight. "Aren't you glad we've come?"

"Yes," Miss Marple says, "but I'd *almost* rather they let us walk. It's not such a great distance. Horses, you know. I do wonder if we put too much trust in such giant, unruly beasts . . ."

But she is ushered firmly into the back seat of the sleigh by another liveried member of staff with a red, frost-nipped nose. "We have had new snow up here, Madame. . . . It is very thick, difficult for walking. And be especially careful after dark too . . . it turns so quickly to ice."

We are whisked along an avenue of firs, the snow whispering beneath the runners of the sleigh, faces tight with cold in the freezing air. Then the trees recede and the Grand Alpine stands majestic in front of us, blazing out in all its glory, emanating strains of music and the voices of unseen guests. I take in the fairy-tale gothic towers at either end of the building, the painted red shutters, the hotel's name picked out in ornate gold letters that stand on proud stilts above the central part of the leaded roof. The light pours rose gold from every window:

a warm and welcoming contrast from the freezing gray wilderness without. Two liveried footmen stand either side of a revolving door, ready with gold luggage carts.

A bustling terrace is just visible around the corner, facing the majesty of the peaks above. I made sure to read the brochure from cover to cover so I would have a working knowledge of the place from the outset. There is the famous red gondola, tracking its way up the mountain, also a couple of chair and button lifts; the very latest technology and a sharp contrast to the romantic timelessness of the sleighs. The serpentine groove twisting down the mountainside must be the infamous Verglas toboggan run. Scattered across the broad white slopes are tiny, colored dots—the skiers—like hundreds-and-thousands shaken onto the cream top of a trifle.

As they step down from the sleighs each guest is handed a small cup of hot chocolate by a red-and-gold-uniformed member of staff. The chocolate is dark and glossy, so thick it hardly moves when you tilt the cup, and delicately spiced with cinnamon. I can't remember ever having tasted anything as rich as this: certainly not since the war.

"*Oh*," Mrs. Bantry says, in an awed voice, after taking a sip. "It makes you question whether the sad affair we have in England really *is* chocolate. No wonder it was booked up every weekend besides this one!" She pulls a face. "Though I'm not sure Arthur would approve of all this. He was very upset with the Swiss for their neutrality. And then . . . well, he really didn't like spending money. I'm sure he would see this all as rather profligate. But I live in such a small way now that he's gone. I'm not extravagant in anything else. And with his death . . . it was a reminder of how very fleeting our time is. Of all the things one hasn't done, you know—"

She halts at the sound of a far-off mechanical howl. I turn and can just make out the red gleam of the distant train, gathering pace as it enters the trees, then disappearing out of sight as it begins its journey back down the mountain.

Mrs. Bantry says, "It does make one feel rather—odd. To know that now the train has gone we're rather marooned up here. I am glad to be here with you, Jane. Your company is always a comfort. And you, Diana, you are so very *capable*." Then she frowns. "Listen to me! How melodramatic I sound. But once one has had the experience of waking up to a body in one's own library, one never really loses the sense that just about anything might happen."

CATHERINE NARRACOTT

The Wife

Through a gap in the curtains of our room I can see a row of small peaks—like the frill of white lace on a collar I once embroidered for myself in needlework class at Cheltenham Ladies'—and a little of the glacier, which I am surprised to learn is not blue and clear but mainly covered in snow and a rather off-putting dirty white at the bottom. Higher up it curves up around the mountainside and is lost to sight.

A charming view, I will write in my letter to Mummy. *And a beautiful room*—if a little masculine—its dark wood paneling and coffered ceiling mercifully softened by patterned rugs on the floor and richly upholstered armchairs.

My husband sighs. "It's no good," he says. He rolls away from me and lies back against the pillows. He is cross; I can feel the crossness coming off him like heat. I don't say anything, I know it won't do any good. And all the while I can't help feeling a little relief that it is over for the time being.

"It doesn't help," he says, "that you society girls aren't taught anything about how to please a man," he says. "You think it's enough to lie there like a plank of wood staring at the view."

It's odd: really my whole education has been about how to please a man. But of course, I don't say any of this. *Poise, grace, and a smiling face*. I do not think I had realized it would be possible to be so lonely when married to someone else. "Love will grow over the years," Mummy said.

"Shall I make you a drink, darling?" I ask, as he begins to light a cigarette. There is a cocktail table in the corner of the room beside a sweet little chaise. A good society hostess knows how to observe others, to learn to anticipate their needs. My husband seems a man who needs a drink.

He runs a hand through his red-gold hair—his crowning glory. It is growing a little thin but I think only he and I know, because it is only noticeable from very particular angles. "Fine. Yes, please. A gimlet."

As I cross the room I feel watched by the portraits on the walls—oils of various serious-looking women and men in traditional Alpine dress: full skirts and brown woolen trousers, plentiful embroidery, *supremely* unflattering hats. I catch sight of myself in the gilt-framed looking glass above the cocktail cabinet. The surface is a little foxed but what stands out are my dark hair, my dark eyebrows, my pale skin. I have learned to bring out these features with clothes: pastels and grays make my skin look luminous, while I avoid white and strong colors because they wash me out. My wedding dress was a very light pink, which Mummy thought a little non-U, though she also understands the importance of making the best of oneself. I am pretty, I know, but a cold sort of prettiness. Not the kind that excites a man.

My pink lipstick is still perfect, which at one time might have seemed odd to me. I had an idea that when a man made love to you it should be "kissed off." That must have come from the romance books girls passed around at chalet school. But then all my knowledge of the world before marriage came from school. Cheltenham, Switzerland to finish, then coming out as a deb.

I do know how to make a good gimlet at least; or indeed any other cocktail my husband might happen to ask for. I was always a diligent student at school. I was the one who read all of the books, did all of the homework. I've taken the same approach to being a wife, always, really from the moment I arrived at finishing school. I paid attention; I learned exactly how to set a table, to write an invitation. The preparatory work is all so important. It has brought me a strange kind of satisfaction, being good at it.

But when I get to the cocktail cabinet, I let out a little scream.

Anthony comes out of the bathroom. "What is it?"

"There!" I show him the offending item on the brass tray. There among the other items—the shaker, the bitters, the Rose's lime and the atomizer—is a small jar with a white label and angry red letters reading: RAT POISON. An icon: skull and crossbones. *Danger of death.* A prettily ornate silver spoon is stuck into the white powder inside, as though inviting one to take a scoop.

He stalks across the room to take a look. "Rat poison?" he says, reading the label. "But what on earth . . ."

"I—I just found it here," I say. "Just sitting there with the spoon stuck into it, as though it were another cocktail ingredient. Oh, it's horrible!"

There is a long pause as he stares hard at the thing. "A foolish prank," he says, finally. Confidently, even. My husband is very good at sounding confident; I suppose it is what makes him such a successful politician. But he has been something of a target of "Red" activists, of late, and I know it has rattled him more than he admits.

"A very *macabre* prank!" I say. "And who on earth would do such a thing? We don't know anyone else here. It makes my skin crawl. I think we should tell the hotel, don't you? Move rooms? Because perhaps if someone else has a key for this one . . . the thought, that someone could just come in here whenever they wanted . . . in the middle of the night, say, while we were sleeping, oh it's horrible, just horrible—"

"Stop," he says, cutting me off. "You are being completely hysterical." He doesn't raise his voice. My husband almost never raises his voice; he doesn't need to.

I nod. "Sorry, darling."

"I'll call Reception." He picks up the receiver.

To a stranger he might seem completely unconcerned. My husband is known as a cool head in politics, even when other men are shouting at him across the House. Daddy was not like that at all; he would work himself up into rages about things. But he *is* perturbed. I can see it. He slams down the receiver. "No answer," he tuts. And then, in a hiss: "Bloody backward establishment. Come on, we'll go down."

Just before we leave the room, I see him glance back at the offending jar. Yes: definitely perturbed.

Downstairs in Reception, I feel I am being watched. I glance across and see three unmistakably English women standing there. One of them, the littlest and oldest—a frail-looking creature with fluffy white hair and a coat that can only be described as Late Victorian Provincial—is studying me. I give her my most gracious "old-dear" charming smile (I am a politician's wife, after all) and she smiles back. The elderly women like me: often even more than they do my husband. I remind them of a time when things were done properly, when women behaved themselves, protected their delicate skin from the sun, and their delicate hands with gloves that matched their hats. I am to them the very picture of duty, honor and decorum and that is perhaps an accurate representation of how I have lived most of my adult life. I look like an angel in the house.

"You, my dear," my husband likes to say, "are my secret weapon." I remember how I was filled with pride the first time he said it.

Anthony is asking the man behind Reception about us changing rooms. "Actually," he says, "we'll take the suite; if it's available. Yes, yes, fine if it's a little dearer. Though," he murmurs to me, "really, they should give it to us for no extra cost. Rather too fond of the gold here. That's why they stayed neutral in the war, no matter what they might claim about pacifism. To the highest payer the spoils."

"Darling," I whisper, touching his arm, "I know I am so *very* stupid about such things. I thought . . . well, with our having to let Mrs. Grady go just the other week . . ." Mrs. Grady was our housekeeper, who was very efficient, if a little less refined than the one I grew up with, who Mummy got straight from one of the Royal households. "And . . . what with having to sell the Rolls . . . can we really afford it?"

"Of course we can, *darling*," he mutters, with a smile, though his jaw is tight. I see the quick glance he makes about the room, to check that we have not been overheard—the prospective leader of the Conservatives, and perhaps one day of the country, cannot be seen to have any financial irregularities in the cupboard. Then he lowers his voice. "I expect to be coming into a little money soon enough. An investment—it's about to pay out very handsomely."

It would be the first time any of his investments have come to good. My husband brought a small inheritance to our marriage, and I, a substantial sum. Alas the remaining pot is nothing like what it was. Not that anyone would know it, of course. Whilst my husband is widely recognized as a very brilliant man he isn't all that clever with money. He is very good at spending it, though. Sometimes I have wondered if he is the sort of man Daddy might have called a bounder, for all his Good Works in politics and his war record. Sometimes I have even allowed myself to wonder whether if *I* had been the one to invest it, we might have done better. At school I was told I had a fine head for numbers. And I have been brought up to enjoy and require money. That is how girls like me *are* brought up.

But "Oh," is all I say, "really? Well, that's lovely news."

He chuckles. "It's more than lovely, my sweet. It will change *everything*."

DIANA GLASS

The Help

As I hand over the passports to be checked, I gaze about me at our surroundings: a mix of the grand and the rustic that seems peculiarly Alpine. At the long desk before us three receptionists work busily away, all dressed in the red and gold regalia of the hotel. Patterned Persian rugs reveal glimpses of an intricate parqueted floor, chandeliers coruscate above our heads and wood paneling makes the whole room glow with a rich amber light. Antlers bristle from brackets and pine branches intertwine in picturesque arrangements about sconces. The scent of their resin fills the air, mingling with woodsmoke and the various perfumes worn by the guests. Paintings showing forbidding mountain scenery are hung all about and to the right, huge windows display the real thing: a view of three white peaks that seem to fit the apertures so perfectly they seem hardly real, as though they too have been painted on the glass in *tromp l'oeil.* Staff flit hither and thither in what seem almost choreographed movements, collecting luggage on golden carts, leading guests into elevators or to the bank of phone booths tucked away beyond the Reception desk.

"Look at that funny little dog!" Mrs. Bantry says.

I watch as an older gentleman with something regal about him—perhaps the long, fur-trimmed cape about his shoulders—walks in with a tiny dog in tow, spilling snow onto the richly patterned rugs at the entrance. One of the staff dashes over and begins to clean the snow from the animal's fur with a brush that looks specially made for the purpose.

"That," murmurs a little man with the authoritative air of a hotel manager, appearing as though from nowhere, "is one of our most distinguished guests. Prince Gustav of Yugoslavia. And Heracles."

It takes me a moment to understand that the latter refers to the dog.

Now the hotel manager begins his introductions. He is a compactly rotund, neat-looking man with a luxuriant moustache and a slightly fastidious manner.

"The whole resort is built upon its tradition first as a site of holy pilgrimage and then as a spa resort," he tells us. "And though we find ourselves situated a little way up the mountain we have a spa par excellence here: all of the latest *thérapies* available." He pronounces "therapies" in the French way. "There is skiing—two marked runs and some excellent *hors piste* on the glacier," he looks at us doubtfully, "and of course never forgetting the Verglas toboggan run. It was the English that brought it here. Late in the last century our founder persuaded some English guests to stay for the winter—*gratis*—to show them the beauty of the mountains at that time. They introduced the toboggan racing as a way to pass the time. Then of course the skiing followed." A tight little cough. "Do any of you *mesdames* . . . ski?" He looks as though he can hardly bring himself to ask such an absurd question. "Or . . ." he says, with the same pained expression, "sled?"

"Oh, I used to go sledding as a girl," says Miss Marple. "Didn't you, Dolly? But I rather think the relatively gentle Downland slopes don't quite compare to the sort of thing you have here, Monsieur."

"Indeed," the manager says, swiftly. "Perhaps you would rather . . . spectate? In two days' time we will have our first race event of the season. You *have* heard of the Cresta Run, in St. Moritz?"

Miss Marple shakes her head. "I am afraid," she says, very apologetically, "that you will think us very stupid. But speaking for myself, I am so very unworldly . . ."

"Well, Madame," says the manager with a rather studied patience, "you will discover that ours, like the Cresta, is made by hand from the snow and ice itself. A very beautiful piece of design. Speeds of forty miles per hour have been achieved on it. It is open to all, *unlike* the Cresta, which is barred to women and . . . to all ages. But I think perhaps—"

"We will spectate," Miss Marple says, firmly, reassuringly. "Won't we, Dolly?"

"Goodness, yes," says Mrs. Bantry. "I have come to look at mountains, to be among mountains, not to hurl myself down them risking life and limb. If man were meant to travel at breakneck velocities down slopes of frozen water, one does rather think the Lord would have made him with skis or a toboggan attached."

The manager gives a tight little smile. Behind it I sense something sorrowful, as though he wishes we were more glamorous, like the couple who have been talking to his colleague at the next desk along.

"Well, we have an excellent library and reading room. And the spa—I think perhaps that will be more to your liking. It is situated just a little above the hotel, only a twenty-minute walk away, so"—he casts another dubious eye over Mrs. Bantry and Miss Marple—"it should be easy for all to access."

I think he continues to talk them through the facilities, but I have stopped listening. I'm watching the couple at the next desk. She wears an elegant interpretation of mountain attire: wool slacks and a powder blue cashmere sweater with a small gray fur tippet around her neck that sets off the immaculate chignon of dark hair pinned up from a long, slender neck. She brushes invisible threads from her shoulders with a manicured hand and the lights catch and glitter on a huge diamond on her ring finger. Everything about her speaks of refinement. It's impossible to imagine her bleeding or sweating like the rest of us. She moves with precise, economical movements, back straight as a ballet dancer's.

He, meanwhile, is patrician of profile and elegant as she, but in an entirely masculine vein: broad-shouldered and long-legged, his hair a reddish gold: handsome as the hero of a wartime poster with a well-molded chin and strong brow. It's not like me to stare at men like some schoolgirl but I find it hard to take my eyes off him.

"Isn't that . . ." Mrs. Bantry is looking at them too. "I'm *sure* it is. Jane, do look! Isn't that man something in politics? Something . . . Narracott." To Miss Marple: "Oh, what was his name . . . Alistair?" Miss Marple looks blank.

"Anthony," I say. "Anthony Narracott: new candidate for leader of the Conservatives. He works in the War Office, so I occasionally see him about the building."

"Yes!" Mrs. Bantry exclaims. "Of course it is." She turns to Miss Marple. "But Jane, I'm embarrassed that neither of us could name him!"

"Well," Miss Marple says. "I'm afraid I'm rather ignorant about that sort of thing. I just like to know that the country is being well taken care of and my taxes well invested. The ins and outs of Westminster are a different matter. If you were to ask me who the new mayor of Much Benham is, then I could tell you everything about him. Sir Hodgson—a fine cricketer and collector of rare orchids, something of a roguish little boy in his youth but very much a reformed character . . . at least one certainly *hopes* so. Goodness me! Here I go, twittering away and you undoubtedly know all this anyway, Dolly, and you, my dear"—this to me—"have I'm sure no interest whatsoever in the subject. Oh dear . . ." Her fingers flutter in the air like startled birds for a second and then settle upon the clasp of her sensible handbag.

She is the very picture of a slightly dithery village spinster, prone to rambling and finding herself in confusing conversational cul-de-sacs. But I remember that assessing look on the train; those soft china-blue eyes suddenly turned as bright and cool as ice.

"Anthony Narracott's rather impressive from what I remember,"

Mrs. Bantry says. "Wartime hero—escaped a prisoner-of-war camp, the story goes. Oh—"

I look up and realize he is approaching our group. He limps slightly, but there is an elegance to the movement, like a panther with a thorn in its paw.

"An old war wound," he says as he draws near, with a rueful smile. "Gives me more trouble in the cold. But luckily it doesn't give me any jip skiing or even climbing. In fact, I think it's positively good for it! May I introduce myself?" He does so, with a great deal of modesty. But surely, I think, he senses that we're all aware who he is. "What an unexpected joy it is to hear other British voices in this out-of-the-way place!" He smiles graciously at us all. "What brings you here?"

I turn to collect the passports from the receptionist, but can still overhear the conversation. He is so interested, so solicitous, asking Miss Marple about the village she hails from. "Near Much Benham, you say? I think I *have* heard of it. I'm almost certain. Well, what a pleasure to meet you all. I am sure we shall all become *great* friends staying here together."

He turns back to his wife, who is looking at a spot beyond us, through us—one of the mountain scenes on the wall, perhaps—as though she is completely unaware of our existence.

Just then another man enters the room. His eyes are fixed on Anthony Narracott. He is as coarse as Narracott is elegant: large and ungainly, a snub nose that looks like a mistake in his wide, pitted face. Every item of clothing he wears seems ill-fitted, either too tight (his trousers) or too loose (his jacket, with the creasing and shapelessness of cheap old wool). His expression is wary. I sense he is enjoying having the opportunity to size up the other man before he has been spotted in return.

CATHERINE NARRACOTT

The Wife

My husband walks back to me, smoothing his hair into place. Just before he spoke to the three women, he ruffled his hair with one hand, making it stand up in small tufts, like the rumpled head of a much-loved schoolboy. I have seen him do it many times before.

"Not quite what I had expected of our fellow guests," he says in an undertone, "three moth-eaten old dears. What can they be doing here? Not skiing, surely: one of them looks about a hundred and a day . . . that little puss with the white fluffy hair. Doesn't look all there, does she?"

"They're not *all* old," I say, looking at them. "One of them is probably in her thirties." With the right clothes and better *coiffure* she might even be attractive: tall and slender with dark-gold hair.

He waves a hand; that makes no difference. Perhaps to say thirties *is* old—for a woman. My husband turned forty a few years ago, but is still described by the newspapers as "boyish." I am twenty-two, and yet I have only a few more years left of being a truly "young" woman. I can feel it . . . as though there is an hourglass trickling sand inside of me. I'm lucky that I'm petite, with good skin; I can fake it for a little while longer than some.

"What difference does it make," says Anthony now, "if they all dress like elderly spinsters?"

It's true: the clothes *are* dreadful. So many women just don't know or care how to make the best of themselves. They don't realize how helpful clothes can be for giving a good impression.

"But darling," I say. "Don't you always say it's the old dears that are the most reliably Blue?"

"Yes," he smiles ruefully. "Tory heartland. Don't want anything to change. Can't bear the thought of the new estates blemishing their beloved old villages. Want everything to go back to how it was before the war, the Good Old Days. All whilst living off their wealthy relatives and contributing nothing to society besides gossip. Well," he chuckles, "as long as they keep putting the cross in the right box!"

I shiver. The large entrance doors have been thrown open again, letting in a rush of freezing air and several people with luggage, who must have been on the later train up. One of them is coming in this direction—apparently making straight for us. A hulking, stooped, ugly figure: a similar age to Anthony but that can be the only thing they have in common. Where my husband is handsome and sleek, everything about this man seems *misshapen*. There is something battered-looking about him, as though life has knocked him around. There's also something lopsided about his face. It takes me a moment to realize this is partly because his right earlobe is missing.

"Darling," I whisper. "Who *is* that man?"

"Ah," Anthony says, "did I not mention Bruno to you?"

"Who?"

"Bruno Crane! My old brother-in-arms."

I shake my head. He has not said anything to me about this man.

"Ah! Sorry, it must have slipped my mind. Yes, Bruno has come along to do some ice-climbing with me, for old times' sake!"

"But—" Before I can say anything, this Bruno Crane is looming over us. His breath is sour. It makes me think of poor diet, of hidden illness. All of my husband's acquaintances dress and speak like him, went to the same schools, have the same voting records, attend the same clubs. Bruno Crane I can tell, even before he opens his mouth, is not one of them. The best society hostess learns to observe others, to learn to anticipate their needs from tiny unspoken cues. It has made me rather good at reading people. And this man does not make any sense beside my husband.

"Anthony," Bruno Crane says. "How are you, old man?" He sticks out a meaty hand and clasps Anthony's arm—so tightly, in fact, that my husband is momentarily unbalanced and trips a half step forward before he rights himself. I look at those thick fingers gripping the smart fabric of Anthony's jacket and can't help thinking of a drowning man seizing hold of a piece of driftwood in a stream.

Then Bruno Crane turns to me. "And . . . Catherine? I—I don't believe we've met." He frowns. "Forgive me. I—I didn't know you were coming."

"No," I say. "I think we are both surprised."

I note that Bruno Crane's eyes dart nervously toward Anthony, a little like an actor in a rehearsal who is still slightly unsure of his lines and relying on the prompt to fill in. "Well. It's—it's an unexpected pleasure to find you here."

But he doesn't sound very pleased. It's clear he is lacking in the social grace, the polish, the charm that smooths my husband's every interaction, that makes him such a good politician.

The look I catch him giving Anthony over my head is more than questioning. I see, I think, *anger* in it.

I turn to Anthony just in time to catch his look in return. It's a warning. He is giving Bruno Crane a warning. I know this look because I've seen it before. *Don't say the wrong thing. Don't say too much.* He doesn't have to send it my way very often, of course, because I am so good at keeping up appearances.

I wait for my husband to explain the confusion and I think Mr. Crane might be waiting for the same thing. But he doesn't. Instead, he says: "If you need any nylons or perfume, darling, I'm sure Bruno can be of assistance. Isn't that right, Crane?" But before the other man can reply: "Fancy a climb this afternoon, Crane? Shake off some cobwebs? There's a short one up the rock face beyond the glacier that should only take us a couple of hours."

I open my mouth, about to say that I thought we were going to try and do a ski run before the end of the day, then close it again.

Bruno Crane isn't as good as my husband at concealing his emotions. It is quite apparent that this idea of an ice climb does not appeal to him, that in fact he can probably think of nothing worse. And yet he nods. "You're on, old man. I'd love to."

SYLVIA SINCLAIR

The Star

"How about this, baby?" I say to Herb. I'm sitting on a stool in a secret room of the main bar, hidden behind a painting; I asked for somewhere private where the rest of them wouldn't all gawp at me while I had a morning pick-me-up. Sometimes it gets too much, you know, the attention? Apparently, they call this place the Stübli because it's done up like a rustic Alpine joint, all low beams and low lighting and red-checked cloths on the tables, furs draped over the backs of the chairs. Red wine stains on the floorboards. At least I *think* they're red wine. Bet this bar has seen some things. Funny, it reminds me a little of the saloon set in the Western I did with Greg Peck.

Herb just looks at me. "No, I know what you mean, baby. All this dark wood: a little macho and gloomy. And these *photographs*." Men up mountains holding skis, looking all heroic and stern. "Give me the baby pinks of the Beverly Hills Hotel any day." Still, after a few cocktails I suppose I wouldn't mind climbing onto that fur-covered bench there and curling up like a babe in the womb. Oh, why did I have to think of that? Too much like the one I—but I was sixteen, for Christ's sake. Pretty much a child myself . . .

Where the hell did I put that drink?

"Oh, Herb," I say, "what are we doing here? Have I gone totally gaga? Well, you know me. When have I *not* behaved like this when I'm in love? All in or not at all, that's me."

The barman hands me a cup of the velvety hot chocolate they do here—I'm already addicted to the stuff (probably no better or worse for me than other things I've been addicted to). "Thanks, sweetheart." Can't help trying the bit on the young fellow: girls out, shoulders back, little purr of thanks. Even in the low light I see his cheeks flush, and the cup trembles a little in his grip. Nope. Not quite past it yet.

I take a long sip. Very nice: he's added the tot of rum I asked for. I turn back to Herb. "I'm so glad you're here, baby. I think I really *would* go gaga on my own. And you're a good listener . . . for a dog. Better than most people. Better than men-people, anyhow."

I chuck him under his whiskery chin and he closes his eyes. I drain the little cup, stay on the stool until the record on the gramophone finishes and the needle starts to hiss, then I jump up. I can never stay still for long. If I do, the little black moths start settling on me.

Up in my suite I go to the mirror, spritz a little Shalimar (good enough for Rita, good enough for me), powder my chin. "Give me the lighting at the Beverley Hills too," I say. "These harsh mountain rays—there's nowhere for a girl to hide." I turn to Herb. "Am I past it? Be honest with me."

I dress, put on my dark glasses. I had a prescription put in, so at least while I'm wearing them I can actually see something. The rest of the time I mainly just bump into things and pass it off as klutzy. When I'm not on-screen they're kind of my signature, the glasses. Because here's the thing: I'm actually a little shy. But I learned long ago I can hide it by putting on a disguise, playing the part of Sylvia Sinclair. The glasses help. So do the martinis.

"Right, baby," I turn to Herb, who raises his furry eyebrows as I open the door. "Here goes nothing."

BRUNO CRANE

The Friend

Narracott wasn't joking about the climb. Barely had time to leave my bag in the room before he was dragging me up here. It is so much colder at this altitude, a couple of thousand feet above the hotel. My head spins. We've tackled the wall of rock that rises up behind the glacier: short and fiendish. I felt every extra pound of flab. I'm not fit like I once was. War keeps you trim. Despair and indolence do not.

Narracott was first on the rope. There were times, below him, when I had to try not to remember that all that lay between me and oblivion was Anthony Narracott and an inch of hemp.

But no. For the moment, at least, I think I'm useful to him.

Now we're sitting on a largish ledge of rock and I don't feel much less uneasy. The white peaks of the surrounding mountains seem to enclose us. There squats the ugly great blancmange of Mont Blanc. Over there among the highest and most forbidding peaks is L'Ours Noir (or Orso Nero) Pass: France in one direction, Italy in the other, though at this time of year the route would be bordering on suicidal.

Far below is the hotel, the dark of the pine forest and then through a canopy of drifting clouds the town itself even farther down . . . my head swims. Vertigo might be one of the few mental weaknesses that *hasn't* plagued me in my lifetime. But in this moment, I'd rather be almost anywhere else. Come to think of it, it might be more the company than the drop.

It's so cold that it's hard to talk. Narracott doesn't seem to feel it at all. Is that any great surprise? He always was an unfeeling b—. And when there's something in his sights, he'll stop at nothing to pursue it.

"I'd have thought it would keep you fit," Narracott says, as I sit here gasping at the freezing air. "All that running from the law. How *is* the," he smirks, "*import-export* business treating you, Crane?"

Truth is, not well. The black market's sewn up by the East End boys now. I'm a lower-middle-class recluse nibbling at the edges, just about keeping my head above water: too respectable for them, not respectable enough for polite society.

"You're just as much of a crook as I am," I mutter.

"What's that, Crane?"

"You heard me."

"Come on, old boy. Just a bit of friendly ribbing between chums." He takes a swig from his flask.

"What've you got there?" I ask him. "Scotch?"

He chuckles. "After a snifter? Wouldn't you like that? No, coffee. The real stuff, pure Arabica. Can't drink enough of the stuff, especially after all that nonsense ersatz chicory stuff in the war and the rubbish we still get at home. I've worked out a little system: drop my flask off at Reception, they fill it up for me and it's waiting by the time I've got my boots on in the ski room. You could get them to make you a pot, old chap. Here, try it! Puts hairs on your chest."

He proffers the thing at me.

"No," I say. "Can't stand the stuff."

"I insist," he says. "You'll like this." He shoves the flask at me so forcefully that on reflex, I take it. "Go on, man," he says. "It'll warm you up."

"I don't w—" And then I find myself giving up. What's the point? I realize I have no choice. Or rather, I can carry on resisting and he will carry on insisting, for the next few minutes. Or I can just give in now. I take the damned flask. He watches me, eagerly. And I think: he is enjoying this.

I sip it and of course it might be the best coffee ever produced but to me it tastes like the bitterest poison. He has always enjoyed little demonstrations of his power, little scenes like this. Finding new ways of humiliating me.

I hand the thing back so violently that a little slops over the side. I wipe my mouth. I feel like a fool, both for being made to drink it and now, acting like a child.

He screws up the flask and draws a great breath into his lungs, then throws out a hand at the view. "Not a bad place to have this little chat, eh? I thought we'd want to make sure we were somewhere we couldn't be overheard."

"I can think of better places," I tell him.

I drag my gaze away from the drop only a few feet in front of us. The quick way back down. A frozen waterfall just below then a sheer wall of granite with a few small outcrops. I let myself think about it for a second. A chap falling might hit rock once, twice, before his broken body came to rest at the foot of the glacier, where the thing splits into huge chunks of frozen ice and moraine.

"Take a look through these," Narracott says, handing me some binoculars. I do.

"You see it?"

"Yes," I say. "I see it." A small shadow in the rock, on the other side of the glacier. The sight of it gives me a dark feeling, a tightness in my chest. There is a cloud hanging above the peaks that looks just like the image of a howling wolf. Though I know it's just foolish superstition it sends a chill through me that has nothing to do with the cold.

"Tomorrow night," Narracott says.

"You don't think tonight?" I ask, trying to sound devil-may-care, as though my heart isn't beating fit to burst out of my rib cage.

He shakes his head. "Tomorrow we'll have a full moon. There's a real dump coming after that, which will make it nigh on impossible. So it has to be tomorrow."

I try to decide whether I'm relieved to have another twenty-four hours, or whether I'd prefer it just to be over, so that I can be far, far away from this place. Oh, how I wish I could have said no to this little reunion. But the honest, nasty truth is I *need* this. I need it so very badly. And at the same time being here takes me back to a time when I saw into the darkest recess of my own soul and it terrifies me.

"I have been asking you about coming here for five years," I tell him. "There have been times I've been damn near desperate. What's taken so long?"

"Oh," he sighs, as though we're discussing a game of golf we haven't managed to play. "Life's been busy, old fellow. Getting married, joining and working my way up the greasy pole in the Party . . . And to be quite honest . . . it hasn't been worth the risk, you understand?"

"Well, why the rush now?"

"They've opened the hotel back up, for one. That made it feel like we shouldn't wait any longer. And things have got a little—tighter—recently. Catherine's trust . . . not what I thought it was, etcetera. Poof! Nearly all used up."

"I've been thinking," I say.

"Always dangerous," he says. "Hope you didn't hurt yourself." His voice is light but when I look up he's watching me like a marksman.

"I'm thinking there're a lot of people staying in the hotel at the moment," I say. "I'm thinking someone's going to see something."

"We don't have a choice. We're just going to have to be very careful."

"And you brought Catherine? You brought your *wife*? What were you thinking, man?" He holds up a hand as though to shush me but I race on. "That was never the plan. You never said she would be coming too. That isn't what we agreed. We said we'd keep it clean, surgical. Your wife being here could jeopardize everything . . ."

He simply waits there now, watching me, as though waiting for me to run out of steam. How can he look so relaxed? I had forgotten this about him. The appearance of grace under pressure. I suppose it's what makes him such a good politician. The face of an expert gambler. I have no such face, worse luck.

"Have you quite finished?" he asks, tolerantly, like a parent waiting for a child to end a tantrum. "Look. Catherine got the idea into her head that she wanted to come. Used to ski as a child, misses the Alps, London and Paris so dull at this time of year, that sort of nonsense. And there has been some talk about how it would be good to be seen and photographed with the wife a little more, in the run-up to the Party leadership bid. Besides it just *looks* better, doesn't it? Less *odd* than two men on their own. Less worthy of suspicion. I find these days that I am very . . . observed. Besides, she's had some *women's troubles* of late—has been up and down to a clinic in London. Her doctor, a veritable old battle-axe, called me up and all but insisted I take her away with me for her nerves. As it is, now you're the one that looks odd, old fellow. Always alone, Crane. Always alone. Any woman on the scene?" And then, before I have time to answer, "No, I imagine not."

He could have got a message to me. He could have told me to bring someone. But perhaps it suited him not to. He's right. What this new arrangement does instead is make *me* look strange. The lone wolf tagging himself onto a husband and wife's skiing trip.

"But how are you going to make sure your wife doesn't get suspicious? You're going to be keeping some odd hours. If I were her, I'd have some questions to ask."

"I think you can allow me to keep my house in order," he says, with a sardonic smile. "Besides, my sweet little wife has a yen for a certain little pill that knocks her out for twelve hours a night. If anything is to threaten our plans here it is going to be your love affair with alcohol."

"You can hardly talk of affairs."

"Oh that," he waves a hand. "All in the past!"

He actually doesn't know, I realize. He doesn't know who else is staying here. It is delicious, sitting here for a moment with this power over him, possessing, for once, greater knowledge than he.

"You have heard who's also here, haven't you?"

"Who?"

"Sylvia Sinclair. She's a beauty," I say, "perhaps *just* on the turn. They get a little windblown, don't they? But still quite something."

"What?" he manages. He looks suddenly like a man facing a firing squad. "But what in God's name is she doing here?" Then he swears, once, but profusely—the word seeming to ring off the rocks about us. It is rare to see him so rattled. He is always so in control. Then he looks back at me. "Did *you* do this? Is this your work? If so, you're a—"

"Why would *I* have done it?" I ask. "And how? I don't have any silver screen sirens in my address book."

He shakes his head. "Oh, for God's sake. No, of course it wasn't you. You don't have the brains to be so devious."

As he looks at me I feel the full force of his scorn. It comes to me now in a rush. He needs me . . . for now. Just as it was before. To do his dirty work for him. I am a useful idiot. For the time being, that is. And when I am no longer useful, what then?

DIANA GLASS

The Help

I meet Mrs. Bantry and Miss Marple on the terrace behind the hotel to enjoy the promised "afternoon alphorn concert" I suggested they might both enjoy. I've unpacked both my own and Mrs. Bantry's cases in our respective rooms. My room's almost a third of the size of my employer's but still elegantly appointed with its little writing desk and view—I was pleasantly surprised by this—up the mountain toward the glacier.

I hand Mrs. Bantry the shawl I have brought down for her. "Thank you, Diana, dear . . . though I'm not sure I shall need it!"

I see what she means. The terrace is bathed in the full glare of the afternoon sun. The sky above the white peaks is a cloudless, gas-flame blue and the mountains encircle us; I have the sense of sitting inside a cut-crystal bowl. The music is just beginning: the trio stand at the far end of the terrace in William Tell felt caps and embroidered waistcoats, playing the huge wooden instruments, the trumpets of which rest on the floor in front of them. The deep sound is mournful and at times surprisingly majestic: swelling to encompass the vastness of the landscape, echoing off the surrounding rock and snow.

After a moment I realize that the tables out here are ringed around an ice rink. Mrs. Bantry makes a cry of delight at the sight of the ice-skating waiters, who in their frock coats glide expertly among the tables carrying—one-handed—trays laden with drinks.

There is a bar built out of hard-packed snow and atop it sit bottles of champagne in silver buckets, platters of smoked oysters, pungent mountain cheeses and cured meats. The guests sitting at the bar on their wooden stools have a glow about them: cheeks ruddy from sun exposure and good food. After the privations of rationing, the pinched gray faces on the Underground and the wet London streets, it feels as though I have fallen into another universe. It is hard not to stare.

"Well," Miss Marple says. "I had always thought a London hotel the very height of luxury. Bertram's always seemed to me second to none, but even they have not managed ice-skating waiters. It makes one wonder how much they have to practice before they are trusted with a full tray."

"Arthur wouldn't like this at all," Mrs. Bantry says, as one performs a rather showy pirouette to whoops of applause, all while balancing a champagne bucket and coupes, "no, not at all." If I didn't know better, I might say she sounds almost gleeful. "He would think it terribly European and flamboyant."

"But look how quickly they move among the tables. So I suppose," Miss Marple says thoughtfully, "he might at least approve of the efficiency."

All around us sit our fellow patrons in their furs and gleaming sunglasses, drinking steaming hot chocolates and coffees. A bartender flourishes a cocktail shaker and pours a syrupy stream into a martini glass.

"I think these people must be what they call the *café society*," Mrs. Bantry says, looking about her avidly. "Aren't they frightfully glamorous?"

I lift my camera and take a few photographs of the peaks that seem to surge above us.

"I wonder," says Miss Marple, "if your photography is a little like my birdwatching."

"What do you mean?" I ask.

"Well, that it often proves a useful way of satisfying one's curiosity."

I manage a laugh. "Well, I take pictures of landscapes and animals. You make it sound a little . . . prurient."

"Oh, I didn't mean that. Only . . . I wondered if you ever experience the same thing I do. One goes to observe one thing, but people *will* keep getting in the way."

"Are those . . . nuns?" Mrs. Bantry asks. They are: two nuns at the far end of the terrace reclining on a couple of deck chairs, wearing dark glasses like everybody else. Finishing their coffees they stand and shuffle away.

"What on earth can they be doing here, do you think?" Mrs. Bantry asks, watching them go.

A man sitting nearby can't help answering; he leans over and in an American accent says: "It's an old pilgrimage site. It's what people came here for first: the holy waters of the spring."

"Oh, thank you!" says Mrs. Bantry. "I think I do remember something on that, now I come to think of it. Where is it . . ." She pulls a Baedeker from her handbag and rifles through the pages. "Ah! Here we are. Yes: the first visitors came for the healing waters, which according to local religious legend were blessed by the spirit of the Virgin Mary herself, several visions of whom have been reported locally, over the centuries. As such, the Virgin remains an important site of religious importance, particularly for orders that are dedicated to her."

"Something this place has in common with St. Mary Mead then," Miss Marple says.

"I believe they get a special rate to stay at the hotel," the man says.

"Different accommodation, dear," his wife chimes in, "dormitories, I heard."

"Well how simply wonderful!" Mrs. Bantry exclaims in delight. "It does make it feel worthwhile, doesn't it, Jane? All the discomfort of traveling. Nuns! One really doesn't see many of them at home. I wonder where all our English nuns can be? Do you know, Jane, I can see you making a good nun. Anglican, of course."

"I'm sure you mean that as a compliment, my dear," Miss Marple says. "But I'm afraid I'm too interested in people as they *are* to be all that interested in altering them for the better."

"Oh," Mrs. Bantry says. "Yes, I see what you mean."

Our hot chocolates arrive, topped with cream as white as the peaks beyond.

Mrs. Bantry takes a sip and sighs happily.

"Ice-skating waiters and sunbathing nuns," she says. "Now I have truly seen all there is to see of life and can go to my grave happily—not that I'm planning to do so any time soon!"

We all sit in silence for a while, contemplating the view. I allow myself to enjoy the warmth of the sun on my upturned face, and experience several moments of brief, thoughtless bliss. Then Mrs. Bantry speaks again: "Goodness . . . can that be . . . ?" She turns to Miss Marple. "Jane, do you think it is . . . ?"

She is staring at a figure who has just arrived and is settling herself on one of the sunbeds: white silk headscarf, silver mink coat and large dark glasses. A couple of inches of platinum blonde hair is revealed by the headscarf at the front. A gigantic shaggy gray dog flops onto the ground beside her—an Irish wolfhound—rests its head in her lap, and closes its eyes in apparent bliss. The woman drains half the martini glass in one go, somehow managing to appear elegant while doing so. Then she summons one of the ice-skating waiters. As soon as the poor man glides close the dog leaps to its feet and lets out a volley of barks that seem to echo off the surrounding peaks. The man wobbles, losing his balance and control of his tray stacked with glasses, looks almost ready to keel over, and then with magnificent poise manages to right himself without dropping a single glass.

Several of the sunbathing guests cheer, as though all of this was performed for their entertainment.

"What *is* her name?" Mrs. Bantry says. "Jane, you must know!"

Miss Marple peers mildly at the woman. "Oh, my dear—if it's

anyone *fashionable* or *celebrated* I am utterly useless. I will say that I think that particular hair shade must be a great deal of work to maintain."

"Oh, Jane, you really are no use."

Mrs. Bantry turns to me. I shake my head apologetically. I dislike letting her down, even in this small thing; I take this job seriously.

"No, I've *got* it!" she declares in triumph. "It's Sylvia Sinclair, of course. The Hollywood actress! And here, in this out-of-the-way place in Switzerland. What on earth can she be doing here? She's often in those odd magazines one gets at the hairdressers. One does spend so much time waiting around that one ends up reading them. Though perhaps now I think about it, she's appeared less often of late. There's a whole crop of new stars in Hollywood. Even Sylvia Sinclair has become old hat." She sighs. "Well, it seems to be what happens in other walks of life to any woman over thirty-five."

She darts a little look at me, as though worried she may have caused offense. I want to tell her it doesn't signify. I resigned myself to being a spinster for life a long time ago now. I haven't thought of myself as eligible for anything for a very long time.

"Still," Mrs. Bantry goes on, "she is like . . . an *icon*, isn't she? Like—a medal of St. Christopher—oh, I don't know if that's dreadfully blasphemous. Or . . . the King. Gosh, and perhaps that's treasonous. But you do see, don't you? Instantly recognizable: that very blonde hair, the dark glasses, that magnificent ermine. Just think of the cost! I've never seen one that luxurious. One feels one would know her anywhere, at almost a hundred paces. All of it says 'film star' quite as distinctly as a crown says 'royalty.'"

Now the woman finishes her martini in a second languid gulp and then stretches in the sun like a cat.

We all watch surreptitiously as she calls the waiter over again who returns a few moments later with a pair of binoculars, which she trains on the cliff face opposite us.

Miss Marple is looking around at the other guests. "There seem to be a great many people using their binoculars," she says. "How wonderful to be among so many other keen birdwatchers. Diana, will you ask what they are watching for?"

"If you don't mind my answering, Madame," says a prematurely gray man in—I'd guess—his thirties at the next table, "they like to watch the climbers, up on the mountain." He stubs out his cigarette in the snow with a hiss. "It is more of a pastime in the summer months, of course, when there are more routes open." He grimaces. "It is a difficult face, that one. Sometimes one falls and then they all get very . . . animated. It is"—he seems to be searching for the right words—"a little like a sport for them. You have heard of the Eiger Birds? They do the same thing there: they like to see climbers perish on the Mordwand, the 'Murder Wall.' It is similar here."

Miss Marple's mouth pinches in disapproval. "I would like to say that I am surprised. But there is something about tragedy that attracts people, like . . . like carrion birds. After that murder at the vicarage we had a sudden expansion in the congregation."

Then she lifts the binoculars to her eyes and trains them upon the mountainside. "There are two of them up there now," she says. "Look."

She passes them to Mrs. Bantry and then they are handed, in turn, to me. Through the lenses I find the two figures up there on the face. They appear to be standing upon a ledge of some sort, above a frozen waterfall of bright blue ice. With all their attire—the goggles, the woolen hats—it's impossible to make out any distinguishing features: only that they are two men, of approximately the same height.

As I continue to watch, something strikes me as odd about their position. One of the climbers seems to be standing a little behind the other and this lends an immediate precariousness to the situation. It occurs to me that it would take one small movement from the man behind—one small *push*—and the unthinkable could happen. From here they are doll-sized and of course nothing can be seen of their faces, and yet from the way the man behind is holding himself I am certain that he, too, is contemplating this fact. I am transfixed. I can't look away. I have effectively become one of the people that we just learned about . . . waiting for something awful to happen up there on the mountain. Is anyone else seeing this? I watch as the man behind takes a step forward; then another. And now he actually raises his arms, palm of his hands outstretched. I don't believe it. He's going to do it—he's going to shove the other man over the ledge. From this sunlit terrace, to the soft sound of the alphorns playing, we're all about to witness a horrific tragedy. A murder.

Miss Marple lets out a small exclamation and when I glance at her I see that she is looking up there. She isn't even using binoculars: her eyesight, in spite of her advanced years, must be quite something.

I look back through the lenses. Ah. There has been no disaster while I glanced away. In fact, the one standing behind has moved farther back, his hands at his sides now, as though there was never any risk at all, as though he never appeared to briefly consider pitching the other man to his death. For a moment I wonder if I imagined it . . . until I place the binoculars on the table in front of me and catch Miss Marple's expression. She, too, knows what nearly happened up there on the ledge.

CATHERINE NARRACOTT

The Wife

It is cocktail hour, but my husband is making a call to London in the telephone booth in the lobby. While I wait for him, I step out alone onto one of the terraces outside the great hall, pulling my shawl about me. My face tightens from the cold: even better for the complexion than an ice bath, I should imagine. This side of the hotel looks down toward the valley, tiny lights shimmer up from the village far below. They are like a reflection of the scattering of stars above, very bright in the clear night sky. It's hard to believe that snow is supposed to descend on us soon.

I check behind me—no one there—then reach into my little beaded evening bag and draw out my little silver cigarette case. It's so slim, so discreet, that looking quickly you would mistake it for a compact. I light one clove cigarette and draw quickly on it. The taste is delicious and forbidden: Anthony hates me to smoke, as he says it looks too "fast" for a Tory wife. Feeling like a naughty child I blow a series of gray rings into the cold night air. Someone taught me to do this a very long time ago—or so it feels—though I am still young.

"Mrs. Narracott." A voice, just behind me.

In my surprise I inhale far too much smoke and cough as it catches in my throat. Then, gathering my wits, I fling the cigarette off the balcony.

An untidy young man with fair hair and glasses stands there, blocking my way back into the hall. He has not made any effort to dress for the evening, or even for the elegant surroundings of the hotel. The collar of his shirt is stained and the lenses of his spectacles seem smeared. He has some sort of nasty-looking rash creeping up the side of his neck. I have an innate distrust—instilled in me by Nanny—of people who don't care for their personal appearance. I take a step back, then realize I am up against the ironwork balcony of the terrace.

"Who are you?" I ask, studying his face. He has a little dimple in his chin that gives him an oddly boyish appearance. I don't know him. But at the same time I know I recognize him from somewhere. Then I have it: "You were at the station!" I say. "In Paris . . . but you were on the opposite platform." An unpleasant thought: Did he follow us here?

He doesn't acknowledge this: "There are things you should know about your husband," he hisses. His wide eyes and general dishevelment give him a crazed look. He is blocking the door back into the great hall. "Things about his past I bet he'd love to keep hidden."

"Please," I say. "Leave me alone." I hate a scene, even if we are the only ones out here. "Let me pass," I say. "Or . . . or I'll scream." I won't—because that *would* be making a scene—but he doesn't know it. I step toward him, purposefully. I can be steely when I need to be. He steps aside but as I pass him he touches my shoulder and I flinch, because I hate being touched by strangers. "He's not who you think he is," he mutters, menacingly. "I think you should know. He's a bad—"

I slam the door on him as I step back into the welcome warmth and light of the great hall, and then for good measure I manage to fasten the catch on this side, leaving him mouthing on the other side of the glass. My heart is beating fast as I try to decide whether or not to tell Anthony, who I can see now emerging from the lobby at the end of the great hall. I hope the young man isn't going to make any trouble here. It is really not what we need.

A few minutes later we step down into the hotel's basement dining room. It's so charmingly rustic down here. The whole thing seems to have been dug out of the mountain rock itself. Torches burn in sconces along the stone walls. A Swiss folk band plays in one corner: a trio of rather beautiful young women with braided hair playing on a couple of fiddles and an accordion. Candles have been lit upon every table. The guests' faces gleam. My husband walks through the middle of the room to our table, nodding and smiling at people along the way, limping a little as he goes. I follow, feeling nervy and out of sorts after the scene on the terrace.

"Catherine!" a woman calls. I turn and look. Oh—Harriet Hodgson, who I haven't seen since Cheltenham Ladies'. I don't specially want to talk to her, but she's seen me now; I don't really have a choice. I move to their table, smiling my politician's wife's smile. "Goodness me," she says, "don't you scrub up well! And you married Anthony Narracott. My husband," she nods to the balding, much-older man opposite, "thinks he's absolutely wonderful. Don't you, darling? Oh"—when he fails to hear—"never mind. But goodness me. You've done so well for yourself. After . . ." she giggles, "that little scandal with the gardener!"

I stand frozen in mortification, willing her to be quiet.

"Oh," she puts a finger up to her lips. "Sorry, was that indiscreet of me? But I think half the girls were in love with Kit. Those *shoulders*! Those piercing blue eyes. But then I suppose your husband has very attractive eyes too . . ."

Luckily Anthony is out of earshot, talking to some other diners several tables down. I tell Harriet that it's wonderful to see her and that I hope we can all have a drink together tomorrow evening—

then am extremely relieved to hear we can't because they leave in the morning.

Finally, we take our own seats. Then I start. The shabby young man who I just left on the balcony is descending the staircase, staring at my husband like a cat that has just spotted something moving in the long grass.

Anthony must have caught my expression because he turns and looks. "Good Lord," he says, but rather humorously, as though it doesn't give him a moment's pause. "That fellow looks as though he'd like to skin me alive. I wonder what I've ever done to him?"

My husband's observer looks quickly away, apparently realizing he has been caught out.

When our food comes, I carefully cut a line down the middle of everything on my plate and push each half to one side: trout, potatoes, vegetables. The waistband of this skirt is a little tight. *Never let the dress out*, Mummy always says. Mummy, at fifty-five, has a marvelous figure. *It is the beginning of the end: the way dignity and husbands are lost. Keep it as is and bring* yourself *in.* Finishing school was all about bringing oneself in in various different ways. Smoothing out any rough edges. After the gardener, Mummy and Daddy decided I needed a little of that.

Anthony chews on his steak. It smells divine. Just for a moment I have the *strangest* fantasy of picking up the remainder with my two bare hands, and tearing into it with my teeth, letting the blood and cooking juices run down my chin onto the brocade of my dress. Sometimes the divide between doing and not doing seems as frail as cobweb. As if I might just brush it aside and tumble headfirst into disgrace. Perhaps everybody feels like that. To distract myself I count to thirty as I chew a tiny morsel of fish, until all moisture has gone from it.

"Bruno Crane," I say, reaching for a topic. "How did you say you met?"

"The war," my husband says.

"But darling . . . you seem so unlike one another."

He takes a sip of his wine. "There are things that bind men together at such times." He doesn't elaborate any further on this. Then I see his eyes caught by something behind me. I turn to look.

A woman moves through the room. In the candlelight everything about her seems to gleam; as though she herself is a source of light. Her hair is bleached such a pale blonde it is almost silver. She has poured herself into a clinging sheath of black velvet that makes my eau de nil Jacques Fath (bought before the money ran out) look like a little girl's party dress. An expanse of pale décolleté spills over the restraint of the bodice like a just-risen soufflé. Two diamond drops glitter at her ears. It's a ridiculous outfit for dinner in a ski hotel. Attire for a film premiere or soirée. Like magic, as if acting under an enchantment, every head turns toward her.

She is the sort of woman Mummy would call *garish* or *simply frightful*. The sort of woman who looks like she eats the whole plate.

I watch her take her seat. She looks as though she could eat that waiter alive. He looks as though he'd enjoy it.

She glances toward our table and I am sure I see her wink, so quick that if I had blinked myself I'd have missed it. Anthony begins to cough, making a great show of covering his mouth with his napkin, reaching for the water.

"Who is that?" I ask, lightly, giving a little nod in her direction. "I just *know* I recognize her, but . . ."

"No idea," he says, reaching again for his wine.

"But darling," I say, smiling at him, "you are funny! You aren't even looking in her direction! So how *can* you know?"

"The truth is," he says, sawing at the chunk of meat in front of him, "I'm finding it hard to let anything draw my attention away from this magnificent steak . . . I can't think when I last ate like this, if ever."

"Oh, darling *do* look," I say, touching his hand with mine.

He sighs and throws a casual, fleeting look over my shoulder while I watch him closely. "No," he says. "Sorry! I haven't the faintest idea."

"Ah," I say, as though I've just recalled it. "She was in that film, the one set on an Atlantic liner. There was a scene where she dressed as one of the officers, to escape notice—"

Every man in the cinema had sat up a little straighter when she appeared in those navy breeches, that snug jacket with the straining gold button work and epaulettes.

"Oh," he says carelessly. "Was she? But they all look the same, those platinum types. Don't they? The Jean Harlow mode."

"You have to at least admit that she's rather magnificent looking," I say.

"If you like that type," he says. "My tastes are different." And in "different," I hear *refined*. It is meant to be a compliment. Except oddly enough it makes me want to pick up the steak knife and brandish it at him.

"I wonder what she can be doing in an out-of-the-way place like this," I say. "It seems a strange place for a Hollywood star. Do you think she's filming something here? Oh, like that skiing scene with Gregory Peck and Ingrid Bergman!"

"I really don't care," he says, his tone dangerous. "You are boring me now, Catherine."

I fall silent. I know better than to say anything else.

He sniffs the air. "I can smell cigarette smoke."

"Oh?" I say, lightly. "There are probably lots of people smoking down here. Look at that fellow!"

"He's got a pipe," Anthony says, his voice low and a little frightening. "It's not pipe smoke. I can distinctly smell clove cigarettes."

Luckily there is a distraction as our plates are cleared and then the pudding brought over: a delicious-looking tart with a caramel-colored top.

"*Nusstorte*," the waiter says, with a flourish.

I realize the problem straightaway, simply from looking at my husband. As the thing is placed in front of him he begins to wheeze and cough—in earnest this time.

"Please," I say, "take it away immediately." The waiter hovers, looking confused. "But it was ordered specially." People are turning to look at us, at Anthony, who has his napkin clamped to his face.

"*Who* ordered it?" I ask. "Who did this?"

The waiter looks flustered, confused, embarrassed. "I'm sorry, Madame, I don't—"

"Just take it away," I say. "Please."

The waiter scurries off with the offending plate.

Anthony removes the napkin. He smiles and puts up a hand. "I'm all right now, folks!" he says, slightly hoarsely.

The other guests return to their food.

"Darling," I say. "That was *sinister.* Who can have done such a thing?" Anthony never makes public reference to his allergy. The limp is one thing—heroic—whereas this is an entirely different quality of impairment, something old-school tie sorts might associate with weakness of character. So I lower my voice to ask: "Who would know about your . . . problem?"

"I'm sure it's just a stupid mistake," Anthony says.

Someone rushes up to the table all of a sudden. It's the young man I saw on the terrace.

"Oh," I say, shrinking back from him. "No. No, go away."

Anthony gives the young man a once-over. "Can I help you?" he asks. But his expression says: *you had better have a jolly good reason for being here.*

"I need to speak to you," says the young man, as though he and Anthony were already acquainted. "Please. I tried earlier—" He looks at me.

Anthony glances at me, questioningly.

"He . . . accosted me," I say. "It was most unpleasant. He said he had things to tell me about you . . ."

Anthony turns back to the young man. Then he smiles, less like a proper smile and more like an animal baring its teeth, and for a moment the young man looks a little wrong-footed, takes a step back. Then he seems to rally and moves forward again. But as he opens his mouth to speak, my husband cuts him off.

"If you don't mind," Anthony says, "as I am sure you can see, my wife and I are enjoying a private dinner. You couldn't really have chosen a worse time."

"But—"

"In fact," Anthony says, standing up from his seat and looking down at the young man from his superior height, "we have to be going, don't we, Catherine?"

Anthony places a hand firmly in the small of my back and steers me away. You wouldn't know it from the grin on his face, but he is disturbed. The only tell is that he has forgotten to limp.

"Sure he's a Red," he mutters as we reach the other end of the room. "You only have to look at his clothes and the lunatic light in his eye. God knows how he got in here. Best not to even give them the time of day. About as much use as engaging with a rabid dog." Six months ago, my husband was shot at in his car by a Communist lunatic as he was driven through London. "Been in far stickier spots in the war," is how Anthony dismissed it. But I suspect it worried him more than he likes to admit. He has limited his personal appearances since . . . and sometimes he cries out in his sleep.

As we leave the room I glance back. The young man is still watching us, mouth set in a grim line. Then as I watch he raises a hand and points at my husband's back—almost, you could say, like someone sighting a gun.

BRUNO CRANE

The Friend

The knock on the door comes at ten p.m. I've just finished a delightful meal of tinned pilchards. Can't afford to eat in the dining room every night (or any night to be frank) so I smuggled some cans in my luggage. It's a usual dinner for me, in fact, in my sordid Bermondsey lodgings. How did it come to this? I'm a grammar school boy, middle class . . . or just about. Thankfully my poor old pa is dead already or he'd die from the shame. He worked himself to the bone to give me a proper education. Was so proud that his boy was learning Latin!

The knock comes again.

I let Narracott into the room. "You all right, old chap?" I ask him, as I close the door. "You're wheezing . . ."

"I'm fine!" he snaps. His face pinches. "It stinks in here. Smells like . . . cat food." Then he looks me over. "Your cuffs, man," he says.

"What about them?"

"They're dirty and . . . are they frayed? Could you not have found it in yourself to buy one new shirt? For God's sake! Thought you spivs were meant to scrub up better."

I resent the term, but it's not altogether wrong. That's what I've been reduced to: hawking the odd counterfeit bottle of perfume to women in nightclubs, cigarettes at railway stations. Somewhere along the way I fell through the cracks . . . I couldn't settle to anything, after the war. And, as I say, I've got the wrong face, even for peddling black market rubbish. The ear doesn't help. Those women in the nightclubs, they scuttle past me. Men walk to the other end of the railway platform. Worse, I took out debts to buy the stuff. And now I can't shift it . . .

"Moping, Crane?" Narracott's voice snaps me back into the present. "Hurt your feelings, did I?"

I meet his gaze with a small shock. He hates me, almost as much as I hate him. We are bound together by this; him to me as much as I to him. I have a sense of myself as a millstone around his neck. His ugly, shabby shadow.

"You weren't at dinner," he drawls.

"Of course not!" I say. "I can barely afford to stay here."

"Ah," he says. "But you'll be at the Casino tonight, no? Losing what's left on the baccarat?"

"It's no nobler if it's via the London Stock Exchange," I bite back. "Or with women."

"Sounds like a touch of the green-eyed monster there, Crane."

"Hardly. You've got your wife and your mistress here under the same roof. And I remember you boasting to me once about all the girls you had on the go . . . the couple of tarts you'd got in *trouble* in the past."

"Yes, and I always sorted them out. Paid for my sins. Little extra pocket money to take care of it, right as rain. Whereas you—I don't think you've ever paid your debts, have you? Well, you'll be able to now if you *don't do anything stupid*." He looks at me carefully. "What's that look? Don't tell me you're getting cold feet."

"Look, I'm as desperate as a man could be. But I can't help thinking . . . do you really think we should?"

"What on earth do you mean, Crane?" His voice is dangerous.

"I suppose . . . I keep thinking the stuff might be—ah—cursed in some way."

A long pause passes before he answers. When he does it carries the full weight of his scorn. *"Cursed?"*

"Yes. Because of how . . . it was obtained."

"Ha!" A short humorless bark of a laugh. "I don't remember you having too much conscience that night. Didn't think you had it in you. It *was* necessary, of course. Here's a thought," he says. "I suppose you could say that this was one gamble that turned out all right for us both, no?"

"Don't speak of it like that. How can you?"

"Well you're here," he hisses, turning nasty. "Aren't you? What would you ever have done without me? You'd be dead yourself. Yes, that's the truth of it. You'd be dead in some dark and godforsaken corner of Europe, if it weren't for me."

"You shot me," I hiss.

"For God's sake, man! It was over half a decade ago. You're acting as though it just happened."

"You don't forget such a thing in a lifetime. Your own friend, shooting you in the head. How do you think I'm ever going to trust you after that?"

Every time I look in the mirror I see it. I feel it, too; the white-hot sting of the bullet. I'll never forget it. He gave me no warning until after it was over.

"It wasn't in the head," he says. "Don't be so bloody melodramatic. It was your ear."

"Which is attached—"

"And it needed to be done," he cuts me off. "I shot myself, too!"

"You lost a toe. No risk that you might kill yourself shooting off your little toe."

Though of course he plays up to it for all he's worth: that absurd heroic limp, which has won him so much favor with the electorate. He's gauged it perfectly: there never was a more aesthetic injury. Not like those poor chaps who lost whole limbs, who had half their faces blown off. No, he's the noble warrior, slighted, but not bested. A small reminder at all times of his heroism, his sacrifice. I wouldn't be surprised, truth be told, if the wound didn't give him any trouble at all these days. "Meanwhile," I say, "you were less than an inch from killing me."

"Goodness, Crane. The expression on your face is positively frightening. Penny for them?"

"Sometimes I wish you *had* killed me," I say.

He rolls his eyes. "What is this?"

I open the doors to the balcony. Look down at the snow. Wonder, idly, if the fall from here would kill you. "I think every day about what we did. I've thought about throwing myself off here several times since I arrived . . ." My voice is rising to a shout now: "The S pill. The one they gave us. I still have it."

"For God's sake," he says, angrily, scattering sparks and ash from his cigarette. "What are you talking about?"

"I'm not finished. Every day I take it out and I look at it and I think: it would have been better if I had taken mine. If you had taken yours—as we were *meant* to do in such a situation. And every day I wonder if it might be better if I *did* take it. Take it now, I mean."

He follows me out onto the balcony. "Why would you say such a bloody morbid thing? And for God's sake keep your voice down."

I drop my voice a little, but I'm rather enjoying making him sweat. "And the thing I cannot comprehend is how it is that I wake each day with the bone-crushing guilt and horror of it, and you wake each day thinking that *you're* just the thing our country needs. Does it not keep you awake at night? When you are just as culpable as me. No, more so—"

Suddenly I can't speak as he has seized me by the front of my shirt. Now the charm has fallen away and I see the lethal ruthlessness that sits a short distance beneath the surface: like a granite bluff beneath fresh snow. Even though I know of its existence it is still shocking to confront. He grapples me back into the room and closes the doors to the balcony.

"I think you would be wise," he hisses, spittle flecking my cheeks, "to hold your tongue. Either you are in or you are out, here. Which is it, Crane? At the moment you are proving a liability . . . and I cannot have that." He scoffs. "You're far too much of a coward to kill yourself. No, if you meant it, you'd have done it by now. You're just as greedy for the stuff as I am. You know it."

DIANA GLASS

The Help

Mrs. Bantry, Miss Marple and I are playing three-handed bridge in the library, with its large windows on the northern side of the hotel. On floor-to-ceiling shelves the emerald and green spines of old books glow richly in the warm light of the fire. A terrier and a red setter snore beside one another before the hearth, lending the room a faint domesticity, as of an exquisitely furnished private home. Except for the odd snicker of firewood the sounds are all low and soft: the murmur of voices, the slow turning of pages, the shuffling of cards.

In daylight the library windows look down upon the town far, far below, over the ledge of rock clustered with thick dark pines, but for now all I can make out are the nearest trees, branches briefly silvered by the light of the moon whenever it appears through the clouds.

"Diana is a genius player," Mrs. Bantry says. "Even a match for you, Jane." She smiles at me. "Besides all her brilliance at keeping my affairs in order it has been wonderful to have someone to play a rubber with every so often." She lowers her voice. "And she loses with rather more grace than that fellow. He looks in desperate straits!" We follow her gaze to the young man in question, hunched over the cards he has strewn on the table. I watch as he takes off his glasses and rubs his eyes, the image of dejection.

"I think they may have been playing for money," Miss Marple

says, in a slightly scandalized tone. "And if I'm not mistaken that young man has been there most of the afternoon. Oh!"

She glances up because another man—the old English army type we saw on the train—has marched past us to the window and cracked it open. "Hot as blazes in here," he bellows.

"He's right," Miss Marple says. "One wonders if they really need *three* roaring fires."

We continue our game. But then there's a sound from outside. From above, I think. Voices, seeping down to us through the freezing evening air from the open window.

"—throwing myself off here several times since I arrived. The S pill. The one they gave us. I still have it." Almost a shout. Then the other voice lower, more muffled and then: ". . . every day I wonder if it might be better if I *did* take it. Take it now, I mean."

There must be some twenty or so people in this room but any conversation quiets instantly.

I see guests catching one another's gaze, raised eyebrows. Muttered conversations begin. Some seem embarrassed to be forced into the position of eavesdroppers. Others seem rather thrilled. I watch Miss Marple across the table and she sits very still, cards clutched in her hands but with her head tilted at a slight angle and a gleam in her eye that reminds me of a blackbird tracking the progress of a worm.

"S pill. . ." Mrs. Bantry says. "What is that? Diana, do you know?"

"I think," I say, "it means a suicide pill. The sort of thing one heard about in the War. Cyanide."

Miss Marple shakes her head. "Such unpleasantness. And to shout about it so loudly for all to hear. The rest of the conversation was muffled. They must have come onto the balcony, I think, just for that part. But of course, it rather makes one wonder—"

"What?" asks Mrs. Bantry.

"Well, whenever someone talks very loudly about something it makes me wonder if, perhaps, they *want* to be overheard."

She falls silent and seems to drift into her own thoughts.

SYLVIA SINCLAIR

The Star

I've run a bath in the beautiful tub beneath the windows. From here I can see the very top of the mountain silvered by moonlight and I suppose if you were somehow looking down from the peaks you would see little naked me, dropping my robe, stepping into the tub and—whoops!—there goes a little of my martini. Oh well. Plenty more where that came from. Still, I lick some of the spill off my forearm.

Sometimes I find it hard to turn it off, you know? The sex? The showgirl thing? I've been playing her for so long. And then when I'm all on my lonesome and I realize no one is there to see the beacon I'm beaming out—flash flash flash, whump whump whump, come and get it boys!—and I realize I can turn her off, I frighten myself that there's nothing left without it. Like what's left is just the shadow behind the light. Who was I before Sylvia Sinclair? Was I anyone at all? I truly can't always remember. Sylvia isn't the name I was given as a babe, I'll tell you that much.

The martinis don't help with that, of course . . . the remembering. Nor does the lovely, scrummy, sparkly pick-me-up dust I keep in my little silver compact. Oh, but at the same time, they've been just about the only thing keeping me stitched together over the years. I've thrown the windows open to the night, to let the clean cold mountain air inside. Haven't smelled air like it since I was a girl. I shiver a little at the cold and also at the zing as the stuff I've taken—whiter and finer than any powder outside—hits. Makes me feel alive.

And this martini, too. I take another slug. The slick salty slipperiness of it: sex in liquid form. Who am I *kidding*? It's superior, baby. Better than most, anyhow. Although I've had it better of late.

I lower myself into the tub without spilling a drop from the glass, sink down into the scented bubbles.

Right on time: the knock on the door. "I'm in the tub!" I call.

Pretty well everything I've ever achieved or taken for myself has been through men, it's had to be. That's how I've got here. Or there, because there is a little higher than here. There's been a little bit of a backslide of late. Men are the ones with the power in this world. They've all been pimps or johns, sometimes a little of both. And it's worked for me. I had the goods, they were selling and buying. Until said goods started to approach their expiration date. And oh Lordy, there's nothing like the contempt of a man for a woman he no longer finds desirable.

So the last few years, things have been a little more dicey. New girls on the block. That clock a tick-tock. Bank balance on the drop. You wouldn't think it, of course, from the suite in the Alps, the vintage champagne on the dressing table in its ice bucket (I started on that before the martinis). But I've always been good at playing a part. Thing is, I can only play it for so long. Can only afford to play it for so long, in all senses. But I'm saved, now. Saved by falling in love, can you believe it? It's changed everything. I can see the way ahead now.

As if on cue, Anthony opens the door and steps inside. I see his mouth go slack at the sight of me, all squeaky shiny clean in the tub.

"How the hell did you get a key?" I ask, mock horrified. (I told them to give him one if he asked. They must know the man's here with his wife but they're good and discreet in these fancy hotels.) I smile to let him know I'm teasing. He doesn't smile back. Instead he closes the door and strides across to me. "What the *hell* are you doing here, Sylvia?" he hisses.

"You know," I say, leaning my chin on my hand, "I was wondering when you'd come, baby. I've been waiting and waiting. Have you put her to bed yet? Children get so tired at altitude, I heard."

He frowns. "Sylvia—"

"Sorry," I press a finger to my lips. "Naughty, I know. I'm just *so* excited to see you! Come over here," I say, low and velvet, "and help me with the parts I can't reach." Funny: I see his little flinch of revulsion. It's in his breeding, I guess. Even while he wants me, he's still kind of appalled by me. Women of good character—*ladies*—don't speak like me. I know his wife doesn't. But if he wanted to be spoken to only in the proper and decorous way then he wouldn't have come calling, would he?

"I told you not to come," he says. "I told you there was a change of plan: that it wasn't a good idea."

I shrug, sink back into the bath. "Must not have got the message! The globe-trotting, you know. I'm all over the place, baby." I pout. "And it seemed like such a *fabulous* spot! Can't a gal have a holiday? I work so very hard."

Actually, I haven't been working *all* that hard lately. I'm being asked to play the mother now, and I've refused so far. Once you do it's pretty much a hop-skip-and-jump to Old Hollywood Hag territory.

"I sent several messages, that I had to come with my wife instead."

"Oh yes," I say. "The *wife*. Sweet little thing, isn't she? So that's your type . . . in wives. Could've guessed, I suppose. Looks like butter wouldn't melt. Whereas me," I let my mouth fall open just a little, "that butter wouldn't stand a second's chance. *Everything* melts with me." Subtlety has never been expected of me. Good thing too; it's not my strong suit. And just for emphasis I rise up out of the bubbles enough just to remind him of what he's been missing.

I've still got it, haven't I? I'm like that painting of the goddess coming out of the waves, except you betcha that little slip of a thing isn't a 35-22-35. *Sex incarnate*, that's what the papers call me. And those critics (most of them, anyway) haven't even experienced me in the flesh.

"So interesting," I purr, "to learn your taste in wives and how it differs from your taste in mistresses."

"Stop it." His mouth is a tight line. Quite a cruel mouth when it isn't smiling, with that hard-molded cleft chin not helping matters any.

"What, baby? I mean it. She really is like a delicate little English flower. One that blooms prettily for a season, then fades."

I remember that voice on the other end of the line when I called his apartment that day. Those tight-clipped little British vowels. "Ken I esk hew is korling?" Giving nothing away. Or not at first. But she knew from the moment she heard my voice on the line who—what—I was, right enough. And I could picture her right then and there, down to the little pearl studs at her earlobes. I swear to you I could *hear* that she was a brunette. Petite. Neat. My total opposite.

"Hey," I say. No, I *purr* it. "I have an idea. Why don't you join me in here? I'll wash that frown from your brow."

"I want you to leave, Sylvia," he says now. "I'll pay anything outstanding on your bill."

He can't pay. I know this, now. Didn't at the beginning, of course. At the beginning he showered me in fabulous baubles and vintage champagne and lovely little red boxes from Cartier. Then somewhere along the way it shifted; gradually it started being me who had to pick up the check. And glitz aside, I'm not rich. I've made some money in my time but I'm pretty damn good at spending it, too.

I shake my head. "I'm not going anywhere. I've spent the last four months freezing my sweet ass off on a Cinecittà set and I deserve this vacation."

"I'll . . . I'll pay you. You're really going to mess things up for me here." He tries to go for a softer approach now. "I'll make it up to you, darling. A weekend at the Ritz—"

I wrinkle my nose. "London?"

"Paris! Like we did last autumn. Remember it, Sylvia . . . wandering through the Tuileries—"

"Sorry, baby, that all sounds perfectly lovely. But it doesn't mean I'm leaving this place early."

He snaps back to mean in an instant. "You'd better watch yourself, Sylvia. A man has a right to protect his situation."

"And just what in the hell do you mean by that? Were you *protecting your situation* that night at the Carlyle? Bet your little wife doesn't offer to li—"

He cuts me off. "For God's sake, Sylvia. Don't be so crude."

"But that's just what I am, baby. You know that. And I know that that's exactly what you like. You don't complain about me being crude when me being *crude* suits you!" I smile at him. "Perhaps it's a good thing she's here," I say lightly. "Perhaps now everything can at last come to a head!"

He stares at me. "What on earth are you talking about?" he says, cold as the ice in the champagne bucket. "What on earth do you mean, 'come to a head'? I'm sure you haven't taken leave of your senses but just for a second there it certainly sounded like it . . ."

I'm quite enjoying this now. Having the power for once. Because I've never really had power. Not even at the height of my career. "I'm just saying, maybe this is meant to be. Maybe it's time. It can all come out. I love you, baby. We could *be* together. No more sneaking around . . ."

His eyes seem to have darkened: to literally have changed color. "For God's sake, Sylvia. Don't be ridiculous."

"But—"

"You think that would play with the voters? The statesman and the showgirl?"

The showgirl. Huh. But I get it. Course I do. I'm an operator. I've only got to where I am by understanding the rules of the game. Still, sometimes it's fun—or maybe fun is the wrong word . . . more like satisfying in the way you might lance a boil—to prod him like this.

He thinks he has all the power. Sometimes it's nice to remind him what a big old mess I could make of his life.

"Well, baby," I say, "nothing's immutable. Even marriage. Even *your* marriage."

He laughs, but there's no humor in it.

"You know this is all getting rather tedious. You're boring me. Yes. I've already got a wife to be bored by. Your role is meant to be something else. You're meant to be fun, sweetheart. You're a geisha, my sweet, a courtesan. You're a twentieth-century Moll Flanders."

I pick up the big, beautiful, heavy cut glass ashtray from the edge of the tub and weigh it in my hand like a pitcher. My first husband was a pitcher. Made love like a pitcher too: all hard and fast and expecting to hit the target first time. Expected wild applause at the end, too. Anyway, you know what? The ashtray feels good in my hand. Powerful. I can feel the alcohol swimming through me, mixing with the white stuff. It feels delicious, you know? And just a little bit *dangerous*. Even *I* don't know what I'm going to do next.

Except then I do, just a second before I sling it at him. *That* feels good too. Sometimes I don't think before I act. Like that time I slapped Bogie for real in a screen test and thought that was it, that I was toast, until he laughed and that film, the spark between us, was the thing that made my whole career catch light.

The ashtray seems to hang in the air forever before it smashes into the wall, missing Tony's head by a couple of feet. He just stares at me, stunned, for a second or two, mouth opening like a koi carp and looking all gormless—he's many things, this man, but he ain't gormless. Then his face twitches and I think for a moment *he* might laugh too, like Bogie did. I didn't aim it *at* him, after all. And I think: he's in on the joke. But then I see: not a laugh. A snarl. Next thing I know his shadow has fallen across the little shield of bubbles above my stomach. Next thing after that and I'm underwater. And all those lovely scented bubbles are in my mouth, my nose, stinging my eyes and I go to scream but of course it just makes me suck in more water. His fingers clamped about my throat, forcing me down. And this, *this* is the thing about men. Even the smaller ones (and he is not one of the smaller ones) are so terrifyingly strong. So much stronger than me. And so many have such violence in them.

I'm scrabbling at the sides of the tub. As I feel the last little bit of air seep out of my lungs I can see it all: the headlines, the gossip. I know how this plays. He's going to drown me right here and maybe all they'll find is the white powder on the vanity and the empty martini glass and think I'm just another silly little starlet who couldn't handle losing the limelight and did herself in.

This, then. This is how it ends—

BRUNO CRANE

The Friend

Everything is fine and dandy. All of my problems have vanished with a lucky hand. I have just won five thousand-odd pounds at the vingt-et-un table—yes me, the dunce, the dolt, the idiot!—and the Casino of St. Celeste is the most beautiful place I have ever been. The colorful spin of the roulette wheels, the bright stacks of chips, the gold fixtures gleaming. Look at me . . . five thousand pounds and I'm a poet! I remember as a boy pressing my face against the Christmas windows of Fortnum & Mason and everything inside gleaming festively and wishing I could fly through the pane and alight in that glorious Neverland. I am there now. I have made it.

I'm not usually a gambler. I have always known I wasn't born with any luck. But it was worth a try tonight. A last-chance attempt at freeing myself from this place. And I've pulled it off!

Now I can tell him I won't do it. That he can't *make* me. That he no longer has any hold upon me and if he wants it then he can go whistle. The thought . . . like feeling the weight of someone's boot lifting off my neck.

The people here are beautiful too, the gathering of faces about the table like a heavenly host. The good looks of the prematurely gray-haired fellow beside me don't annoy me like they normally would. The ruby and diamond necklace of the woman sitting opposite me seems like a dazzling smile. I am surrounded by a warm golden light, as though nothing I can do can possibly turn bad. I feel godlike. I can walk away from this place and never look back. I can tell Narracott that I don't want it, don't need it. I never have to return to the darkness, the hidden place, the blood and horror and shame—

Don't even think of it. Stay here with the warmth, the perfumed bodies—feel the champagne fizzing through my veins. Maybe just a little more? To really see off the darkness . . .

"Champagne!" I call. "Champagne for the whole table. You, yes, you, man . . . what's the best you have? Three bottles of that." They all cheer, all these beautiful people. They are looking at me like they love me. It has been a long time since I have been looked at like that by another human being—it feels as though the last time I felt it I must have been a small boy, with my mother. Has anyone ever really loved me since?

Look at me, turning maudlin! Of all the nights to succumb to melancholy this is not it. *This* is the turning point. I always knew my moment would come. And nothing that has come before this, nothing I have done—days and acts of despair and violence—none of that matters now. I am ready to step into this glittering golden future. I sweep up the teetering pile of chips, so many it is difficult to gather them together, so many that I can hardly hold them all at once and some Casino lackey runs forward with a velvet tray for me to use to carry them.

I will take them to the cashier, exchange them for a sheaf of real banknotes. I can see him there, sitting in his cage. I wonder how many lives have been changed in here with a click and whirr of his till.

There's a young fellow across the table who catches my eye. Hang on. I've seen him somewhere before. Did he follow me here . . .

No, for God's sake, Crane. You're being paranoid.

I glance down at the velvet tray. Funny thing, the pile of chips doesn't look . . . well, quite so impressive, if I'm honest. Yes, if I shake them out the layer doesn't even cover the surface. There are large gaps, the velvet showing through. Other people have won even bigger hands this evening. Perhaps even *much* bigger hands. Yes . . . I pass the roulette and there's some chap sitting there with almost double the number.

No, I remind myself. Five thousand pounds is a great deal of money. A life-changing amount. When did I last have my hands on that kind of money? Imagine how that'll feel, having the notes snug in my wallet. I can breathe a little easier just thinking about it.

Although . . . just a little more would be nice. Just a little more would *really* solve all my problems. Is five thousand really as life-changing as all that? Because when all is said and done, when I've paid off my debts . . . it would keep the wolf from the door, that's certainly true. But does it banish the wolf entirely? If I had a little more, I would be truly secure. More than that, I could call myself a wealthy man.

I hear the whir of the roulette wheel. And I think: I could sit down there and in a matter of minutes I could double my fortune. Double it! Ten thousand pounds. Just imagine that. That would be a *real* number.

This third bottle of champagne is doing its work. If I don't think about the possibilities of losing . . . if I don't glance at the darkness, I will be all right. To think of losing is to lose faith, so *just don't think* . . .

Besides . . . I don't know that I believe in God these days, if I ever did, but someone is smiling upon me tonight. It would be almost churlish to go to the cashier now. To step out into the dark and cold, when all of life is in here, in all its warmth and zest and beauty. It would be like giving up. Like . . . volunteering for an early grave.

That thought brings with it thoughts of the frozen earth, of the things that lie beneath—

Apparently, my feet have already decided for me, because I am nearly at the roulette table, and just like that there is a space for me. It's meant to be! The croupier glances up at me expectantly and smiles. They never smile, these people! It is a sign. In his smile I read a promise. He's with me too. He is my friend. All will be well. I will make sure of it. I push all of my chips forward on the baize.

Then I glance up and realize the croupier isn't smiling now. He has the bland if slightly sorrowful expression of an undertaker, of Death himself, and I'm filled with dread. But it's too late.

The wheel spins.

DIANA GLASS

The Help

Everything looks different in the morning light. The valley far below is sunk in deep blue shadow but up here the sun scatters every surface. The snow appears beside the path the brightest, most perfect white—its surface marred only by the tracks of nocturnal animals both clawed and hooved.

Mrs. Bantry said she would rise late and breakfast in her room but I've already been up for a couple of hours, using the time to explore the hotel and its grounds. I've walked the three floors of bedrooms and all the communal areas below, learning how they connect to one another. I've found the hidden rustic bar beyond the main bar, the ski room and lockers beneath the hotel, the padlocked cellars for the (extensive) wine collection, and even the cheese cave, where the Grand Alpine matures its own Vacherin. Before this I paced the twenty-minute walk to the spa building, and had a quick look inside the small bare chapel tucked away to one side of the hotel, where the nuns congregate. Now I know the geography of the place I can be even more efficient in my duties here. It gives me a pleasing sense of order and control, knowing the lie of the land.

Now, I walk toward the small train platform, the light covering of snow on the path stiff and squeaking beneath my boots. I am going to take a train down to town in search of some Darjeeling—Mrs.

Bantry's favorite. I am determined to complete this small task. I like to feel useful. I am not sure I have felt truly useful for the last few years.

"Good morning!"

I turn to see Anthony and Catherine Narracott. He carries, chivalrously, both pairs of skis over his shoulders. His hair glints reddish-gold in the sun. He looks like a hero from a wartime poster: all vitality and derring-do, or an advertisement for Alpine tourism. In his hand he holds a steaming flask. His wife, meanwhile, is a vision in a tailored gray wool jacket and ski salopettes, a dove-colored cashmere snood about her head and slanted dark glasses shielding her eyes. I suspect she might be wearing them even if the sun weren't shining. There's a sphinxlike reserve to her. It has a presence, seems to surround her like an invisible shield. I wonder if even her husband gets beyond it.

"Not skiing?" Anthony Narracott asks me.

"No," I say, my gaze going back to him. "I'm taking the train down."

He frowns at me. "Have I seen you somewhere before?" Then: "Wait—I've got it! You're traveling with the two elderly treasures, yes? A granddaughter?"

"Paid companion," I say, waiting for his expression to change as his estimation of me falls. To his credit it doesn't.

"What does that involve?"

"Oh—running errands, providing conversation, helping out with itineraries, that sort of thing. At home it's more secretarial work and things like booking this holiday . . ."

"Noble work!" I don't *think* he's being facetious. Then he peers at me. "My wife was right. You *are* younger than I thought."

"Oh," I say, and can't think of anything else. What is one supposed to say when a man makes such a pronouncement?

"Well. I do hope you have a chance to get out on the slopes.

Nothing better for the soul than racing through thick powder on a winter's morning. Have you spent any time in the mountains before?"

"A little," I say. "But it was rather different to this." I gesture to the hotel in all its quiet luxury.

He chuckles. "Well, yes. There is nowhere quite like this." He points at the camera around my neck.

"A photographess! Of what?"

"Excuse me?"

He smiles, but there is nothing of the charming politician in this smile. It is a vulpine grin, showing too many teeth. "What do you like to photograph?"

"Well—landscapes, mainly. Some of the wildlife, too."

"Oh? But what wildlife can there be at this altitude?"

I stand a little straighter. "That's what I'm looking to discover," I say. "Chamois, marmots . . . mountain quail, that sort of thing."

He nods. "Ah," he says. "How fascinating."

"And apparently there are wolves in these parts, too."

I see a change come over his whole body at this. A predatory stillness. "What was that you said?"

"Wolves. They're rare, but apparently there are still a few about—I read it in one of the guidebooks to the area."

"Gosh." He grimaces theatrically. "Well, do watch out if you go into the trees alone."

I wonder if he means this to sound as menacing as it does. And all the while his pretty little wife stands there, looking completely disconnected from her surroundings.

"I will," I say. "Thank you. Enjoy your ski."

"Yes," he says, "come on, darling!" And then, to me, "I'm determined to make the very first gondola every day."

The two of them walk off toward the gondola station. I wonder if they know they have a follower. Fifty yards farther on I spot a bobble-hatted figure stalking after them, using the trees at the side of the path as a kind of cover. It is the young man from the bridge table,

I realize: sandy hair covered by the hat but the slightly dirty-looking glasses still in place. He is so fixated on the Narracotts that he seems barely aware of my presence.

Then a horn sounds and the mountain train emerges from the tree line a little way down the slope. A few moments later and it is pulling alongside the platform. I hurry to meet it and yank at the handle of the door to the nearest carriage. It sticks at first and then swings open heavily, abruptly, as though it has had a great weight leaning against it. I'm not someone who is easily shocked—I think anyone who lived through the war has had some part of themselves cauterized to horror. But I can't help the small scream that escapes me as a man's body plummets from within the train carriage, knocking me off my feet and landing on the platform with a sickening, inanimate thud.

DIANA GLASS

The Help

For a moment I stare at the motionless figure lying face down on the train platform, becoming gradually aware of the sound of my own panicky breathing in the silence of the morning.

Just as I begin to wonder if he's ever going to move again, I see Bruno Crane stir, then groan. He clambers unsteadily to his knees, unfolding with all the grace of a broken umbrella, his eyes bleary, nose just beginning to bleed from the impact of the fall. As he staggers to his full height he pitches forward and takes hold of one of my shoulders to steady himself; I lurch away from him, hardly able to contain my disgust. As though he's unable to support the weight of his upper half without help he folds forward at the waist and vomits clear liquid onto the snow-covered platform. A small pause, a belch . . . and then he vomits again.

Finally, he straightens, wiping his mouth.

I should get on the train. I should just leave him here, now I know he's not dead. But for a moment I just stand here, transfixed.

The driver's cabin is opening, evidently the man has seen the commotion from the train. It's not going anywhere for the time being. I'm caught between the urge to escape into the carriage and a kind of voyeuristic fascination.

Now he finds his voice and is pathetically apologetic.

"Missed the last train back up from town. Had to spend the night in the Casino. I suppose there are worse places to find oneself." He attempts a smile, but in a horrible contrast his eyes are those of a badly wounded animal. He has the look of a man who has spent the night, Prometheus-like, having his liver pecked out. I could almost pity him.

I board the train back down the mountain to the town. Returning to ground level feels a little like reentering the real world once more, after living in some enchanted kingdom. It feels slightly easier to breathe, and I don't think that is just the altitude.

I find an odd selection of shops: one selling wooden cuckoo clocks, several selling religious ornaments, a couple selling hats, gloves, and slippers, made from the different pelts of mountain animals, and one selling—improbably—clothing for maids and kitchen staff; though perhaps it's not all that odd, considering the concentration of hotels opening in these parts. Unfortunately for Mrs. Bantry, though, no shops selling tea, Darjeeling or otherwise.

I catch sight of a couple of guests from the hotel; we nod to each other like members of a secret society. I even spy the actress, trying on a fur hat as the owner of the shop wrestles with her Irish wolfhound.

Back up at the hotel once more I find Mrs. Bantry sitting with Miss Marple on the terrace behind the hotel, drinking steaming, white-frothed coffees. I hand Mrs. Bantry yesterday's papers (the most recent I could find in English) and apologize for returning without the asked-for Darjeeling.

"Oh, not to worry," she says. "I'll simply spend the whole week drinking these, which the nice young man on ice skates there," she indicates one of the gliding waiters, "tells me is called a 'cappuccino,' after the Capuchin monks. Speaking of the clergy, look over there! Can it be? Yes. Nuns! Skiing nuns."

There they are, descending the slope above us: five, no, six nuns, black shapes looking for all the world like giant crows swooping down the mountainside.

"One doesn't think of nuns skiing," Mrs. Bantry says. "I suppose there is no reason why they shouldn't. I wonder what they're all doing."

"They're returning from Terce." This is spoken—rather pompously—by the purple-faced, gray-whiskered old army type who threw open the window in the library last night. "They always do it at the statue of the Virgin up there. Have to go up on skins because the gondola isn't open until ten past nine. Surprisingly athletic! I say, are you all English?" He gives us a little salute. "Colonel Chapman, very pleased to meet you all."

"Terce?" Mrs. Bantry asks.

"The third hour of prayer, dear," Miss Marple says. "Usually about nine o'clock, I think." And then, by way of explanation, "I grew up in a cathedral close, you know."

"Yes," Colonel Chapman says, looking a little annoyed at being unable to supply the explanation himself. But he makes up for it by saying: "Here it's the most important hour of prayer, because it was around then, they say, that the vision of the Virgin appeared on the mountain to some goatherds. They observe Terce at the statue up there."

He points and about halfway up I can just make out a silver form stationed atop one of the rocks, reflecting the morning sunlight.

A little while later, at Mrs. Bantry's insistence—"Please, go, Diana! I shan't need you for hours. I'll be happy here in the sun with Lord Peter Wimsey . . . oh, though perhaps you could book me one of the therapies in the spa first?"—I borrow some skis from the hotel and take the gondola up the mountain. My fellow travelers are a middle-aged couple and a man around my own age. I recognize him as the man with the prematurely silver hair from the terrace yesterday.

It takes a little getting used to, trusting in this metal box suspended so high above the white slopes and the bristled tops of the few pines that have managed to grow above the main tree line. They didn't have anything like this in Scotland, where I learned to ski in the late thirties: there, whatever you wanted to ski down you had to have climbed yourself. I try not to think about how insubstantial the coupling mechanism looked compared to the cabin itself. I'm not the only one: the man in the couple next to me makes nervous little whimpers at every sway. His wife seems to be counting down the stanchions until we reach the top in order to keep him calm.

From up here, in the mid-morning sunlight, I can make out the brightly colored forms of skiers floating down the white slopes like confetti. I feel a thrill of adrenaline at the thought of joining them. Will I remember how to do it? Will I remember how to be the version of myself who would think nothing of throwing herself headfirst at danger?

Now I can make out the upper reaches of the glacier too—the parts that are hidden from the hotel by the mountainside. There I can just make out a small dark shape that seems to cling to one of the rock flanks of the glacier. I wish I had binoculars. I take out my camera and look through the viewfinder, which offers me some magnification. A kind of mountain hut, I think, or climber's refuge.

A sudden swing of the gondola sends me careering forward; my skis falling with a clatter. I seem to be moments away from crashing to the metal floor of the gondola myself when I'm caught from behind.

"Are you all right?"

I turn to see my rescuer—it's the man with the silver hair. His eyes are a curiously dark blue, almost navy. He wears a red patterned Alpine sweater beneath a sheepskin jacket. His accent is unplaceable—it could be French or French-speaking Swiss.

"Yes," I say. "Thank you. I was mainly worried about my camera. But we're both in one piece."

He smiles at me. "I'm glad to hear it. You don't want to fall *before* you've even got to the snow." He takes out a gloved hand. "Christophe."

I take it. "Diana."

"*Enchanté*. You too are staying at the Grand Alpine alone?"

"I'm here with my employer. She's kindly given me the morning to ski."

"Well, enjoy it today." He points. "You see that strange light on the horizon there, toward Italy? Almost purple?"

"Yes," I say, peering. It *is* an odd color . . . the mauve of a fresh bruise.

"That means snow—and a lot of it. Soon, perhaps tomorrow."

"One doesn't think of snow being bad for skiing!"

He shrugs. "It is if you can't see beyond your ski tips. Or you can't move for fear of being buried by an avalanche. In the past, the mountain people—my people—would see a light like that and know to stay indoors."

CATHERINE NARRACOTT

The Wife

My skis whisper as we plummet down an avenue of firs, the trees running together in a blackish blur. The air is a freezing rush against my face and the snow a cold embrace: the powder knee-high and yet almost weightless. This must be the closest a person can come to flying. I could shout with joy. In the winters we skied every single day at the Swiss school—I loved the freedom of those afternoons on the mountain. And hours upon hours of ballet lessons taught me excellent balance and control.

We pass the tall woman with dark-gold hair, the elderly ladies' companion. She is an excellent skier, fluid and economical, not at all showy—somehow exactly as one might expect from the look of her.

As we stop at the top of a ridge, my husband turns to me. "Darling," he says, solicitously, "you might want to try using a bit more weight in the downhill leg in your half-christie."

"Oh," I say. "Thank you. I'll try that next time. You're right, of course."

He isn't. I know that would overbalance the whole thing. I never fall and I can match him turn for turn. Actually, I'm the better skier by some distance. He leans back, and he is too showy with his turns. But of course I would never tell him.

We continue downward. And then . . . I'm not quite sure what comes over me but suddenly I find myself shifting my skis to a near-vertical line and overtaking my husband. The whole slope is open and empty in front of me. The speed and the freedom of it! I can hear Anthony calling to me but for several glorious arcing turns I pretend that I can't hear him. Then I realize I am being foolish and sweep to a stop.

"For God's sake, Catherine," he says, as he joins me, more crossly now and breathing hard because I think he's been trying to keep up with me. "You're totally out of control. You should stay behind me. This slope is steep, and there are some nasty bumps. You don't want to get caught out and take a tumble."

"Of course, darling," I say. "You're absolutely right."

This is what he wants, so of course he will get it. I have been trained to be the perfect partner in life, after all. That's what finishing school is, really. A polishing of a raw green girl (though I was never *very* raw and green—Mummy saw to that) in plaits and pleats into the refined form of A Society Wife.

I know the right forms of address for all persons of importance; I know the topics of conversation to cover with a bishop and a duke and even a member of the Royal Family. I know how to run a household of tens of staff (even if we can't actually *afford* them these days). Most importantly of all, I know to follow my husband's lead in all things. I know what happens if we don't both do what he wants.

I let him guide me down the rest of this slope and, on the next, teach me how to approach the moguls (though I long ago learned to turn on instinct—when the mogul "tells" you to—and not always between them, as he does, which inevitably leads to one getting further and further out of control).

We stop at a little refreshment kiosk halfway down: a sweet little structure shaped like a miniature chalet with deck chairs and wooden tables arranged in the snow outside. Several of the other Grand Alpine guests are there: I see the elderly ladies' companion, a couple of the nuns who seem to ski as well as anyone else here, and—I experience a sudden jolt of alarm—the young man with the glasses who bothered us yesterday, a red bobble hat covering his sandy hair. Oh no. I don't tell Anthony I've spotted him, lest he react badly. My husband is currently looking at a map of the area that he has unfolded on his lap, studying it hard, no doubt plotting the rest of our skiing itinerary. We order two hot chocolates.

"Hasn't been near any nuts, has it?" he asks the member of the hotel staff behind the counter. "And a tot of rum in it, please. Little wartime trick," he tells me. "Keeps the wolves from the door." He peers at me. "You still look half asleep! Did you take one of your little pills?"

I nod. I have many little pills that all do different things. A year ago, Anthony made an appointment for me with a very discreet Harley Street doctor. The one all of the society wives go to, apparently—though you would never know it. I was having some trouble coping, I suppose you might say. He gave me some pills for my low blood pressure (I get very dizzy if I stand up too fast). Also for sleeping, because I'm not very good at that. Then my pills for the morning—to counteract the drowsiness from the night pills—and some more pills for the afternoon to counterbalance the morning pills and calm me down. It felt lovely and easy for a while, like having a little nap in the passenger seat and letting someone else do the driving. There really isn't a condition my doctor won't prescribe for. Sometimes, when I've been a little bored, I've wondered about inventing some, just to see what he comes up with.

I take out the little silver box with the little "wake-me-uppers" in, pop one into my mouth and wash it down with a few sips of hot chocolate. I leave the rest to grow a rubbery skin.

We sit for a while looking at the view of the peaks opposite—still majestic but more forbidding, without the same covering of trees. I cast about for interesting titbits of conversation. I tell him all about the galleries I visited in London a couple of weeks ago. For a long time, I rather wanted to pursue painting myself—I know I have a good eye for color and form. But Mummy says proper women painters are all "sapphic hairy types who stink of turpentine" and I should confine myself to "the odd watercolor."

As I walked through the rooms of Impressionist landscapes, I made notes in my little Asprey notebook—I checked them this morning to remind myself. *Be culturally informed but never* intellectual, *sprinkle knowledge but never* flood.

"Christ," Anthony says, his gaze wandering over my shoulder. "Give me the Old Masters any day. Is that what you do after you go to the clinic, then? Moon about over some artists who didn't know how to hold a paintbrush properly?"

Even though he's wearing a pair of dark glasses for the snow glare I sense his eyes aren't on me. While he stubs out his cigarette, I look behind me and see a figure in a white mink jacket, cropped at the hip, and salopettes so outrageously tight one wonders at the engineering of the seams, particularly over the hips and seat. She must have been hidden from us before, reclined in one of the deck chairs. Her lips are painted the same ladybird red as the gondola making its ascent above the slopes. Her cotton candy platinum hair seems a little dirty against the pure white of her fur and the fresh snow. Her shapely bottom protrudes as she fastens her skis to her boots.

"Oh!" I say. "Darling: there's that woman again. The actress. Sylvia Sinclair."

"Oh," he says. "Is it?" Funny thing, he is barely glancing at her now, where before he was looking intently.

"What a very odd outfit," I say. "To wear for sport. Still"—I say this as she begins to move—"I suppose you could hardly call what she is doing *sport*." She is inching forward in a kind of crouch, knees together, her behind thrust out, arms crooked and back rounded. Hardly the glamorous silver screen siren the world knows. "You have to wonder," I say, "how she actually managed to get up here in the first place, if that's how she skis. It's so steep, above us and—"

"Can we stop talking about that bloody woman!" He cuts me off, his voice sharp. Then he seems to catch himself, softens and says,

"I don't want to blather on about some Hollywood floozy. It's a—a pleasure—to have this time alone together. I'm so glad we arranged this little holiday."

"Well, I think I rather invited myself," I say.

"Nonsense!" he says, with a chuckle. "I *insisted* you came!"

This isn't true and I have no doubt that he knows it, too. In fact, I recall that when I first suggested I accompany his skiing trip he seemed distinctly put out. But I suppose all married couples have these little pretenses, these little white lies they tell one another—and most of the time they signify nothing.

There is a sudden commotion a few yards away: a large cloud of powdered snow and a tirade of unsavory and very unladylike curses as Sylvia Sinclair clatters to the ground, skis crossed. Every skier at the kiosk is watching her—every skier except my husband.

"Oh darling, look, she's fallen over! Should we help her? We're the nearest . . ."

"No!" he exclaims, then clearly realizes he has been too abrupt. "She shouldn't be here in the first place if she can't ski."

"Darling," I say, putting a hand on his arm. "Not so loud! She'll be able to hear you."

"I don't care!" he almost shouts. "Perhaps it would be better if she did. Frankly it was utterly stupid of her to come. She is making an embarrassment of herself! She shouldn't be relying on others for help. It is entirely irresponsible." This time, it seems, he almost *wants* her to hear.

"Darling," I say. "You're . . . you're not being very kind." I for one can't just stand here and watch! I stumble over to her through the snow and offer a hand. She takes ahold of it.

I pull her to her feet with difficulty: she weighs a good deal more than me. As I do I catch a scent: bold, blowsy floral notes over-laced with a frankincense smokiness.

Funny thing. It isn't the first time I've smelled it.

"Thanks, sweetheart," she says. Her voice, breathy. The lazy

American drawl. I think of the voice on the end of the phone that day in my husband's London apartment. The breathy little-girlishness of it.

The London apartment: I never stayed there but the tedium and quiet of the countryside had got to me. I'd come up to do some shopping in the sales while Anthony was at Chequers with the PM and at the last minute I borrowed the keys from his desk drawer, in case I missed the last train home.

The phone had rung. I can't tell you what it was that made me answer it. I'd never pick up at home: it's always been the work of our housekeeper, Mrs. Grady . . . until a couple of weeks ago when we let her go. There is nothing more bourgeois than answering one's own phone.

The voice on the other end—breathy, a little girlish but at the same time all sex—asking if my husband was at home. "Is Tony in?" she asked. *I'm* not even allowed to call him Tony. And then, "Who's there?"

I drop her hand. Then I look over at my husband. He has begun putting his skis back on, facing in the opposite direction, as though nothing at all were happening just a few yards behind him. It would be far less telling for him to have turned and watched the interaction. After a moment, he actually pushes off and continues down the slope without me. He could give no clearer sign of a guilty conscience.

CATHERINE NARRACOTT

The Wife

We are skiing among the trees now. No time to think, only to react. I quite enjoy the slight danger of not always being sure one can stop in time, the whip of branches against one's face and shoulders when you get too close. Everything about my life has been so safe; I make sure to enjoy the thrills when they come my way.

Anthony gets a little way ahead, going so fast that I think he might fall. Then we come out of the trees and emerge onto a wide piste. I look up the slope before crossing it to make sure that I'm not on a collision path with another skier, when I see a familiar figure at the top. He's some hundred yards above us but the bright red bobble hat marks him unmistakably as the young man with the glasses.

When Anthony stops to catch his breath I pull up beside him, and say: "Darling, there he is again! That young man. Look—" I point. "He's skiing down toward us." He seems to be calling something to us, but the wind funneling down through the gaps between the fir trees snatches any sound away before it reaches us. I look over at Anthony. He, too, is watching the steadily approaching figure.

"Oh, for God's sake," he says. His tone is one of vague annoyance but this time I notice that he appears a little spooked.

I've never seen my husband quite like this, in fact. It's almost unnerving, to see the change in him, from the assurance of only a few moments ago. "Who is he?" I ask. "Do you know him?"

"It's nothing," he says, but his lips have gone taut and pale, like someone suffering from a chill. I can't stop looking at him. It's almost fascinating. "Cut it out." His voice is a whiplash. "Stop mooning at me. Come on," he mutters. "Let's go."

"But shouldn't—"

"Let's go," he barks, and before I have time to respond he has swung his skis around and plummeted down the slope, leaving me stationary, staring after him. I have no choice but to push off in pursuit.

After a few moments I glance behind me at the bobble-hatted figure and realize that he has definitely closed the gap between us. He seems to be skiing like a madman: almost without turning, plummeting down the slope. There's no question that he's in pursuit of us.

Should I stop, and ask him what it is he wants? No, I think that would be too foolish. We're all alone here out on the mountain. He could be a madman, for all we know. I am sure that he's trying to catch up with Anthony, not me. But all the same, he could conceivably have some sort of weapon . . . a knife. A gun? Anthony is always telling me how unworldly I am. How naive about what people are really like.

The sun has completely gone—when did it get so cloudy?—and the light is so flat and gray it's difficult to see the slope beneath my skis.

Anthony has already disappeared around the curve of the slope, into a thicker layer of cloud. Soon I too have descended into the cloud and all of a sudden I can't seem to get my bearings at all: it's even hard to tell whether I am really going down or simply sideways across the slope and it's making me feel a little queasy.

But I'm tougher than I might appear. Hunting on a seventeen-hand thoroughbred in the depths of winter will do that to a person. So I keep going, keep skiing, keeping pushing forward, downward, trying to turn only when I really have to, trying to keep up the speed as much as I can, until I see Anthony as a faint figure in the distance, crouched low. Suddenly, though, he disappears again. Where has he gone? I thought I saw him swerve to the left—but I can't be sure. The cloud swirls around me and a few fat flakes of snow have started to fall—my lenses blurring with them so that it's even more difficult to see. The shifting cloud seems to reveal something up ahead. There is something strange about the slope, a dark area far below that seems to appear and disappear, a striking contrast to all the white, and one that my eyes and mind can't quite make sense of. But inside of me, some clever knowing part I don't hear very often—a little voice saying: *watch out*. And then suddenly the light changes again; the cloud and snow clearing . . . and I realize that I am in very great danger. Only a little way ahead the slope falls away in a huge drop . . . and now I see the void that goes all the way to the valley below.

Worse: the thick powdery snow beneath my skis has begun to move. Shifting all as one, taking me with it as though I am standing on a raft being pulled along a river.

I throw all my strength into turning in a stem-christie, my legs burning; I even let out a little scream from the effort of it. And somehow, *somehow*, I manage to extricate myself from the moving snow, gathering pace now as it spills over the cliff in one huge mass. Legs trembling, I just manage to point my skis in the right direction and continue down the run which, I can finally see, curves around to the left.

I ski slowly, catching my breath, running through all that just happened. I nearly skied off a cliff. It was only ten yards ahead of me. If I had been slightly less observant, or the cloud slightly thicker . . . everything would have been wiped away just like that. I think of all the things I have ahead of me, the things I have planned for my life.

And where is Anthony? He had the map of the area: he carefully studied the terrain at our hot chocolate stop. He would have known about the drop, wouldn't he? Or . . .

No. There he is, a dark figure waiting expectantly a little way beneath me. And the young man? He had almost caught up with me last time I turned. I glance back up the slope, but the swirling cloud covers everything.

I manage to stop beside him. Now I realize how much my legs are trembling. "I—" I can't seem to catch my breath . . . I gulp at the freezing air. "The cliff . . . I nearly skied off it."

"I told you to turn," Anthony drawls. "Before we set off. And I was shouting to you, just now."

"I didn't hear you," I whisper. I didn't. I don't remember him telling me and I didn't hear any shouting. "Perhaps the wind . . ." I say, faintly. But there isn't much wind. The cloud, then? Can cloud muffle sound?

"I *shouted*," he says. I know that tone. It's an end to the conversation.

He peers beyond me. "No sign of our friend. Think we managed to lose him. Good. Just as I hoped. With a bit of luck, *he* won't be bothering us again."

"Anthony," I say. "Oh, how horrible . . . just think, what if he skied off the cliff? He might not have known to turn, either."

"Well darling, you know what they say? The only good Red is a dead Red."

"But Anthony," I say. "*I* could have died."

"Oh, don't be hysterical," he snaps.

We ski back to the hotel. It's not difficult to ski slowly now. It's actually difficult to stay upright, stay moving. My legs feel shaky. The truth is, I don't believe my husband shouted at all. What did he mean to happen?

SYLVIA SINCLAIR

The Star

I'm feeling blue. Sometimes I'm so high on life and yes, on the white stuff, that I want to take a big bite out of everything and everyone, to just . . . eat them all up. And then other times the little black moths come and you wouldn't believe how heavy such tiny things can be if they settle in their thousands. When that happens I can't move, or get out of bed, for days and days. And everything seems hopeless . . . me most of all. They've visited less, recently, since I met my lover. Less since I've had a plan. But this evening they've returned with a vengeance. Best thing to do when I'm feeling like this is to hide from them, to get into character, become someone else. Celluloid and stardust: my medicine.

I'll cover the bruises on my neck with some panstick and setting powder, though I'm half-tempted to leave them bare and make Tony sweat that I might expose him. I hate the idea of being pitied, though, that's the trouble. I douse myself in Shalimar. The white satin. Like a whore-bride. Yes, that's the one for tonight. It's too tight, I've put on weight lately: all this mountain cheese and meat aren't helping a broad but really, I'm lucky as it mainly all goes on the assets. I have to lie on the bed to do it up. The girls are hiked practically up to my chin and the skirt is so damn tight I can only take little mincing steps, but men like a bit of a totter, I've learned (or at least the fellas I've always gone in for).

A knock on the door.

"I shouldn't let you in," I tell him. "Not after last night." I point to my neck. "Come to admire your handiwork?"

"Sylvia, I'm so sorry." To his credit, he looks it. It's unusual for a man like Tony to be in this position. I quite enjoy the power of it for a few moments, making him grovel. It would be better if he were literally on his knees, but you can't have everything.

"I always choose the bad ones," I say. "I'll never learn. And they all say they're sorry, so sorry, like you, and I believe them, and fall for the same old schtick. Well, not this time, baby."

"Please, Sylvia," he sounds agonized. "Look I—I lost my head. But seeing you today on the mountain . . . and next to my wife—"

"Where *is* that little wife?"

"She's been in the hydro—the spa I think they call it here. Look. The problem is, up until now I've been trapped. It's all been her money. But from right now things are going to change. Once this comes off, I won't be tied to her any longer. I want *you*. Do you understand?"

"What happened to"—I put on a snooty English voice—"*the statesman and the showgirl?*"

He waves a hand. "Doesn't signify! We can leave all of that behind. Westminster, all of it. We can go to the Bahamas, to Rio, spend our life on a luxury cruise liner, whatever takes our fancy. We can join the café society, the idle rich. You can stop prostituting yourself out to Hollywood, because let's face it, it hasn't been very kind to you of late."

"And how are we supposed to do all this?"

"It's as I told you before. I'm about to come into an inheritance, of sorts."

"When?"

"Very, *very* soon. I just need you to behave for me." He presses a forefinger to my nose. "Good things come to good little girls who wait."

"Baby, I'll be good as gold," I say.

"What?" He looks thrown for a moment, then he recovers. "Oh. Glad to hear it."

I pout at him. "Shall I tell you what color *culottes* I'm going to wear down to dinner this evening, beneath my dress? I want to make sure you can't think about anything else."

A sleepy, stupefied look in his eyes. Yes, I've still got it.

I let the question hang in the air.

"Tell me," he says, after a long moment has passed. Begs.

"Nothing!" I say. "Absolutely nothing. It ruins the line of the dress. And this particular dress"—little shimmy—"is very, very snug."

He throws his head back and groans. "I can't wait to have you all to myself, all the time."

"You promise, baby? You're not just telling me a pretty story? You really mean all of that?"

"I mean it, my sweet."

A moment later the door closes behind him with a click.

It's all going to be smooth sailing from now on. It's like something from a film. One of the ones I'd have been cast in a decade (and a half . . .) ago, all big-eyed ingenue who gets her happy ever after. It's all going to be OK. Because my love is here and finally, against all the odds, in spite of all the obstacles standing in our way (marriage vows and money, mainly) we're going to be together.

As a just-before-curtain-call wardrobe adjustment, I make a tiny rip in one of the shoulder straps where it attaches to the bodice, leaving only a few flimsy threads to hold it. That thin strip of fabric will be no match for my proportions. When it's going to go, only the Lord knows, but go it will. I've always known how to make an entrance.

DIANA GLASS

The Help

"Aren't those hideous?" Mrs. Bantry says, pointing at the wall. "All this elegance," she indicates the surroundings of the hotel's great hall, where we are having a drink before dinner—the oils of mountain scenes on the silk-covered walls, the thick carpets upon the floors, the low, inlaid mahogany tables between the elegantly upholstered chairs—"and then they choose to put those up!"

I look and see what she means. Just above us leer several hideous faces: yellowish teeth bared, eyeballs bulging, horribly realistic hair sprouting wild and matted from scalp and ears. The features are grossly exaggerated and distorted and yet at the same time slightly too lifelike; the skin has a convincing texture to it, the irises seem to follow one's movements.

"Can those be . . . real teeth?" Mrs. Bantry asks.

"Yes, Madame," says a waiter, appearing as if from nowhere. And then after very slightly too long a pause: "*Animal* teeth, Madame. Bovine, you know. Or sheep, depending upon . . . availability. The hair is real too." He grins. "Horse."

"Gracious," Mrs. Bantry says, apparently making a heroic effort not to look too repulsed. "But what *are* they?"

"Trolls, Madame," he says, proudly. "Mountain trolls. We like our trolls in Switzerland."

"Do you . . . really?" Mrs. Bantry says, a little faintly. But soon her attention is caught by the Narracotts passing through the hall on their way to dinner.

"She reminds me a little of Gertrude Dunlop from St. Mary Mead," Miss Marple says.

"Oh," Mrs. Bantry gives her a *look*. "Do you mean the one that ran away with that trampolinist at sixteen?"

"Yes," Miss Marple says, and then, "she was rather babied by her parents, do you remember? They couldn't really accept her dressing up. Seemed to keep her in almost little girls' clothes, didn't allow her to go to any of the local dances. That repression, you know . . ."

"But Catherine Narracott's a grown woman," Mrs. Bantry says. "She's a wife."

"But doesn't she give you the impression of a little girl? It isn't really about one's station in life. It's a state of mind. She seems to me like a pink and white girl who has seen very little of the world. And I am sure he has been happy to keep her that way. I'm sure it suits a man like that." This last said rather darkly.

"Jane!" Mrs. Bantry says. "Here was I, thinking only what a handsome couple they made. And all the while you . . . well, you never cease to surprise me."

"Look, and they don't talk to each other." She's right, they pass the length of the hall in complete silence. "They sit there at mealtimes hardly saying a word to one another. I eat most of my meals alone, of course, but that seems to me to be true loneliness."

"Oh, but Jane, plenty of very content marriages are like that. Arthur hated talking, particularly at mealtimes. Said it gave him indigestion. And really, we were very happy in our way." Mrs. Bantry's eyes, for a moment, seem to grow a little filmy.

"Of course, my dear," Miss Marple says. Very briefly, her small frail hand touches Mrs. Bantry's across the tabletop.

"Do you have . . . anyone, Diana?" Mrs. Bantry asks, turning to me.

"I don't," I say. "I—was engaged once. But it . . . didn't last."

I have forgotten the smell of his skin. For a long time I could still summon it to me. It smelled like a life lived outdoors, like the scent of the rain-soaked ground after a drought. I can no longer conjure it on demand, as I once could. So too, I have lost the precise feel of his fingertips on me, the husk of them, fingers that had done battle with earth and stone. I have not had anyone since; probably I never will. I am alone and that is less lonely, somehow, than any alternative to him.

I take a sip of my wine.

The light in the room shifts suddenly, bathing us all in a roseate glow. It has begun to snow lightly, I see. And a strange optical illusion has occurred: the peaks of the mountains have turned deepest crimson. On longer inspection it's a trick of the light: the snow and the very rock itself have been stained red by the setting sun.

"I think it's called Alpenglow," I say.

Mrs. Bantry shivers. "It seems a little eerie—even portentous. Like a blood moon. Don't you think, Jane?"

"I'm not sure," Miss Marple says. "I find the actions of human beings are usually far more predictive of coming danger than any natural phenomenon."

CATHERINE NARRACOTT

The Wife

"How was the spa?" my husband asks across the dining table. As he reaches for the salt I catch a scent. He has worn the same cologne for as long as I have known him: D.R. Harris's Marlborough. But this is more feminine. It's completely feminine, in fact: bold, blowsy floral notes over-laced with a frankincense smokiness.

I take a deep breath. I tell him about the spa: the hammam and the Finnish sauna, the solarium with its charming view of the glacier. I am surprised at how calm I sound.

And all the while my hand grips the thing I brought down from our room so tightly my palm stings.

I can tell that he is not listening to a word I say. He isn't even trying to pretend any longer; he's gazing over my shoulder. And she is there, I know. Just a few tables away. I saw her come in, with that huge shaggy beast trailing behind. As the saying goes: it takes a lot of money to look that cheap. I understand exactly what he sees in her, of course I do. She is everything that I am not. The platinum blonde of her hair with its nacreous sheen, the chignon like a silkworm's cocoon. The extravagance of her silhouette; I learned that she buys her dresses two sizes too small on purpose. I can smell her scent; that funeral wreath floral miasma that lingers in the corridors and stairwells of this hotel like an unquiet ghost.

In the past I have always looked the other way. Played the good little wife. But this time . . . this time it's different. I am trembling, my hand in a tight fist, remembering that breathy voice on the end of the telephone in his apartment. I was so tempted to put the phone down. Turn a blind eye. But I didn't. I had to know more.

"Is Tony in?" she had asked.

"No," I said, tightly. Still resisting the urge simply to slam the receiver down. Then I took a deep breath and said, bright and glib as a secretary about to leave for the five o'clock train, "I'm . . . his secretary. Can I take a message?" I *knew* that if I'd said who I really was the line would go dead. And I wanted to hear more. Even though I was also very frightened. I think I must have gone a little mad. It was like that urge you get as a child to pick the scab, though you know it will bleed.

"Ah," she whispered. "No, that's OK, honey. Shame." But she was shame*less*. And yet there was a real sadness in her voice. Not just the disappointment of finding him gone. No, this was something that came from within the stranger on the other end of the line. I could tell. As dark and deep as the voice was high and airy. "Oh no," she said. "Wait. Say that . . . yes—could you write down that New York was fun? And that he should check the new shows in London's West End for the spring. No . . . he'll be too busy. Tell him: *The Cherry Orchard*."

"Of course," I said, clenching the pen so hard that it was really a wonder the bones in my fingers didn't snap.

"Can I ask who is calling? And may I take a number?" I said. "So that I may ask him to return your call?" I noted down the number on the pad beside the phone.

"Tell him it's . . . tell him it's 'Sylvia Baby.' And he can reach me at the Dorchester."

Afterward my palm ached; I had been holding the receiver

so tightly that it had bitten into my hand. I'd had my suspicions. But—oh, I only really learned this then—there is such a leap between wondering and *knowing*. Perhaps I was naive. How many women, married to powerful men, find themselves in such situations? And yet it made a mockery of my life, of everything I had tried to be.

I look at him now, chewing a morsel of his goulash, the beautiful line of his jaw only just beginning to soften in middle age.

I have been so good, up until now, at hiding the unacceptable parts of myself. A splitting into three selves. Public. Private. Secret.

As if on cue he looks back at me.

"Darling," he says. "You're wearing the most alarming expression!"

This is the moment. My hand trembling violently, I produce the diamond drop earring: an exact match for the ones she was wearing while skiing earlier.

"I found this," I say. "In our bed."

My voice is a little too loud. People at the neighboring table turn to look at us. Oh, but I'm not going to stop now. I am just beginning. I throw the earring onto the table; it bounces onto the floor so he is forced to bend down and scrabble to pick it up. More diners are staring now and like ripples spreading outward in a pool the tables beyond them turn to look too, and on and on until I can feel the whole room's rapt attention upon us. Usually, I hate making a scene. I never make a scene; this is all very new and exposing for me. But this time, I *want* everyone to see.

He tries to bluster his way out of it. "That's . . . that's yours, isn't it?"

I give a hard shout of a laugh. He *must* know I only wear clip-ons; pierced ears are frightfully vulgar.

Clearly realizing that isn't going to work, he says: "I have absolutely no idea how that got there. It's—it's not possible." He seems genuinely astounded. He gives such a good impression of total innocence.

"Really?" I ask, all scorn. And then, my voice laced with disdain: "It's *hers.*" I jerk my head toward the actress's table. "I can *smell* her perfume on you."

"Darling," he hisses. "Please. Not here. Let's go to our room. There will be a perfectly reasonable explanation for this . . . I can give it to you, if only you let me." His politician's voice, smooth, easy charm.

"There can be no other explanation," I say. I turn and gesture toward the actress's table. "She was in our room. That American . . . whore." I hear him catch his breath. I have never spoken like this before either. He probably did not even know that I had it in me. So *indecorous*, for a politician's wife, the wife of Anthony Narracott, to be speaking like this. But I am beyond decorum. This must all be said now. "She was wearing these at breakfast. Then one materializes in our bed, no less: I found it when I came back from the spa. Where were you?"

"But this is ridiculous," he says. "It—I wasn't even in our room . . . I was out."

"And where *were* you?" I ask.

My husband, always so self-possessed, reddens.

"I can turn a blind eye," I say. "I *have* turned a blind eye. All I ask in return is a little discretion. But you have humiliated me. Now it's your turn."

"Darling," he says, his smile firmly in place though only I can see that his teeth are clenched behind it. "Darling, you are humiliating *yourself.* What do you *want*?"

"You must tell her to leave," I say. "I can't bear it . . . her sitting over there, flaunting herself like that. It's so unseemly."

"Baby," a voice drawls. I turn to look. That beautiful, pitiless face. The red-lacquered lips hitched to one side in the characteristic natural sneer, which takes her from merely pretty to something more complicated: darker and yet more compelling for it. She caresses the dog's head in her lap as she speaks to me. "You're making a spectacle of yourself. Don't take it so hard. All's fair in—what is it?—love'n'war, and all that. And nobody can tell me to leave. I'm a paying guest here, just like you. Or perhaps I should say: your husband."

I stand now, on shaky legs. Then I march over to her table. I am vibrating with nervous tension, as though my whole body is in revolt against my own actions. I am so overwrought, so beyond any of my usual codes of behavior that I hardly know what I am going to do, just that I have to do *something*. In a sudden moment of wild inspiration, I pick up the martini glass in front of her and I sling an arc of viscous liquid into her face, the wafer twist of lemon peel landing in the middle of that generous décolletage like a strange ornament.

She gasps and blinks up at me through wet eyelashes, the dark makeup already beginning to run. "How dare—"

There are exclamations all around us. And part of me—the finishing school pupil, the good girl, the good wife—is mortified. But another part of me—the part that has always been there, only suppressed, the part that has wanted for so long to find her voice, to make a scene, an ugly, shameful scene—is rejoicing.

And then my hands are seized from behind, wrists hitched together, the delicate bones bruising. The martini glass falls from my hand . . . there is the sound of glass shattering. I stop breathing, stuck with pain; like a fox with its paw caught in a snare.

"That is *enough*," he mutters in my ear, his voice quietly violent. "You are to stop, now."

He has never spoken to me like this in public before . . . but he has never needed to, because I have always been perfect. It does what he intends. It stops me in my tracks. I step away from the actress's table; feeling the eyes of the room on me.

"Go," he says. "Go and sort yourself out. Now. You have done *enough*."

SYLVIA SINCLAIR

The Star

I step into the bathroom, to clean myself up. That, out there, that wasn't the good kind of attention. It's the other side of the coin. People looking for all the wrong reasons. I could hear their thoughts as if they'd spoken them aloud. *Whore.* See, I always think my skin's grown as thick as the crocodile handbag I'm taking my compact out of. But it hasn't. My old friend is still there under everything: the *shame.* I look in the mirror. Lancôme's best is sooty beneath my eyes and there are streaks in my powder. My eyes are stinging. Normally when I'm hurting from martinis like this I've had a little grace to enjoy it and it's at least the morning after. I pick up one of the towels to undo the damage.

And then the stall to the toilet opens and she steps out. "The little wife," Catherine. I can tell she's been crying, but on her there's no makeup to streak and it only looks picturesque, in the way that young women look picturesque when they cry. She's not even that much younger than me! But a decade—and the rest—is a hell of a lot for a broad. And we're two different types, too, the two types of woman you're allowed to be: whore and virgin. I know this because a director once told me. Can't have you and Lizzy in the same picture, he said. It'd turn the whole thing into a goddamn bordello. Need a Grace Kelly opposite either of you to cool it all down.

I gaze into the mirror. The contrast between us, side by side at the sinks like this, really doesn't favor me. The lighting in here isn't kind. I'm seeing shadows in all the wrong places (did you know Blanche DuBois was only thirty? Thirty!). Anyway, it does all the right things for *her.* Bounces off that perfect skin, those high cheekbones, that little upturned nose. She reaches for the tissues to dab her eyes.

"Hello," I say.

Her eyes meet mine, and widen in shock.

"Nice show in there, sweetheart," I say. I just can't help myself. I lift up my hands and do a little miniature round of mock applause. She opens her mouth but no sound comes out, as though she's too outraged to even find the words.

Somewhere behind us, a flush from the stall.

Then: "Don't you dare speak to me," she manages to hiss, whirling on her heel. "I'd do all of that—what did you call it, *show*?—again . . . and more. You should be watching your step, *sweetheart.* Because you won't get him, I tell you. I'm a lot stronger than I look. He's mine, for always." And then, like the icing on the cake: "*Whore.*"

"Oh baby," I say, with a smile, as a mousy English woman (maybe around my age but frankly who can tell she's made so little effort) steps out of the stall, careful not to make eye contact with either of us. "You can cry all you like, but he's already mine."

She slams out of the bathroom, the door swinging behind her.

BRUNO CRANE

The Friend

It's so much colder out here on the ice in the dead of night. The snow is hardening in the freezing air, a lethal slick beneath our boots on the well-trodden pathways near the hotel.

"Heard about the little scene in the restaurant earlier," I say. "They're not going to make a complication here, are they? Your two women?"

"Oh, for God's sake, Crane. You look after your house; I'll look after mine. But no. I put Catherine to bed like a good girl, made sure she took a nice dose of Veronal . . . it's just her nerves getting to her. She apologized to me, in the end. But you see, don't you, old man? One can't dine on cucumber sandwiches forever. Actually, maybe you *don't* see. I'll clarify: No *full-blooded* male can. Every so often, one needs some red meat. All women are a Catherine or a Sylvia in some formulation. A Virgin Mary or a Mary Magdalene. And it's just a damned shame you can't get both together. It would be so much less work if one didn't have to roam beyond one's hearthstone. It's just bloody inconvenient, when it comes down to it."

We continue to tramp away from the lights of the Grand Alpine, using just the blue glow of the full moon as Narracott doesn't want to use torches in view of the hotel. We have reached the glacier now. I hate the idea of crossing it in the dark, the hidden dangers of the ice. I thump my gloved hands together to stop them going numb.

My teeth are starting to chatter. So cold that my head feels like it's in a vise, as though my toenails have been ripped off. They tortured people like that, in the war.

"So how exactly are we going to get the stuff out of here?" I ask. It's something I have been mulling over, alone in my room. "Can't imagine it's going to be easy with your wife here. Especially not now."

"Ah, ye of little faith! I've got someone here. Going to do the whole transaction in situ. Much cleaner that way, don't you think?"

"There's someone at the hotel?"

"Yes."

"Who?"

"Oh, never you mind, old chap. Think it's safer for you if you don't have that information. Don't you worry your ugly little head with such matters. My contact would prefer that the fewer people know about their identity the better." He taps his nose. "Let me take care of that side of things. Less risky to you that way."

Is it? As far as I can tell I'm taking a pretty enormous risk as it is, with all of this. I don't like this secrecy. I'm not sure it benefits me; Narracott has all of the information and I have only a rough sketch. The suspicion I have had about this whole endeavor grows.

Is this how he edges me out? His banker, whoever the fellow is, cuts him a check? It might not even be a fellow. It could be anyone at this whole bloody hotel, other than perhaps the old dear who seems always to be knitting. It could even be her! Now I come to think about it, she *looks* as though she has a secret.

I don't voice any of this. Instead, I ask: "Presumably they take a cut, too?"

"Fifty percent for me," he throws back, "thirty-five for you and fifteen for our banker's commission."

I stare at his back. "I don't get half? But I never agreed to that! Why should you get the lion's share?"

"It was my inspiration. My plan."

But I risked just as much that night.

And a little voice inside me whispers: *100 percent sounds a damn sight better than 35. That would sort out my troubles once and for all . . .*

He swings round to face me and I feel caught out, as if he might be able to read my train of thought. "Penny for them?" he asks, peering at me through the gloom.

"Nothing," I say, but my mind is racing. If he's just sprung this on me, what other tricks might he have up his sleeve? I need to keep my wits about me. Perhaps think up a few tricks of my own.

"Come on, you old sack of potatoes." He sounds jovial enough but there's an edge. In the light of the full moon the white flank of the mountain glows like radium. We need the moonlight, but we don't want to be spotted out here if we can help it. I have the sudden idea that we must look rather like two small boys, sneaking out for some larks in the snow. But there's something perverse about all of this. Narracott has a pistol in his jacket, too. I can see the shape of it in his pocket, the gleam of metal when he turns.

There is an unearthly groan from somewhere high above us; the sound of ice calving. I try to gulp down my fear of the glacier. I don't remember the ice being so *loud*. It creaks and moans and growls like some ancient monster. The darkness only seems to amplify the noises. This part of it is meant to be riven with crevasses. There could be one mere inches away. I could be standing on a snow bridge right now, moments from the ground giving way beneath my feet.

Would Narracott send for help, if I fell? How would he explain what we were both doing out here in the small hours? Best not to think about it. Best not to think too hard about anything. Focus on putting one foot in front of the other. It's hard going. The snow holds beneath the foot in places but gives out in others; I sink to mid-thigh every other step.

Then I hear something that makes my bladder clench with terror. A high, keening cry, which seems to ricochet among the surrounding peaks, the walls of ice and rock ringing like tuning forks.

"Did you hear that?" I ask Narracott.

"What?" He glances over his shoulder and his breath, white vapor in the night air, comes in fast pants. There's a loud creaking sound from somewhere up the glacier. "That's the ice," he says. At this moment, as if on cue, there is a hideous cracking, like the sound of a giant's bones splitting.

"No, I heard—" But what *did* I hear? It's hard to be sure. Maybe it was the ice? But it seemed a different quality of sound . . .

Now Narracott shines his flashlight up toward the rock wall of the glacier, the lowest flank of the mountain that rises above it. "There it is," he says, and now I can see it: the small cabin built onto a shelf in the rock there. The refuge. The ice has sunk back over the years: it's higher above the glacier than last time I saw it.

We bought the mountain hut in 1943, from a local climbing guide, with our watches, two packs of cigarettes and one of our pistols (mine). He probably thought he'd swindled us, because no one was climbing these routes and the hut was falling into disrepair. That suited us just fine. Better than fine. As Narracott said, we didn't need anyone nosing their way in there.

We begin the short scramble up the rock. That sound—again. A high whine, or howl. "There! Did you hear?"

"For God's sake," he says, crossly. "That was definitely just the wind."

He opens the door to the hut. There is a sudden, brief bright light . . . from somewhere behind us, I think.

"Did you see that?" I ask him.

"What now, Crane?" He comes to the doorway.

"A strange . . . flash."

"A strange flash," he repeats, mockingly. "Sure you aren't getting cold feet, old man?"

"No—I really saw something." Now I voice the thought that came to me the first time I heard that strange howl. "You don't think . . . you don't think there could be one of them *here*, somehow?"

"Spooking at ghosts now, Crane? They're all dead. We made sure of that. *You* made sure of that." He says all of this as though daring me to challenge him. "No. There are small electrical storms up here all the time. Even in the summer. You must remember that! Now for God's sake get in here and help me. It's not going to be easy. Earth stood hard as iron and all that."

I follow him into the musty darkness. The smell; hadn't even realized there *was* a smell, but it clutches me by the throat and drags me back through the years. We lived here for several weeks, after all, before we "escaped from the prisoner of war camp" and rejoined our men. I feel as though I might vomit.

"Steady on, old chap," he says, catching me by the upper arm as I pitch forward. And then, almost kindly, "This, now: this is the easy part. This is you taking what is yours."

For one insane moment I'm struck by the fear—or is it almost a kind of hope?—that it might have gone. That someone might have watched us, or found it by accident. It would be a great blow in one respect, but at the same time it would mean I could continue to believe that all of it only really happened in the realm of nightmares.

"Naughty, naughty," he toes the ground, showing a patch where the floorboards have been lifted up. "Look here. Someone had a go. Lucky we took precautions."

He takes a hammer from his pack and uses the claw to pry out several nails from the boards in the floor. "Come on, help me."

Once we have the boards loose the rock itself is exposed beneath. Or what appears at first to be the rock but is actually an amateurishly made floor put together from loose fragments of rock and stuck fast with homemade cement.

"Here." He thrusts cold metal into my hand; a pickaxe. "Come on, man. Do get on with it. Now is not the time to grow a conscience, Crane." And then: "Most of them would be dead by now anyway," he says, casually. "You know that."

"No, I don't. And neither do you."

And then, like a fox that can't resist toying with its prey: "What was it? Bullet through the back of the head? One of the most cold-blooded things I've ever seen."

I'm as shocked as if he'd just shot *me*. "That wasn't me," I say. "That was you."

He scoffs. "I saw you do it, you idiot. You can't go playing the innocent now. Remember being pretty shocked at the time."

My heart starts racing, my head swims; I lurch against the wooden wall for balance. I squeeze my eyes shut, try to remember. Oh God, but I don't want to. But it *was* him, wasn't it? I'm sure it was. But now I'm not absolutely certain. That night is all darkness, a kind of murky, bloody horror. I've spent the last five years purposefully not thinking about it, not remembering. Was my part in it even worse than I thought?

Everything since that night has felt more like a waking dream than real life. It was his idea. Does that make it better? No, I think the opposite. Because I was still there, I still did it. At least I suppose one could find a perverse kind of audacity—perhaps not courage—in his role in it all. My part, meanwhile: that was all cowardice.

Narracott's voice snaps me back to the present: "What's it going to be, Crane? If you're too lily-livered I'll happily bid you adieu here and take your share."

"No—"

"Then can we please carry on with the task in hand? It's too bloody cold to stand around waiting for you to have your next crisis." And then, his tone turning hard again. "Get on with it, or get out."

My eyes go to the shape of the pistol in his jacket. It has just occurred to me that he wouldn't merely let me leave. Of course he wouldn't. I don't have any choice.

I grip the pickaxe and he hefts his and together we begin to work on the floor. Finally, something begins to appear . . . a piece of hessian sacking. The sight sets my skin seething. Horror and excitement fight for dominance.

This is why he needed me. The job would be too physically exhausting for one man. It seems to take forever. Soon enough, every swing of the pickaxe sends pain juddering up my arms. And every so often I am sure that I hear something out there.

Les loups des montagnes . . .

I remind myself that there are no wolves in these mountains any more. They're all dead.

I put all of my concentration into the task at hand. And finally, it's all exposed: the unprepossessing hessian sack, the sort of thing you might store grain in. We found it in an abandoned shepherd's hut, chose it because it was so unlikely looking. The fiber worn and stiff, falling away to reveal a metal chest. Narracott opens this and now we can see the gleam inside—the rich yellow light bright even in the darkness, *especially* in the darkness. Something miraculous about it. Something magical and ancient, this treasure from underground. I understand it, how it has driven men to madness and death and violence.

I lift the first bar from the chest. So cold, so dense. The weight of it is unexpected, quite incredible. I am very aware of Narracott standing just behind me. If it came down to it . . . I'm taller, but he's in better physical condition. But I have less to lose.

A voice speaks inside me: *I want it. I want it all*. The pass over the mountain is too deadly in winter. At this time of year it must be a deathly wasteland of snow and ice. No, it wouldn't work, not for one with my lack of skiing ability. But perhaps there's another way . . . a way that wouldn't have him hot on my tail . . .

"What are we going to do with it?" I ask. "Take it back down with us?"

"Are you mad? No. The best thing is for it to remain here, not in a hotel full of people with few secure hiding places."

"Then . . . why are we here?"

"We had to make sure it was in situ. Before we make the exchange."

"But when—"

"We're going to meet in the morning. I'll let you know the next steps." Has he somehow guessed at my innermost thoughts?

"But . . ."

"Trust me, Crane."

I almost laugh out loud. Of course I can't trust him. I know this better than anyone. Anyone alive, that is.

Sometimes I have thought it's odd he didn't kill me there and then, and take it all for himself. But he needed someone else to back up his story, when we got back to our own troops. And he needed someone else—a mule—to help him with this part. But now . . . now I'm a liability, aren't I? He has to split the pot with me.

Perhaps more importantly, I am the only other who remembers that night. And I've seen him kill in cold blood before . . .

CATHERINE NARRACOTT

The Wife

It must be morning. White light lances in through the gap in the curtains. The sound of church bells—there's a small chapel for the nuns up here, I heard. Perhaps I'm letting my imagination run away with me but it seems there's something foreboding in the sound. *For whom the bell tolls* . . . was that John Donne? I was always rather good on the poets at school. I used to daydream about studying them at university . . . becoming a real bluestocking. Smoking while riding a bicycle. Taking lovers. Rather thrilling at the thought of how angry it would make my parents. I was in love, once, but it was a completely unsuitable match. A gardener, for one thing. In fact, it nearly caused a minor scandal . . . and was the reason Mummy and Daddy thought it would be good to get me as Finished as possible—and married off soon after that.

I turn over and stare up at the ceiling. It really is rather oppressive, all this wood. It feels as though it's bearing down on one. Anthony snores beside me; he snores often, in fact (I would never tell him because he would *detest* knowing it).

A few moments later he stirs. I close my eyes and pretend to be asleep. I can't quite face talking to him yet. He leaps out of bed with one athletic bound, not a stitch of clothing on his body, and prowls across the room. He isn't limping. The limp only really appears in public; especially when, as yesterday, he is speaking to the public. When he wants to remind them of the war hero, given the Victoria Cross for courage under fire. One of the only survivors in a skirmish between a small band of brave British fighters and the Nazis, just over the mountains from here, in occupied France. Funny thing, I've noticed that the story changes a little every time he tells it.

I watch him secretly, through nearly closed eyes, as he crosses to the mirror and smiles at himself. It's a closemouthed smile, the sort you might give someone if you politely disagreed with what they said. Then wider, revealing a few more teeth, and then, biggest of all, the smile he gave the elderly ladies at the Reception. He is practicing these expressions . . . like a dancer practicing positions, an actor, practicing a part. I close my eyes again. I don't want him to catch me watching him. *There are times as a wife*, Mummy used to say, *where one must be extremely attentive to one's husband. And there are other times in which it is really far wiser to look the other way. Becoming the best sort of wife is about knowing when to do which.*

After a few minutes I let out a little sigh and stretch, so he knows I'm awake.

"Good morning, darling," he says. He is being solicitous. "Oh, look at you, sleepyhead! You took one of your pills? You're dead to the world with them. I find it rather alarming at times. When I came back last night—"

"Oh," I say, rubbing my eyes and sitting up against the pillows. "Were you late?"

"Not very. Just a nightcap in the bar afterward, with Bruno."

"I'm sorry about yesterday evening," I say. "The scene . . . in the restaurant. I'm terribly ashamed. I think I had too much wine, and with my pills—"

"We won't talk of it again," he says, a little sharply. "We will pay that . . . that *person* no attention, because that is what she wants. I cannot understand what she is doing here. I think it must be because she wants to make trouble for me. It's what she does. Beneath the veneer of the actress is a . . . a vamp, a seductress." And then, with a great effort he says, in his politician's voice: "I apologize, for any . . . indiscretion on my part."

Then after a pause he stretches: all is forgotten. "Ready for a beautiful day on the mountain?"

"Oh," I say. "But the wind's terrible this morning. Besides, I heard there's snow coming in a couple of hours and I hate skiing in a whiteout. I'm going to the spa."

"Well yes," he says. "You're a perfect bluebird skier, darling, but a whiteout does rather sort the experts from the amateurs."

He proceeds to do his warm-up exercises. Any other human would look a complete fool wearing nothing and throwing themselves into all sorts of strange shapes, but he looks more like an Ancient Greek athlete limbering himself up for the Games. Afterward he dresses in his skiwear and throws open the curtains with a grand flourish. "Time to greet the morning—"

But the last word seems to die on his lips. He *freezes*: it is as though I can see the chill passing over his flesh as he takes in something outside the window.

"What is it, darling?" I ask.

"Nothing," he says, quickly. A little too quickly?

I pull my robe about me and move to stand at the window. Now I can see it too: a flag has been run up the flagpole, which usually flies the Swiss flag. Black, with a central white triangle, the symbol of a howling wolf inside the triangle and letters apparently stitched onto it beneath the symbol, reading:

Les loups des montagnes

It looks like an antique, too: torn and frayed in places, the loose ragged pieces dancing in the wind.

I say the words aloud and I'm sure I see my husband flinch. I am almost fascinated by the effect these words have upon him, the power I feel over him, speaking them. It's so unfamiliar. I say it again in

English: "The wolves of the mountain."

"I know what it says," he says in a hiss, rounding on me. This time the change in him is unmistakable: the dread in his expression.

"Sorry, darling," I say. "Are . . . are you all right?"

"Of course I'm all right!"

"But what a strange thing," I say. "I wonder what it means?"

"It doesn't mean anything!" he cries. "It's some damn fool practical joke." These are almost the same words he used when that jar of rat poison appeared in our room. Then, with a furious yanking motion he draws the curtains closed again and stalks into the bathroom, as though completely unaware of the fact that his action has just given the lie to his words. Why would my husband feel the need to obscure that stunning morning view of the mountains, plunging the room into darkness again, if it weren't for the fact that something in that view had seriously disturbed him?

BRUNO CRANE

The Friend

I'm woken from bad dreams by the hammering on my door.

"You were right," Narracott says, as he pushes his way into the room. He's dressed for a day on the mountain, coffee flask in one hand, skiing gloves in the other.

"What?" I'd been readying myself for some sort of confrontation. Now I'm wrong-footed.

"You were right. I think there is one of them here. I didn't think it possible. I thought you were being paranoid."

He sets down his gloves and coffee cup, stalks to the windows and throws open the curtains. I see the flag straightaway. A rush of blood to the head. But also a kind of triumph. Believe me now?

"What do we do?" I say, urgently. "Have they come for the gold? Do we leave it where it is? Have they come for *us*?"

"Calm yourself," he says, seeming to gain composure with my apparent lack of it. "Just leave the next steps to me. We'll simply do the transaction more rapidly. My banker is ready to do the exchange."

My banker. "Is that where you're going now? To meet him?" I watch him, thinking: *he's going to try and cut me out. I knew it.* And again, that little voice: *100 percent is a damn sight better than 35.*

"I'm going skiing," he says. But he doesn't say he *isn't* seeing this mysterious banker, I notice. "Best cure for a late night and a troubled mind that I know. I've gone out every morning at nine o'clock so far, and it's best I stick to it."

"But . . . but what should we do with the gold?" I cry. "Surely we should move it?"

"Shh! Keep it down, old man. Business as usual—that's the thing! Act as normal as possible. So, I suppose for you that means drinking yourself half to death or moping around here in your own squalor." He can't resist any opportunity to twist the knife, can he? "Let's not lose our heads and do anything rash. Especially not if they're watching. Keep calm and carry on." He checks his watch. "Now, can't keep those mountains waiting." He walks back toward me and picks up his flask. "I have a pressing appointment with the piste. Later we will reconvene. But in the meantime: be on your guard. Do you understand? And leave the rest to me."

DIANA GLASS

The Help

I hurry into the hotel, stamping the snow off my boots and brushing flakes from my jacket; it's snowing in earnest now. I've been on an early morning walk with my camera among the pines as I'm not needed until breakfast. I check my watch. Nine o'clock; Mrs. Bantry will be back from the spa soon.

"Attention!" Just inside the doors a member of staff is removing something unmentionable from the Persian rug near the entrance. I had nearly stepped right in it.

"Oh!" I make a face.

"The actress's enormous dog," he mutters, apparently too irritated to be discreet, "on her way out it stop"—he makes a face of utmost disgust and gestures at the stain—"and she just carry on her way. *Bof*, like that!" He gestures out through the doors.

I wonder what it must be like in such a bubble of Hollywood stardom that you don't even stop when your dog defecates on a rug—ruffling the feathers of the supremely unflappable staff here.

A loud voice seems to carry over the general hubbub. "But what I am asking you is *can* one shoot the chamois?" the old colonel says, leaning against the counter and over the poor receptionist, speaking very slowly and loudly. "You've got their heads mounted on every which wall. Need a license, what! I tell you I have a license. A *Swiss* license? The bureaucracy these days!"

I sidestep a maid carrying a load of laundry so huge it obscures most of her face, a nun, three bellhops, and a group of guests who seem to be deliberating about whether to go out. "Visibility will be next to nothing," one of the men says, worriedly. "I just think we'd be better having a day in the library playing Whist."

"Perhaps you're right, dear," says his wife. "We have the rest of the week, don't we?"

The nearest elevator doors open and I hear: "I said no! *Not* now." It is Anthony Narracott, dressed in his skiwear and followed out of the elevator by the unkempt sandy-haired young man with glasses. All his usual suavity of manner is absent. He looks truly furious as he marches in this direction. I'm standing right in his path; don't even have time to step aside, so suddenly we are face-to-face.

I watch as he seems to recollect himself; it is like watching a mask slip back in place. "Oh, hello," he says, charm fully restored. "The photographess. We meet again. What did you say your name was?"

I didn't. "Diana, Diana Glass."

"Diana. The *huntress.*" He sizes me up, and I feel suddenly as though I might as well be standing here in a bathing suit rather than several layers of cotton and wool. "Yes, I see it. *Do* you hunt?" He turns and hands his coffee flask to the receptionist. "This to be filled up, please. I hope it's freshly brewed today because yesterday," he pulls a sorrowful face, "it was a little stale, I'm afraid." He gives her his most dazzling smile. Then he turns back to me and studies me more closely. I am pinned by that cool blue gaze. I have the sense he is formulating a question.

"I should be going to my employer now," I say. "She wants to take her breakfast at nine o'clock today so I'm actually running a little late."

"By all means," he says, gracefully.

"Monsieur," the hotel manager comes over. "A call for you."

"Oh, for goodness' sake."

He turns and stalks off toward the phone kiosks. A few moments later—with astonishing efficiency—the receptionist places his flask back on the desk, the scent of fresh-brewed coffee filling the air.

A few minutes later I join Miss Marple in the breakfast room. She smiles at me and then produces a cotton laundry bag.

"Oh, Diana," she says. "They delivered this to my room instead of yours. I know the mix-up they must have made—19 and 61—and I knew as soon as I opened it, I knew that they couldn't be mine. I'm afraid I never had such fine undergarments, not even as a young woman—silk and leavers lace. Goodness but they must cost a great deal!" And then: "Sorry, that's rather prying of me."

I take the bag from her, my cheeks warm. "Thank you."

Now she looks out of the window. "It is interesting," she says, "isn't it, how the snow keeps the record? All the night-time wanderings of the birds and mountain animals. Look, that must be a bird and those prints there one of those funny goat-antelope creatures . . ."

"Chamois," I supply, thinking of the colonel and his eagerness to shoot them.

"One wonders what they are all doing. Searching out food of course, finding shelter and trying to kill or not be killed, I suppose. And even more interesting is that it seems the kind of animals that walk on two legs have also been hither and thither. What do you make of these tracks . . . over there, leading off toward the glacier? It looks as though someone, or two someones or perhaps even three, have been up there—but they must have done it after nightfall, because we had that small fall of snow yesterday evening, which covered everything up—" She stops and looks at me. "Are you all right, Diana? You really don't look well."

"Yes, you look definitely peaky," Mrs. Bantry says, appearing and sitting down. "Are you tired? But the beds here are so comfortable! And the mountain air."

"I think it must be the altitude," I say, and it comes out a little apologetic. "I'm not used to it, you see. I'm fine, though. Please don't worry about me."

"The spa!" says Mrs. Bantry. "You should try the spa. I've just come from there—it's lovely and empty at this time of day. Only a couple of other people around, though I have not yet managed to try the hammam: it was full. There's a room with walls of salt . . . imagine! I tell you, Jane, it makes any English spa look a little underwhelming, by comparison."

"Well," Miss Marple says, "I was most impressed by the Royal Spa Hotel in Medenham, in spite of the unpleasantness that became associated with it."

A maid approaches the table to clear our plates. She freezes at the sight of something out of the window and mutters under her breath.

"What is it?" Miss Marple says, craning to see. "Ah, that strange flag?"

"Oh yes," Mrs. Bantry frowns up at it. "*The mountain wolves.* How strange. Whoever did this, it's not very attractive, is it? It seems a little sinister."

The maid suddenly speaks, in accented English and in a rush, as though she couldn't bear to remain silent. "I know who they are," she says, somberly. "Or who they *were.* The wolves of the mountain. They were not *sinister.* They were . . ." She switches into French and her accent is in fact French, I note, not Swiss. "They were very brave people." Her voice seems to tremble a little with feeling. "They fought the Nazis in the mountains, not far from here, but over the border, in France . . . under occupation."

I turn to Miss Marple and Mrs. Bantry, in case they haven't caught it all. "It sounds as though they were some sort of Resistance group, in the war."

Miss Marple nods, as though she had already understood all of this.

"So, what can this mean?" Mrs. Bantry says, gesturing toward the strange sign on the mountain. "The war, as I kept telling Arthur, is over. What role do the Resistance have now? And here, in Switzerland?"

She looks at the maid. Perhaps it is something about her rather imperious British voice, the authority in it (I'm sure she has marshaled many maids in her time) but the Frenchwoman takes a step back, as though she feels she has said too much. "I do not know, Madame." Then she turns imploringly to me, switching back into French. "I was only a young girl at the time. I don't know anything apart from what others have told me. That is all. But when I heard you talking of the flag . . . I felt I had to speak for them. For what they were. My father knew some of them. All lost their lives, in the war. It was a terrible thing."

"Perhaps not all," Miss Marple says, with a glance toward the strange ragged flag, dancing in the wind. "Because how does one explain that, if so?"

We are all looking through the large windows of the restaurant now but as they continue to discuss the flag my gaze is caught by the sight of the first gondola of the day beginning its slow climb to the top of the mountain. The bright red capsule is briefly agleam in the gold rays splitting through the gathering snow clouds. I watch it until the light reflecting from the windows is so bright it scorches my eyes, like a second sun, and I have to look away.

9:30 a.m.
The top of the Grand Alpine gondola

The gondola attendant steps warily into the gondola, just to make sure. He searches for a pulse; finds none. The man, curled on the floor in the fetal position, facing the open doors, is unmistakably dead: his skin cold. His suntan and full head of red-gold hair and look of general vigor and vitality make for an uncanny contrast with death—he seems almost more like a waxwork than a corpse. His eyes, eerily enough, are open. The only other object in the gondola is an empty coffee flask, which has rolled into the shadows beneath the seat. There is a smell of coffee and of something else that oddly enough makes the attendant think of the Hanselmann Konditorei in St. Moritz, where he grew up. Yes, that's it: it reminds him of freshly baked *nusstorte*: the sweet, caramelized nut-filled pastry that was their most famous confection. Perhaps the man had brought a pastry from the hotel restaurant to enjoy with his coffee. The last breakfast he would ever eat.

The attendant realizes that he doesn't want to spend another moment alone with the corpse if he can help it. It's enough to rattle even the most stoic of men.

He takes out his radio and calls down to the hotel to receive his instructions. Simple enough: he must send the body back down in the gondola again, like an unwanted meal in a dumbwaiter. The staff from the hotel will meet it and transport it to the hotel to await the authorities. If left up here in these sub-zero temperatures it would freeze and denature. This is the protocol with all bodies found on the mountain here: claim them before the mountain can take them for its own.

And all the while the dead man stares blindly on, at a view he cannot see through the open doors: toward the majestic Alpine chain and the Black Bear Pass.

PART TWO

DIANA GLASS

The Help

"What is it, Jane?" asks Mrs. Bantry. Miss Marple has suddenly stopped talking—has lifted her nose to the air like a cat scenting danger—or perhaps prey.

"Something's happened," Miss Marple says.

"What do you mean?" Mrs. Bantry says, setting down her teacup.

"The staff," Mrs. Marple says, looking about the breakfast room. "They're all a-fluster. They're excited about something." One of the receptionists has just entered and is conversing urgently with three of the waiters. One covers his mouth with a hand, the other lets out a whispered exclamation. I am sure that I make out the word: *mort*.

"Someone's dead?" Mrs. Bantry exclaims; apparently her hearing is just as keen.

Miss Marple, meanwhile, is already on her feet. She walks over to the small group of waitresses whispering in one corner, moving surprisingly quickly for a woman of her age.

Mrs. Bantry raises her eyebrows at me above her coffee cup. "Whatever is going on," she says, "Jane will be sure to find it all out. People tell her things, you see. Sometimes I think it is as if they can't help themselves! But I think it is also because she seems—as she is—so very *good*."

A few moments later, Miss Marple returns to us. She shakes her head. "A dreadful thing," she says. "Such a dreadful thing . . ."

"What is it, Jane?" Mrs. Bantry bursts out, after a moment. "Don't keep us in suspense, please."

"A guest," Miss Marple says. "Has been found, *dead*."

"Where?" Mrs. Bantry asks, and then: "How?"

"The top of the gondola," Miss Marple says. "He got in alive. Then, at the top, the doors opened . . . and there he lay—dead."

"He?"

"I am sure they should not have told me this," Miss Marple says. "But then, I think they should not have told me *any* of this. The dead man is Anthony Narracott."

"No!" Mrs. Bantry is aghast. "But . . . what could it have been? He seemed so vital. A heart attack, something like that?"

"Possibly." Then Miss Marple gives a little sigh.

"What is it, Jane?" Mrs. Bantry asks. "You've got that look about you . . . I can see it now."

"*Wickedness*," says Miss Marple ominously. "If one has lived long enough with enough experience of the world, then that is what one thinks of, at a time like this. A man in the peak of health and vigor, suddenly struck down? Of course, there are sudden deaths from natural causes. But it just feels . . . wrong." Now she stops talking; her attention caught by something through the window. I see one of the horses that brought us from the station moving slowly through the falling snow with a low-slung sled attached; to the sled is fastened a long dark shape; something wrapped in black cloth. The snow, the bowed head of both black horse and rider against the snowstorm—all combine to create the impression of a funeral cortège.

"The body," says Mrs. Bantry.

CATHERINE NARRACOTT

The Wife

I watch through the windows of the breakfast room. The awful shape of the thing on the sleigh . . . I can't take my eyes from it. There are three men untying the restraints and lifting it from the wood, their heads bent against the snow, which has begun to fall heavily now. The thing . . . it looks heavy and awkward. And then—oh, horrible, horrible—they jostle it and the coverings loosen enough for a limp hand to fall through the gap. It hangs there until one of the men notices and tucks it back inside. The color of it is a kind of purple-blue . . . no skin should be that color.

Everyone is staring, some of the guests are standing. I stay seated, frozen, watching. A group of nuns has formed in one corner of the hall and are praying together. For the soul of the dead.

"Madame Narracott?"

I blink. It's the hotel manager, the little man with the flamboyant moustache. And he's saying something else to me, his lips are moving, but it's like my ears are blocked or I'm standing behind a pane of glass . . . because I can't hear a word he is saying.

Then suddenly I can: "I am very sorry to tell you, Madame," his fingers caress one another, as though he is comforting himself, "that your husband has been found," he purses his lips, gives a little sigh, "he was found at the top of the gondola. He was . . ." He seems to summon all his courage. "Madame, I am very sorry to say that he was found dead."

"Oh." My hand goes to my throat. I can sense a hush falling around me, faces turning to look at me. "I don't believe it," I say, "oh, no, it can't be true. It can't . . ." I stand up, very quickly. The lights are too bright, the faces of the other guests in the room seem to swim around me. Then everything goes black.

DIANA GLASS

The Help

"She's hit her head!" somebody shouts. Catherine Narracott went down like she had been shot, her limbs as loose as a crumpled doll's.

Somebody else is howling: the actress I realize. Her face and palms pressed to the glass. But for once, no one in the room is paying her much attention.

Catherine Narracott lies sprawled on the ground, unmoving, her upturned face ashen.

"I—oh, Diana!" Mrs. Bantry cries. "Quick, won't somebody do something!"

I spring to my feet, ready to go to her, but someone is faster still: the young bespectacled man. He crouches beside her, fingers to her wrist. Then: "Someone find me a chair!" he shouts. For one so young and disheveled in appearance he carries a surprising authority about him. A chair is brought and he lifts Mrs. Narracott's legs onto the seat of it.

"What on earth are you doing, man?" Colonel Chapman bellows.

"I'm a doctor," the young man says, dismissively. And then he corrects himself, looking a little abashed. "Well, a medical student."

He slings that ever-present knapsack onto the floor and opens it, spilling loose change, a couple of copies of the *Modern Quarterly* and a few paper-wrapped toffees. Finally, he seems to find what he is looking for: a smaller doctor's case. Inside I catch a glimpse of various vials and bottles of liquids and tablets. When I glance across at Miss Marple, I notice that she is looking at the bag with an absorbed expression on her face.

The young man pulls out a syringe, fits a needle and plunges it into Catherine Narracott's upper arm. "Adrenaline," he says, to those of us watching, as though an explanation is required—which I suppose it is. "For the shock."

I step a little closer, to get a better look inside the medical case. I can distinctly make out the word *morphine* on one of the bottles. Another has a skull and crossbones warning logo, the kind that denotes a poisonous or hazardous substance. As though he is aware of the pressure of my gaze (and Miss Marple's, for that matter) he quickly reaches a hand over and snaps the thing shut.

BRUNO CRANE

The Friend

He's dead. He's *dead*. I have to keep repeating it to myself as I begin the climb up the glacier. Dead! I feel like I've just grabbed hold of a live wire. The blood's rushing in my eardrums, my heart's going like the clappers. I'm terrified . . . and I've never felt so alive. He's dead and I'm here. I *won*. Turns out he was mortal after all.

Now I'm trying to think clearly through the adrenaline. I'll use the chaos at the hotel and the falling snow as cover. This hike up the mountain is just as hideous as it was last night but, funny thing, my motivation's much greater now. It's all going to be mine.

It's not going to be easy to get the stuff back to the hotel in the light of day, without being noticed, but I don't have a choice. I have to do it now. In a matter of hours (perhaps sooner?) it'll be swarming with foreign police and then I'll have no hope at all.

If I can pull this next part off, I'll be a pretty rich chap. Doubly as rich as I would have been. And his share—well, I think I'm going to enjoy it even more than mine.

Who's the idiot now, Narracott?

Once I've got the gold I have to get out of this place as quick as possible. Can't go back to England, of course. I'll be a wanted man after all this. But what's left for me there? I can start a new life elsewhere. The beautiful thing about gold is, it can't be traced. It can be melted down and made new and universally accepted. Perhaps I can hope for the same thing myself. Can see myself finding a little place out here, in fact. Or, rather, a *big* place. On a lake somewhere. Yes, that will do me nicely. No, I can't speak the language. But I can afford staff now to smooth out any difficulties. Perhaps I can drop out of society completely. Yes, just leave the world behind. Do you know, I really *hate* people.

The snow's coming down heavily and the wind drives the fat wet flakes straight into my face. It's difficult to keep my bearings, but I keep pushing on, one foot in front of the other, sweat rising in spite of the cold.

See, Narracott? The old lump of lard can move pretty swiftly when he needs to.

I take little nips from my hip flask to give me some fire in my belly. Try not to think about how easy it is to go off track in such conditions—even easier than the other night—and end up breaking one's neck in a crevasse. It seems worth the risk, though. Nothing to lose. And everything to gain.

He is really gone. And with him, the only other soul who remembers that terrible night. Even though we were both implicated, even though it would have done more damage to him if it came out, he always held it over me. Then I stop in my tracks, remembering what we heard two nights ago when we climbed up here. Remember the flag with that damned wolf on it too.

Has someone followed us here from the past? I think of the young oddball with the glasses who couldn't take his eyes off Narracott at drinks. Him? But which could he have been? The French youth seems like the only possibility . . . but I was so sure he was dead.

I take another big slug from the hip flask. Can't dwell on all that. Get the stuff and get out of here, that's the answer.

Finally, I see it and I could almost weep with relief: the dark shape of the hut appears through the haze of white. A few moments later I am standing inside. I lift the boards, loose from the other night, and then climb down into the shaft. As soon as I lift the metal chest from the sack, I know something is wrong. It's too light. Even before I open it, I know it's gone. The gold has gone.

The cry is out of me before I can stop it. I could swear that I can hear him laughing at me from beyond the grave. He would enjoy this.

It's as though I can hear his ghostly chuckle ringing in my ears. *Crane, you stupid clown. Did you really think it was going to be so easy? Look at you, you big ugly bumbling idiot.* It would be just like him to have the very last laugh; to come back and haunt me for the rest of my days. I feel rage rise up inside me like the rage I felt last night and this morning, thinking of all the ways in which he has humiliated me. I wish him dead all over again.

I punch the wall of rock and howl.

DIANA GLASS

The Help

"I suppose this snowstorm can't last forever," Mrs. Bantry says. Miss Marple, Mrs. Bantry and I are sitting in the small private sitting room adjoining Mrs. Bantry's bedroom. A maid entered a short while ago to light the little fire in the grate and beyond the windowpane the snow spirals down so thick and fast that it makes one lose all sense of perspective. Snowflakes press themselves in wet kisses against the panes. The mountains have completely disappeared. It feels as though the world has shrunk to encompass only this building and the people within it. I shiver, in spite of myself.

Mrs. Bantry continues: "And then the proper authorities will be here. For some reason I imagine the Swiss police wearing great plumed hats and a sort of colorful jester's uniform . . ."

"I think that may be the Swiss Guard, dear," Miss Marple says, lightly. "The ones that patrol the Vatican in Rome."

"Oh yes," Mrs. Bantry says, thoughtfully. "That must be it."

"One imagines the Swiss police will be very efficient," Miss Marple says.

"Unlike their English counterparts, you mean?" Mrs. Bantry asks.

"I'm not sure I meant *that* precisely," Miss Marple says. "Our men tend to be very clever, I'm sure. Though I wonder sometimes if it is possible to be a little *too* clever. The Great Minds at Scotland Yard like to have their theories, and yet what use is a theory for a simple case of petty jealousy, or rage, or wanton greed? Sometimes a more provincial—well, simple—approach is actually what is required. So many criminals are really so very stupid."

A few moments pass. And then: "It's better being up here, I think," Mrs. Bantry says. "The atmosphere downstairs is positively febrile. People are nervous, yes, but one also senses a kind of prurient excitement which I find extremely distasteful."

She produces a tin of Huntley & Palmers biscuits. "Here, from my emergency supply. In times of strain only English biscuits will do, don't you find?" And then, sitting forward a little in her chair, "So, do you think it could be *murder*, Jane?"

"Oh, my dear," Miss Marple says sorrowfully, "I am afraid to say that I think it a possibility. Even a strong possibility. A man in the prime of health and vigor? The flask . . . we know that it was left on the desk in Reception to be filled with the coffee and then collected. I would like to have a look at the flask. Of course it *could* have been a suicide, but it seems unlikely to me that one would go to all the effort of getting dressed for skiing. And he seemed in high spirits, by all accounts. No, the whole thing carries about it a sense of wrongdoing."

Mrs. Bantry shakes her head. "Such a horrible thing to happen in such a beautiful, tranquil place, too. I know it couldn't have been foreseen, but I feel guilty that I brought us here . . ."

"Please, do not concern yourself, Dolly." Miss Marple puts out a consoling hand. "As you know, some of the most terrible things happen on one's own doorstep."

"All the same," Mrs. Bantry says, "it was my—" But her words are cut off as a scream sounds like a siren from down the hall.

CATHERINE NARRACOTT

The Wife

"Where is it?" he hisses. Bruno Crane stands over me, breathing hard. I can feel the cold from outside coming off him; snow still clings to his jacket, falling onto me in freezing droplets. He's a big man, but he looms even larger now as I lie on the bed.

I came here to recover from hitting my head when I fainted. I thought I would be safe in my own room, at least, but it took him only a few seconds to smash his way in. Just two loud thuds against the door before the lock gave way and he crashed into the room.

I open my mouth—try to scream. But suddenly his fingers are around my throat. He could choke me so easily, I realize "Scream again, little girl, and it will be the last sound you make. Show me where it is. Quickly—" He looks at the door.

I just blink at him. I gesture frantically at my throat. I can't speak.

"You won't scream? You know what will happen if you do . . ."

I shake my head as best as I am able.

He loosens his grip just enough for me to talk. In spite of my fear, I try to speak to him like I would to my husband when he's in a rage, very softly and slowly. "I don't know what you are talking about. You're scaring me. Please. Anthony didn't tell me anything. He never tells me anything."

Then I remember: he'll never tell me anything again. He is dead—

"He took it and hid it, didn't he?" he says, as if I didn't say anything at all. "Didn't want me to get my share. And I'm sure you know all about it. Why did he bring you here, if not, hmm?"

"We came for a holiday!" I say.

"You must know something," he says. "Come on, you snobbish little fool. Oh, yes, I've noticed the way you look at me. Just like he did. You think I'm some vile creature, beneath your notice."

"I don—"

"Well, I can tell you that your husband was far viler than me . . . did you know what he did to get the stuff? Did he tell you the whole horrid tale?"

"Please," I say, "he didn't tell me anything. I don't understand any of this."

He puts his head in his hands and makes a terrible, animal, groaning sound. And then an awful string of expletives. "This is a waste of time! Perhaps you really are as bird-witted as you look. Stay there," he growls.

And then he goes to the chest of drawers and starts heaving them out, flinging out all my lovely things, the furs, the pretty nightgowns and underthings I wore to try and please Anthony. "Oh, stop!" I scream. "Please, stop . . ."

DIANA GLASS

The Help

The echo of the second scream hangs in the air. Miss Marple's hands lift from the pile of wool in her lap like two startled birds.

I leap to my feet, instinctively taking one of Mrs. Bantry's walking poles from the holder beside the door to use as a makeshift weapon. I step cautiously out into the hallway, bearing it in front of me. The scream came from quite nearby, I think, perhaps only a few rooms along from Mrs. Bantry's. A door flies open along the corridor and I see the intense young doctor, clutching a match for the glass paperweight I have on the desk in my room. Eyes wide behind his glasses, hair mussed, he reminds me of a small boy who's woken from a nightmare. He gestures a couple of doors farther down the corridor and together we creep toward the room in question.

We find the door slightly ajar. Catherine Narracott stands in front of the wardrobe, breathing hard, face blanched. Behind her I glimpse a couple of woolen coats half torn off hangers, furs of various kinds—mink, winter ermine and fox—and a tangle of heeled shoes and boots disgorged from the shelves at the bottom. And across the room the chest of drawers has been ransacked too: a froth of lacy undergarments and negligees in various pastel colors pulled free. It is a scene of violation and a strange sort of violence.

"He just burst in here . . ."

She gestures limply across the room, at the figure crouched on the floor, now busy looking under the bed. He glances briefly up at us like a cornered animal, some scavenging species, interrupted while feasting upon a carcass. His eyes are wild, his teeth bared. He looks deranged.

"Disgraceful!" the old colonel bellows. Several other guests push their way into the room behind him: the young doctor among them. "What on earth are you doing?" the colonel shouts at the figure on the floor. "Explain yourself, man."

But Bruno Crane doesn't seem to have heard him. Then in one rapid motion, surprising for such a large man, he is on his feet and rushing across the room toward Catherine Narracott.

"Where is it?" he hisses, backing her up against the wardrobe. I see his spittle land on her cheeks. "You must know something. He was trying to take it all for himself, wasn't he? I knew he would. I *knew*."

"I don't know what you're talking about," she cries. "Oh, get him away from me, please!"

"He stole it all from me. Tell me where he hid it!" He shouts this last into her face. Then he seizes her by the forearms and begins to shake her, apparently still oblivious to his appalled audience. She stands her ground admirably. Then two of the male guests lunge forward to seize Crane and drag him away from her. He writhes in their grip like a captured wild animal.

"Did you do it?" Catherine Narracott cries. "Because you think he stole something from you?"

There is a stunned silence and Crane's eyes widen. This, more than anything, seems to stun a little sense into him. "I didn't kill him," he says.

I hear several people scoff. The scene just now seems to have confirmed his guilt. I look at Miss Marple, though. She is watching him with an expression of, I think, genuine curiosity, as though waiting for him to say more.

"We should restrain him somewhere," the old colonel says. "Lock 'im up until the police come."

"The wine cellars?" a square-jawed American guest says. "They have a lock. The vintages they have in there!"

Bruno Crane wears a different look of desperation now. "You can't do that to me! I'm . . . innocent." He stumbles over the word "innocent," though.

"Pah! You can't even convince yourself, man," the old colonel barks.

They heft him to his feet and begin manhandling him out of the room.

"What is going on here?" We turn to see the mustachioed hotel manager standing in the doorway. "My door!" He notices the splintered frame of the doorway. And then: "What, may I inquire, are you doing to Mr. Crane?"

"Got to lock him up!" the colonel says.

The little manager seems to grow in stature; his moustache positively vibrating with affront. "Mr. Crane is a guest of the Grand Alpine. You will *not* lock up one of my guests," he says, in an outraged tone. "The reputation of this establishment is at stake. In any case I have just received—this minute—some very good news. The Swiss police are not far; they began the journey from Geneva as soon as I reported the tragedy to them. In spite of the wind and snow they will be able to take the train." And then as though he can't resist this little boast: "Our trains travel in almost any weather. They will be here within the hour. *They* will decide who needs to be locked up."

BRUNO CRANE

The Friend

"Here within the hour," the manager said.

I make it back to my room without anyone trying to lock me up. But I could feel the eyes on me as I passed through the corridors, could hear the muttering. It's quite clear they'll all be crowing to the police as soon as they get here with tales of my misdeeds. I have to get out of this place or I'm as much of a fool as a frog that stays in a pan of boiling water. I'll be suspect number one, and then they'll search my room. I've got the couple of bars of gold I took last night while Narracott wasn't watching, at least. It's not much—it's certainly not what I'd hoped for—but it'll pay off some of my debts and keep my head above water for a while. And freedom is a damn sight better than the hangman's noose.

The train is the safest way out of here. There is just the small matter that I have never driven a train before, but how hard can it be? Surely the thing practically drives itself. I gather my belongings, the two bars of gold, thinking what a stupid, trusting fool I was. How I wish I'd had the gall to steal more!

Then I leave this place for the last time.

DIANA GLASS

The Help

"Where can he be going, I wonder?" Miss Marple asks.

She is peering out of Mrs. Bantry's window through her bird-watching glasses. "Look, there—"

I join her at the window and see him: a large, ungainly figure with a large pack slung over his back, hurrying through the wilderness of white.

"It's Bruno Crane," Miss Marple says.

"He's heading for the train station," I say. "That path really only leads in one direction."

"He's trying to escape!" Mrs. Bantry says. "Someone must stop him, surely . . . he can't be allowed to leave!"

But no one seems to be following him along the path; perhaps no one else has seen him leave.

"I'll go," I say.

"No, Diana—he's far too dangerous!"

"I won't do anything foolish," I promise. "I'll just try to get there in time to alert the driver."

I hear further words of protest, but I'm already on my way out of the room.

• • •

A few moments later, after pulling on boots and jacket, I am hurrying through the thick snow that has already covered the path toward the train station. Every step is an effort, my boots sinking through the frozen crust and my lungs burning as I gasp the chill air, the blood-tang of iron on my tongue. The falling snow is a cold assault; it lands in my eyes, mouth and nose. At the same time there's exhilaration in the sense of duty and purpose, of pushing myself like this: something I thought I had lost after the war. I think I am even gaining on Crane—he's not a fit man. But I'm running out of time, because we are already at the station, the train resting patiently beside the platform. Now I watch in disbelief as Crane hauls open the door to the driver's cabin. So that's his plan. He's going to drive the train himself.

"Mr. Crane!" I shout, hurrying after him, my feet skidding a little on hidden ice beneath the packed snow. I suppose I'm hoping just to distract him a little, to buy time.

A figure runs from the little hut on the platform, gesticulating: the driver. I see him speak with Crane and then a brief tussle: Crane throwing a punch and the man falling and lying very still on the platform. And now Crane is climbing into the driver's cabin.

He can't be allowed to leave . . .

I have reached the train now. But I'm too late: there's a screech that echoes off the surrounding rock, the groan of large machinery, and the train begins to move. Very slowly at first, then beginning to gather pace, the windows running together to form a chain of light. I don't have any time to think. I reach out a hand, my fingers brushing a door handle which is ripped out of reach. But there's the next, which I lurch for and miss again, and then the next, the metal smacking against my knuckles, and then finally on the next I manage to grasp hold of the freezing metal. I feel myself pulled from the ground with a wrench that feels like it's tearing my arm from the socket. At the same time, belatedly, I think: *Diana, what on earth are you doing?*

SYLVIA SINCLAIR

The Star

It was supposed to be simple. Come here to be with my lover. Just the small issue of holy matrimony standing in the way. And the small issue of money, too . . . but it was all to be sorted out, here. Things are never quite as simple as they seem though, are they?

Tony is dead. And now this place stinks of death. Stained by it. I'm going to go crazy here, stuck inside sitting around. Things start to catch up with me . . .

For the moment I lie back on the couch and let the little black moths brush me with their wings. See, those moths, they're the ghosts I carry around with me. My dead mama when the drink finally took her, making us orphans (we never had a daddy, maybe that's why I spent so many years of my life going after the paterfamilias type).

My poor dear sweet little brother, lost in the South Pacific fighting a war he didn't even really understand. Only a boy. That loss was the one that really orphaned me, because Mama was never much of a parent to start with.

Then the little baby I lost at not-so-sweet sixteen, who I thought I didn't want because of how I got her . . . until I saw her face and for the few hours that she lived she became my world.

The other kinds of ghosts. The things people do to you if you're green and shy and scared and starting out with a hick accent and a body that's grown too fast for the rest of you, and you don't have anybody looking out for you in the Wild West, otherwise known as Tinsel Town.

The ghost of the girl who came before the myth of Sylvia Sinclair. Little Sally Simmons. I carry her around inside me somewhere. Half a lifetime of pretending to be someone else. It's not good for the soul.

And now a new ghost to join all the others. I need liquor, strong and clear as it comes. But I also need to stay on my game. Ugh, the claustrophobia of it. And all these awful people. I long for the smoky risky sex appeal of some dive bar . . . or Ciro's on the Sunset Strip with the dancing girls and stars at every table and the razzle-dazzle so bright it scorches away the darkness for a couple of hours.

I reach under my pillow and pull out the little bar Tony gave me, weigh it in my palm. So dinky and slim and yet such a *good* weight. Such a pretty, pretty color. Is that why men lose their heads over it? Just like they do over some broads, I suppose. It's no accident that my hair is the palest gold. I think of Tony's words as he handed it to me: *It's you. It is always you. I think you know that. But I need you to be a good girl for me and keep schtum until all of this is over. Here's a little . . . present, to make it up to you. There'll be more where this came from.*

I long to pick up the phone and call my love. But of course, I cannot—it is no longer possible. I sink forward into the cushions on the bed and scream into the goose-down.

BRUNO CRANE

The Friend

The mountainside hurtles up at me through the windshield of the driver's cabin as the train plunges down the track. It feels like I'm clinging to the back of some wild beast and I'm half out of my mind with terror but I've made it out of that godforsaken place at least—and in the nick of time. I've lost most of the gold but I've got my freedom, for now. Seems my ambitions have shrunk to that. At least when you're used to having nothing it's no great shock to return to it.

The train shudders around me. I grip hold of the lever for some pretense of control, though I haven't a clue what I'm doing. Can't quite believe I got the thing started in the first place and it's definitely on the fast side, but I suppose that's what the rails are for. I've no bloody idea how I'll ever stop it, but I'll cross that bridge when I come to it.

For now, I risk a glance over my shoulder at the hotel, receding around the bend. Goodbye and good riddance to that hellish place.

The old cog mechanism is damn loud—clack-*clack*, clack-*clack*, clack-*clack*!—so it takes me a moment to realize that I can hear someone shouting my name.

DIANA GLASS

The Help

"Mr. Crane!" I call.

Bruno Crane is hunched over the controls in the driver's cabin. The train is going fast now, too fast: tree and rock and snow rushing past at a dizzying speed.

"You need to stop the train!" I shout, clinging to the doorframe, dazed with fear.

He throws a savage look back over his shoulder. "What are you doing here, you stupid b—"

"Please," I call again, my voice hoarse. "You need to stop the train. You're going far too quickly; you have no idea what you're doing. You're . . . you're going to get us both killed."

"You chose to get on here, you stupid little fool. That's your lookout!"

He's not wrong. I seem to have left the prudent, cautious Diana back at the hotel in Mrs. Bantry's cozy room, as if shedding a thick coat. I close my eyes and open them again, silver fish swimming in my vision, half-hoping I'll find out this was all a nightmare.

No: I'm really here, trapped on a speeding train with a man who doesn't seem to care whether either of us lives or dies. As we round a bend with a sheer drop on one side, I catch terrifying glimpses all the way to the valley far below. My stomach lurches and for a moment I think I might actually vomit. We are going far, far too quickly.

"Mr. Crane," I say, trying to swallow my terror, to sound calm and rational, "please. Be reasonable. There is no hope of you getting this train to the bottom of the mountain in one piece."

He shrugs, as though this doesn't mean very much to him either way.

I look up and see that we are twenty yards or so from entering the mountain tunnel. Safer, perhaps, than the precipice, but that black hole suddenly seems like oblivion.

"Please," I say, stepping forward. Crane hunches protectively over the controls.

"Stay back!" he snarls. "Don't you dare come any closer."

Some peculiarity of the track causes the train to rock from side to side. I cling onto the door of the cabin and see Crane lose his balance. With a cry he sprawls forward onto the controls . . . and a moment later the train lurches forward with an awful acceleration.

We are hurtling now toward the black of the tunnel.

Then there is a rending, grinding sensation, an earsplitting screech and, just as the tunnel swallows us whole, a strange brief feeling of weightlessness, as when one is in an elevator, moving between floors.

I open my eyes to find the world at a strange angle. Darkness and silence. For a second I cannot remember where I am. Gradually, I realize that I am lying on my side on the floor of the train, looking up at the leather underside of the driver's seat.

I'm very aware of the feel of my heart beating, my breath moving in and out of my nostrils—it seems such a miracle I'm still alive. I can taste blood in my mouth. My temple aches and when I raise a shaking hand I can feel a lump already forming beneath the skin. The train itself is at a slant, reared up on one side. Every so often the lights flicker feebly back on, illuminating shattered glass and a crimson spatter of blood—my own, I think—and everything at the wrong angle. Then they flicker off and all is plunged into darkness again.

A groan comes from somewhere nearby. I sit up groggily and in the next flicker of light see Crane's crumpled form in the void beneath the controls. Very still. The lights flicker off and when they come on a minute or so later he lies motionless and inert as any of the other inanimate objects.

The only sound in the chill air is that of my own breathing.

I squint, trying to see. Is he . . . ?

And then . . . a faint sound. A weak groan that I gradually realize is not coming from my own lungs.

In a brief stutter of light I see Crane stir.

"Oh God," he moans. When he finally sits up his palm is clamped to his head and I wonder if he's badly injured. As his hand drops, though, the cut seems unremarkable. "What happened?" he slurs.

I think of that moment of weightlessness, note the strange angle of the train. Through the shattered glass of the cabin's window I make out a dark wall of rock. It appears that the train wrenched itself from the tracks just as we entered the tunnel and hit the wall.

"The train crashed," I manage. "You must have fallen onto the accelerator. We were going far too fast . . . I think it sheared off the cog mechanism."

"But that means . . ."

He trails off at an inhuman groaning sound . . . some part of the train moving imperceptibly. I feel the metal floor beneath me shift a fraction. There's a percussive, smattering sound, as of small fragments of rock hitting tin. It shocks me to myself. With a supreme effort of will I pull myself together. "It means we're lucky to be alive. And I think we should get out of here before the whole tunnel collapses on us."

DIANA GLASS

The Help

"You're bleeding!" says Mrs. Bantry, as I limp back into the hotel Reception. "Jane, look at her. Where's that young man with all the medical supplies? Someone call for him immediately!"

"I'm all right," I say. "Just a knock on the head." But there's a tremor in my voice and my legs feel ready to buckle underneath me. The pain in my temple seems to pulse: sharp, now dull, now sharp again. I set my teeth against it. "I think I got away lightly," I manage, pleased that my voice sounds steadier now. "As did Mr. Crane."

All turn to look at a scowling Bruno Crane. "Show's over!" he shouts. Then he staggers past us, disappearing into the depths of the hotel.

"Come, Diana," Mrs. Bantry says. "We'll go to the library. You can tell us what happened. But what on *earth* possessed you?"

For a moment I'm not sure how to answer. And then, the truth: "A sense of duty, I suppose."

We move into the library. The events of the last few hours haven't seen the staff slacking: a majestic fire hisses in the grate and in spite of everything the warmth on my frozen cheeks is comforting. With the glow of the flames, the richly patterned rugs upon the floor, a jazz record on the gramophone and the silvery scene beyond the windows—the snow continues to fall apace—it might be a scene of cozy perfection. This safe, warm world is such a contrast to the terror I've just experienced that it doesn't seem quite real.

Some of the guests are reading in high-backed armchairs or playing card games over glasses of liqueur, as though totally oblivious to the tragedy earlier this morning. But we learned this during the war. You can't be in a state of full-blown panic at all times. Normality, humanity—even boredom—creep back in at the most fraught of times. The incongruous element in the room is me, disheveled and bleeding and accompanied by the slow drip of snow melting from my clothes onto the carpet. Gradually, the room begins to notice our little group. The card players lay down their hands, the readers their books, the drinkers their brandies . . . and turn to stare in our direction. Then the hotel manager arrives, hovering anxiously at the edge of it all.

I explain everything that just happened on the train, finishing with the crash.

"You have to be kidding me!" Sylvia Sinclair has appeared from somewhere. "If the train's kaput . . . does that mean we can't leave this place?"

We all look to the hotel manager for confirmation. He gives a little sigh, smooths a hand down his moustache. "I have just come from a phone call with the police. When our train did not arrive to pick them up at St. Celeste, and the driver could not be reached, they came up in the service engine. But when they reached the tunnel they had to stop: it appears that the tunnel has been completely blocked by the crashed train." He seems to have run out of the energy required to polish matters for us. He drops his voice, though, so that the rest of the room cannot overhear. "As that is the only route up and down the mountain, for the next little while we are alone up here. When this wind and snow stop . . . there are some very good climbers among the Swiss police; they can attempt the rock face. But not while the conditions are like this. No. We must wait here until the weather improves."

A collective gasp goes up from everyone in earshot.

"This is outrageous!" a woman cries.

And Sylvia Sinclair is saying: "But I'm meant to be in Palm Springs in a couple of days' time . . ."

"And a killer on the loose!" a man says.

"Monsieur," the manager says, pleadingly, "I must stress that we do not know that . . . it is perfectly possible that Monsieur Narracott died of natural causes."

Amidst the commotion a figure rises from a nearby armchair and moves toward our group: a tall, youngish man with prematurely silver hair. I realize it is the man that I met briefly in the gondola yesterday, Christophe.

"If it helps," he says, in lightly accented English, "I myself am from the police. I did not feel the need to reveal myself before, but I am a detective."

"Indeed!" says Mrs. Bantry, rather imperiously. "You don't look it."

He doesn't, really. He wears a royal-blue knit sweater with a white Alpine pattern of snowflakes and prancing deer, caramel-colored corduroy trousers, hiking boots on his feet, and a red scarf tied about his neck with a panache that an Englishman could never achieve.

There is something almost boyish about him at first glance, belied by the lines etched on his brow and into the sun-kissed skin around his eyes. There is a small silvery scar, like a notch, in the corner of his full top lip.

He makes a little bow to Mrs. Bantry, then reaches out a hand to shake mine. Elegant fingers, lightly calloused.

"Allow me to introduce myself," he says. "I am Inspector Moreau, of the Paris Judiciaire. I am here just like you, for a holiday. But I also happen to be a detective in my own country."

"You're not Swiss?" Mrs. Bantry asks. "You *look* Swiss. But perhaps it is just your knitwear. Knitwear can account for a great deal, I find."

"No indeed, Madame. I am French."

His accent is odd, though: definitely not Parisian. As if in answer to this thought, he says: "But I *am* from the mountains. Whilst I am based at the Paris Judiciaire now, I'm originally from a town not far from here, on the French side of the massif."

"Goodness," says Mrs. Bantry. "Well, we don't have policemen like *you* in England." Clearly age doesn't prevent Mrs. Bantry from being able to admire attractiveness in a much younger man. I think it is those eyes, very dark blue—almost navy—that somehow elevate his looks beyond the ordinary. It is the brightness and cleverness in them, perhaps, but a cleverness that seems as lightly worn as the red woolen scarf about his neck. That and the unusual silver hair. I catch myself. It has been so long since I have thought about another man in this way. I thought that part of myself had died completely. Perhaps I hit my head harder than I thought.

"I am going to try to conduct an investigation of sorts here," he says. "I have already spoken to the Swiss police and they are happy—indeed, eager—for me to begin, while they are unable to do so. When they arrive, I will hand matters over to them."

A pause as the assembled company digests this. Then: "Jane can help you in your investigation!" Mrs. Bantry exclaims. "Really! She is very good at this sort of thing and has much experience with it. Inspector Moreau, meet Miss Jane Marple."

"Pleased to make your acquaintance, Madame," he greets Miss Marple. Then he takes her hand and kisses it. Miss Marple pinkens a little.

"She has solved several very complicated and terrible crimes," Mrs. Bantry says, "including—oh, I still shudder to remember it—the discovery of a body in the library at Gossington Hall, my own home." And then, as though for her *pièce de résistance*: "In England, you know, Sir Henry Clithering, former head of Scotland Yard, trusts her *absolutely*."

Inspector Moreau raises his eyebrows. "The great Scotland Yard?

I am impressed. One English thing for which I have great admiration." He smiles, and it is still difficult to be certain whether he is really impressed or simply humoring her. "My grandmother was English," he says, "an English governess who fell in love with a Frenchman. She taught me the language—though as you discover I am out of practice—and gave me a great appreciation for all things from your country. Shakespeare, cold post-theater suppers, Colman's mustard and Cooper's Thick Cut Marmalade. But above all, for English *people*." He smiles at Mrs. Bantry, who positively beams back at him.

"So, will you allow Jane to help? She is so clever."

"Oh really!" Miss Marple says, deprecatingly.

"Jane, you are too modest." And to the detective: "So, what about it?"

He hesitates for a second. And then he gives a rather Gallic shrug. "*Pourquoi pas?* It is a little . . . irregular, but then everything about this situation is a little irregular. I am not acting in an official capacity here. No: indeed, it would be my honor. Because, you know, as I also learned from my grandmother, women who have had a good experience of life . . ."—I note that he is careful not to mention age directly here—"are an excellent judge of character. My grandmother could always tell when any one of us was lying. It was very . . ."—he grins—"*annoying*. And of course you will be able to speak to the guests in a way that I will not. The English guests because of the language and the culture . . . but also those who feel inhibited by speaking to a police officer."

Mrs. Bantry says, "Jane can get simply anyone to talk to her. Can't you, Jane?"

"I believe," Miss Marple says, "it is simply because I am a very old lady that I present no threat to anyone. So many people seem to have had some sort of elderly aunt figure they have been wont to confide in. I think I fulfill that role."

"I suspect it is more than that, Madame," the French detective says. "I think it is those wonderful eyes of yours, clear as *verglas*. One imagines, and I imagine one is right, that they are all-seeing."

"Oh, well . . ." says Miss Marple, with almost girlish coquettishness, apparently for once lost for words.

It is fascinating to watch the two of them. There is something there: a spark, as though on some level they are kindred spirits. If there weren't such a great gap of years I might almost be tempted to call the attraction a romantic one.

"So." Inspector Moreau clasps his hands together and sits in the free armchair across from us. "First of all," he says to Miss Marple. "We must—ah—*compare our notes*, is the phrase, I think? I have made some investigations of my own. There is the matter of the flask of coffee that Anthony Narracott took with him. Proper analysis in a laboratory will have to wait, of course, but it seems that may have been the cause of death.

"Mr. Narracott had, I believe, an allergy to nuts. So, it might not have been a poison, precisely, but something that was as deadly as cyanide to him alone. An empty bottle of almond oil was later discovered tossed in the snow outside the library windows."

"So it must be someone who knew he had a nut allergy," Mrs. Bantry says.

"But everyone knew, dear," Miss Marple replies, surprised. "The *nusstorte*, at dinner the first night: he got rather cross about it. Of course, it may not have been the almond oil at all. The bottle may have been a plant."

Inspector Moreau nods. "It seems likely that someone tampered with the flask of coffee while he had it filled at Reception, or indeed made it seem that was when the flask was tampered with. Possibly during the phone call that took him away for a few minutes, while the flask waited for him on the side, in which time someone might have been able to slip something into his drink. I have spoken to Monsieur Narracott's office in London. Apparently *they* had received a telegram—purporting to be from Narracott—asking them to call him close to nine o'clock, and if they didn't get him immediately, to keep trying, because it was urgent. When Narracott finally came on the line the whole confusion was discovered: that an unknown third party must have set up the whole thing.

"I have been asking about anyone who was seen passing through Reception around that time. Based on the reports of staff and other guests, no one can remember seeing much of interest at that time. The usual members of staff, numerous hotel guests," he reaches into a pocket and pulls out a small notepad, consults its pages: "a maid carrying laundry. Now, this is interesting because some of the staff claim not to have seen her before; though there *are* many new staff here."

"Diana," says Mrs. Bantry, rather excitedly, "did you not in fact tell me that there was a shop selling garments for maids and other domestics, in the town? And after all, the maids here wear a very generic sort of uniform, the black dress, the white apron, the little cap . . ." She's getting rather excited, speaking quickly, turning now to Miss Marple. "Jane . . . don't you think it a possibility? And the large bundle of laundry used to conceal the face . . . or indeed to conceal whatever it was that contained the poison."

"It is certainly a possibility, my dear," Miss Marple says. "After all, so many people fail to notice the help." She turns to me. "You were there of course, Diana. Do you remember seeing anything else out of the ordinary?"

"No," I say. "Inspector Moreau's account seems . . . about right."

"You are a photographer, I think?" he says suddenly.

"I take photographs, yes. But how did you—"

"Oh, I have seen you on your walks, with your camera about your neck."

"Yes."

"What have you been taking photographs of?"

"Oh," I say, "the surroundings, the wildlife, that sort of thing."

"I wonder . . . perhaps we could borrow your film from the last few days?"

"What?" I say, too surprised to think of anything more intelligent.

"In case you captured anything interesting. The smallest detail may seem like nothing, but could prove to be very helpful," he says. "Even in the most innocuous photograph of a mountain landscape we may find a figure that seems out of place, a set of tracks . . . something caught on the edge of the frame."

"No," I say—then realize this won't do. "I mean, I don't think it's going to be possible to develop them here. We need a proper darkroom, paper—all of that. I would be very upset if the film got damaged being improperly developed."

He opens his mouth and for a second I think he's going to say more. But he seems to think better of it and lets it go—for the time being, anyway.

"I think, then," he says instead, "the next step is to speak with the circle closest to Anthony Narracott. To see if we can uncover anything that does not add up. Or rather, something that does add up to a motive."

CATHERINE NARRACOTT

The Wife

"Madame Narracott, thank you for joining us."

I've been led into a small, dark, horrid-smelling room off the library. I take the armchair indicated opposite the French detective. "What . . . is this place?"

"It's the *fumoir*, Madame. We thought it would be private, nice and quiet."

"Oh." I look about. It's rather like sitting *inside* a cigar box: wood paneling, seats upholstered in claret-colored leather and the pall of old smoke that catches at the back of my throat and makes my eyes water. A humidor cabinet bristles with cigars of all shapes and sizes. It reminds me of the dining room at home after all the women had departed and Daddy talked to his cronies for hours. All around us are very masculine scenes of snowy hunts and heroic-looking mountaineers. The one on the wall opposite, with his swept-back hair and strong chin, looks rather like Anthony.

I smooth the wool over my knees. I hope the smell of stale smoke doesn't permeate the fabric. I have brushed my hair, put on some lipstick and a dove-gray silk shirt and black wool skirt for the interview. It felt important after the horror and upset of the last few hours; it is crucial never to underestimate the power of clothes to restore one's sense of order and control. After that torrid afternoon when I answered the phone to *her* voice in Anthony's apartment I went straight to Fenwick's and bought a fabulously expensive new dress by Norman Hartnell, even though (or perhaps because?) I knew we could not afford it.

"Madame?" Suddenly I realize the detective has asked me a question.

"Oh. I—I was just struck by how much the man in the portrait looks like my husband. But maybe I'm seeing him everywhere . . ."

"I am so sorry for your loss, my dear child," says a high, quavering voice.

I see that, for some reason, there are also two women in the room—two of the three we saw on the first day. The elderly one has a large pile of fleecy wool in her lap and reminds me a little of the maiden aunts at the Season balls who would sit off to the side and cast judgment on the new crop of debs. The other one, the younger woman with the dark-gold hair, sits farther back from the other two at a little table with a typewriter. She gives me a cool look, then starts typing.

"Miss Marple is helping me with my investigations," says Inspector Moreau.

I manage to smile at her. "Thank you," I say.

He indicates the younger woman. "And Madame Glass is making a record of our conversation."

"I hope you are feeling better," Miss Marple says. She turns to Inspector Moreau. "Mrs. Narracott fainted earlier. I had a maid once who was prone to fainting," she says, absentmindedly. "It always seemed to happen if someone surprised her when she was scrubbing the baseboards." And then, as if remembering herself, "Anyway. I am glad you have recovered."

"Thank you," I say. "I am feeling a little better."

She might be a little mad, I think. But as the French inspector begins to ask me about what prompted our holiday, the journey here, etcetera, I find her a reassuring presence—even the sound of her knitting needles clicking together has something soothing in it.

She makes this interaction feel softer, less confronting, more like a friendly chat. One feels that nothing too bad can happen in a room that has her in it. Miss Glass I'm not so sure about. There's something rather austere about her and the ghastly bump on her forehead doesn't soften her appearance.

"Could we start," the policeman says, "with Bruno Crane?"

I shudder, thinking of him crashing into my room earlier.

"I think it was a surprise," the detective continues, "to find him here?"

I glance across at the old woman. The needles are still clicking away but I'm sure there is a new alertness to her posture. She was there in Reception when I was introduced to Bruno Crane.

"Yes," I say. "It seemed *odd*. I couldn't work out why my husband would be friends with a man like that."

"In what sense?"

"Ah," I try to find a delicate way of putting it. "He's very . . . coarse. Perhaps not quite—not quite our sort of person."

"Your class, do you mean?"

"Well . . . yes, I suppose I do. And he also seemed not to *like* my husband very much. I'd say he seemed jealous, or perhaps resentful of him in some way." I think again of him crashing into the room. "What do you think he was looking for this morning, when he attacked me?" I ask the French detective. "He seemed—*crazed*."

"Ah," he smiles at me. "But I was going to ask you the same thing. Do you have any idea?"

"Only that he seemed to think Anthony might have hidden something in our room."

"And did he? Hide something?"

He is watching me very carefully. "No," I say. "At least . . . I don't think so. But you are welcome to search it, if that is helpful. Because if he did—" I hesitate.

"Yes, Madame?"

"Well, I might not have been aware of it. I take some rather strong medicine to help me sleep; it makes me dead to the world. But what could my husband possibly have wanted to hide?" I wait, but no answer comes, so I continue. "No . . . I think Bruno Crane is a little mad. And there's something else. When we first arrived here, we had to change rooms because someone put rat poison in the first one, and my husband thought it was probably Crane who did it."

"I remember that," Miss Marple says, suddenly, "when I first saw you and your husband, in Reception. You were changing rooms."

"Rat poison?" the detective asks.

"Yes. And my husband thought it was *just the sort of joke* Crane might have played. But to me it seemed positively sinister . . . a threat. And I'm sure Anthony was shaken by it, really. Does it seem like a joke to you?"

Miss Marple speaks before the inspector does. "No, it doesn't seem like a joke to me. I think it likely that whoever put the thing there was trying to send a clear message."

"And the first night, in the restaurant, someone had sent Anthony a pudding with nuts in it and of course he was allergic. That, too, felt sinister—targeted. It caused a terrible scene."

"And last night," the inspector says. "There was a different scene in the restaurant."

"Yes," I close my eyes. "That's right. I'm so ashamed to think of it now. I suppose you saw it." I say this to Miss Marple; she gives a tiny nod. "Oh, I wish I hadn't made such a fuss. To think that that was our last night together. And I know there are times, as a wife, one should look in the other direction. But when I found that earring . . . I'm sure she left it there on purpose. That was the thing that really upset me. The *purposefulness*. As though she was staking her claim. It was so unlike me. But then at dinner I had drunk too much wine and something in me just . . . snapped!"

I remember the faces turning to look at me, the shame of it. "Of course," I say, "I see it clearly now. It was *her*. *She* came here to try and seduce him from me. She didn't realize that all she was to him was a . . . a whore." The word is a shock in the quiet of the room. But I don't mind . . . I suppose I *want* them to be shocked. "The satisfaction of a fleeting, base urge. He would never—" I shut my eyes. "Oh, the whole thing was just disgusting. But I did understand it, from his perspective. Anthony worked very hard . . . the pressure of such a job, you know. I am not completely naive." I look at Miss Marple, because I think she will understand this better than the detective. "I do realize such things happen and are even normal at, well, our level of society. In a way it is rather accepted as their due. My mother explained it to me." *There are some ideas about marriage that are very bourgeois. Fidelity being one of them. Better to take up your own hobbies. Gardening is excellent.*

"Still," I say, "I expected more discretion. The earring seemed beyond the pale. But how I wish I had gone up the mountain with him now, even if I couldn't have *stopped* his death, even if it was just to spend those last few moments together. But I chose to spend the whole morning in the spa, instead, because I was still a little angry. I saw your friend there, I think," I say to Miss Marple, who nods.

"Oh yes, Dolly went before breakfast."

"But worst of all, *she* was there too. She even came into the hammam when I was there. Sat across from me as though she hadn't any shame at all. And I . . . well, this sounds childish. But I wasn't going to be the one to leave first. It would have felt like conceding something. After everything she had taken from me, I wasn't going to give her that." I look at my hands in my lap. "I know that must all sound very foolish."

"No," Miss Marple says, "I quite understand. There was a similar situation with the church flowers in my village. I grew some baby's breath specially for the christening of our vicar's baby, but Miss Hartnell told me it wouldn't do because she had some damask roses that would be more striking. Nevertheless, I took the baby's breath over to the vicarage on the day and Griselda loved them and actually didn't want the roses because she found the smell too powerful." She blinks at me, earnestly. "St. Mary's is rather a *small* church."

"Ye-es," says Inspector Moreau, dubiously. "Please continue, Madame Narracott. When did you see the actress in the spa?"

"She got there a little after I did, I think. About nine o'clock—I remember feeling surprised that she was up so early. She seems such a . . . creature of the night." I mean the implication: whore. "So I suppose she must have poisoned him before she got there." At his expression of surprise: "Oh yes, I'm quite sure she did it. Once he'd dashed all her hopes that she could steal him away from me. I'm sure she isn't used to having people say no to her. *And* she seems quite unstable."

Miss Marple looks thoughtful. Then she says, "But my dear, she *can't* have done. If indeed she was in the spa from nine o'clock."

The inspector explains: "The spa is twenty minutes' walk from the hotel and she went on foot. Your husband hadn't even come down to Reception until about nine o'clock. He had his flask washed by the kitchen before they put the coffee in it."

"Oh," I say. "I— Are you absolutely *sure*?"

He nods. "Yes. Unless you are incorrect in your timings—"

"Well," I think quickly, "perhaps I *have* got them wrong! One can't be totally certain about these things! Perhaps she got to the spa a little later than I had thought . . ."

"But," the inspector says, almost apologetically, "she was also seen by several people on her way to the spa at quarter to nine. Her dog"—he pulls a face—"even made a mess on the Reception carpet, on her way out."

I sigh, and sit back in my seat.

He presses on. "Is there anything else you'd like to mention, Mrs. Narracott? Any other interactions your husband had here that strike you as significant?"

"Well, only if it is helpful. There was one person who was worrying my husband a little, though again he tried not to show it . . . the young man who gave me the medicine yesterday, in fact. He worried *me* too, actually. I'm sure I first spotted him in Paris, in the station concourse. And I'm also sure he was originally waiting for a different train; he was on the platform across from ours. I think he followed us here. And he kept following us once here, trying to talk to my husband, who did not want to talk to him. He had a very . . . aggressive way about him.

"Anthony tried so hard to lose him on a run that he nearly skied all of us over a cliff. I know he says he's a doctor but I think he might also be a Red or something. They seem to really have it in for my husband, because he promotes people working hard for their money. He *looks* the type, don't you think? And—I don't want to sound like a snob—he doesn't at all look the type to be staying in a place like this. I certainly think you should have a word with him."

DIANA GLASS

The Help

Every part of the young man seems to be in a state of perpetual motion. He scratches at the side of his neck where a livid red rash has formed. He keeps running a hand through his sandy hair, knocking his glasses askew as he does. Several times he takes them off and wipes them with a grubby-looking handkerchief, but it seems more nervous habit than for any practical purpose because they appear just as smeared as before. Little beads of sweat stand out at his temples. His knee jitters up and down until eventually he puts a hand on it, fingers splayed, as though to force it into submission.

"Could we have your name?" asks Inspector Moreau. "For the record?"

"Charlie Levitt," the young man mutters. Then: "What do you want with me?" he says, raising his chin defiantly.

"We know that you had a number of interactions with Monsieur Narracott here," Inspector Moreau says. "According to Madame Narracott, you were . . . bothering her husband a great deal."

"I didn't kill him," he mutters, "if *that's* what you're asking me. I'm a doctor! I'm in the business of saving lives, not taking them. Have you ever heard of the Hippocratic Oath?"

"I'm afraid your profession doesn't exonerate you," Inspector Moreau says. "Too many doctors, over the years, have been in the business of killing. They seem to be quite good at it, in fact. Do you agree, Madame Marple?"

"Oh," Miss Marple says gravely, nodding, "I'm afraid so. I have very little experience of such matters but I know that sometimes medical people have a god complex. That can be very helpful, in its way. But there can be more sinister implications.

"There was a nurse in Much Benham who looked after a number of elderly residents. It transpired that she was making them ill on purpose, slipping things into their water and food, in order that she could then 'cure' them. One has heard about this happening with mothers—a kind of corruption of the maternal instinct in which the mother is so desperate to provide care that she makes her children ill on purpose in order to make them better. But this nurse, the evil creature, went too far in a couple of cases and actually killed her charges. For some—a very few, of course—the power over life and death goes to their head. That and a ready supply of potentially lethal chemicals. It seems to me that it is two sides of the same coin. Giving life, on the one hand. Being able to take it away, on the other."

The young man, to his credit, looks genuinely appalled. "Well, that's not me! I became a doctor because I want to help people."

"There's something else," I say. The others look at me in surprise. "When you opened your bag, I saw a journal: The *Modern Quarterly*. It's a communist publication, I think?"

There's a longish pause and then the young man erupts. "Well, what of it? Trust me, if you saw some of the things I have witnessed in our *green and pleasant land*—the inequality, the desperate ill health of children from lower-income families—then you might start looking for another way, too."

Inspector Moreau speaks: "Catherine Narracott tells us that her husband was lately a target for Red activists."

"Oh," the young man says, mockingly, "so which am I then? Demon Doctor with a god complex, or Red Terror? I think you'll have to choose one!"

Miss Marple clears her throat delicately. "I think, if I may, I have another suggestion. Long-lost son."

A stunned silence follows.

"What?" the young man splutters.

"It's only a guess," Miss Marple says. "But you have a cleft chin, as Mr. Narracott did, and I believe that is often hereditary. There is a general physical resemblance between you besides. And a heightened allergic response—" she indicates the rash on his neck. "That is, I'm afraid, often something passed down from parent to child."

"How do you know all of this?" Inspector Moreau asks Miss Marple.

"Oh, long conversations with our village doctor, Haydock. But also simple observation of such things across a long life." She turns back to Charlie Levitt. "The question is: Am I correct?"

He seems to jut his distinctive chin defiantly at us. Now Miss Marple has pointed out the resemblance it seems almost uncanny: the build, the general face shape, the similar coloring. All masked by the stark differences in manner: Narracott's smooth charm versus Levitt's nervous agitation. "What do you want me to say?" he mutters, with a shrug. "Yes, fine: I'm his son. His *bastard* son. I happened to be at the Gare de Lyon terminal. I was meant to be traveling through Europe, on the trains. And then I saw *him*. It felt predestined, somehow. Like it was the perfect opportunity. So I followed them here, him and his wife. It felt like my chance to know who my father really was, once and for all. And now I never will."

He takes off his glasses yet again but this time to rub furiously at his eyes.

Miss Marple makes a noise of sympathy, but her gaze on him, I notice, has lost none of its scrutiny.

Now he stands up, giving up any pretense of trying to sit still, and begins to stalk up and down the room. "Wish I'd never come," he says. "It would have been better never to know. When I think how as a boy I'd ask and ask: Who was my father? Why did he abandon us? And finally, *finally*, when I was old enough, my mother pointed to a photograph of him in a newspaper. 'There,' she said. 'Now you know where all your cleverness comes from!' Because that's just like her, never giving herself credit for any of it. She was his Scout, at Oxford. You know—one of the chars, that clean the rooms? She explained it all like it was her silly fault to get herself in trouble. That he had given her the money to . . . well." He grimaces. "Do you know, she actually seemed to think it was all rather decent of him? That it was all her own stupid folly keeping the baby . . . keeping *me*? What a piece of work he must have done on her. If you can believe it, she was actually *proud* of him. She would point to pictures of him in the news, say, 'Look what a great man your father is!' What a dupe."

"Pride in one's parents can be a very powerful thing," Miss Marple says. "It can be character forming. Your mother knows this, I am sure. It was the case in my village, St. Mary Mead. When so many men went away to both wars—and when so many did not come back—the mothers were very careful to keep the *idea* of them alive for their sons and daughters. *You are the image of him. I'm sure you will follow in his footsteps to be a great man like him. He worked so hard. He loved you very much.* That sort of thing."

The young man looks suddenly astounded.

Miss Marple continues, gently, "Mothers are often very clever, when it comes to their children. A kind of instinct, knowing what it is they need to hear, whether that be criticism or praise, or the odd instructive fairy tale. I suspect your mother might not have been quite the dupe you have thought her to be."

"You mean . . . all of that might have been for me? That she wasn't *really* proud of him? She was telling me a kind of . . . fiction? What was it you said . . . a—a fairy tale?" Now Charlie Levitt sits, digesting this. His eyes, I notice, have the glitter of unshed tears. He looks suddenly more like a little boy than a twenty-year-old medical student.

He says, "When I saw him that day at the train station . . . I couldn't believe it. Can you imagine? My father, who I had only ever seen in the pages of the newspapers. I *had* to follow him. I can't afford this place, any of it. I've been using money that was meant to last me the whole year. But it all seemed worth it, to get to know him. That was all I wanted. To get to know him."

He passes a hand over his face and when it drops, I realize that he is weeping, silently. "Oh, how I wish I'd never learned what kind of man he really was. I tried to follow him, the other day on the mountain. I thought it would be a chance to speak to him away from the crowds He fled from me! So first, I learned that he was a coward. Second, do you know . . . I actually think he might have tried to kill *me*."

"How do you mean?" Inspector Moreau asks.

"I think he made some effort to ski me off a cliff. It's the only explanation for how he behaved that day. That pretty much gave me the measure of the man. But try to kill him? I just wanted to know him! Do you know, I never even managed to have a proper conversation with him. And now he's gone and that chance has disappeared forever. You think I'm capable of killing my own father?"

"Monsieur Levitt," says Inspector Moreau, "I really know nothing about you at all. I can't make a judgment like that in one direction or the other."

The young man looks stunned. "But—"

"And that is why we must look toward the facts. Nothing more, and nothing less."

Charlie Levitt blinks, once, twice, as though to clear his vision. He looks genuinely outraged. He sits up in his seat, practically spluttering with indignation. "How can you say such . . ."

"Monsieur, I'm not saying that it *was* you. I'm simply saying that your being his son does not discount you."

Miss Marple clears her throat again and both men turn to look at her. "You say that it was coincidence that brought you out here, Mr. Levitt, rather than design."

"Yes, that's true."

"And you seem to have been under no illusions about your father's character. I mean—even before you came out here. And you don't mention any attempt to get in touch with him before? *Did* you ever try to get in touch with him?"

"No . . ."

"That is the part—forgive me if I am being very foolish—that does not quite make sense to me. After all, you *knew* who he was. He has a public role. It would have been easy enough to seek him out. But you didn't. So why here, now?"

The young man gives a short, humorless laugh. "I don't understand. You're trying to make it out like I had some great master plan? To come out here and . . . and kill him?"

"Oh no," says Miss Marple soothingly. "I believe that it really *was* a coincidence when you saw him at the station. I do *not* believe there was any great plan. But *there* lies the issue. In my experience, if a long-lost child has any desire to establish a relationship with a parent—or indeed the other way around—it happens rather differently. It is something planned and fretted over. It carries much emotional weight. It is not something done on a whim, because of a mere coincidence. You do see the problem?"

The young man gives a laugh and casts a look around the room that says: *Are we really going to humor this mad old cat?*

Miss Marple continues. "You see, it doesn't sound to me as though you really wanted anything to do with your father. And yet you saw him at the Gare de Lyon and it seemed like *the perfect opportunity*: those were your words. An opportunity for what? Not, I think, to get to know him. You seem, Mr. Levitt, like a man of strong judgment and principle"—I see Levitt give a tiny, rather pleased-looking nod of approval at this assessment of his character—"meaning that once you have decided on a thing, it is settled. Is that a correct assessment?"

"Yes," he says. "That seems about right."

"You are twenty years old. You have never tried to contact your father before. Well then why would you suddenly throw away all those principles on a whim? It does not fit. No. You did not *want* to know him. I think ideally you would have had nothing to do with the man. But you *needed* something from him."

Charlie Levitt folds his arms.

"You have a disease, Mr. Levitt."

"What?" Levitt stands up quickly from his seat, as though to better display his youth, health and vigor. "You can't mean this stupid rash? It's just from the soap here . . . I'm perfectly—"

"Not a disease of the body. A disease of the mind, the spirit, and it has affected many clever men. You have been seen, often, playing cards for money. Often losing badly. But that does not seem to put you off: the mark of an inveterate gambler. You have an addiction and you need money to fund that addiction . . . or to cover your debts. Of course, the price of a hotel room here is no small trifle but it would *become* a trifle if you could get your father to really pay out. Imagine the scandal! The upstanding future star of the Conservative party a philanderer with an illegitimate child . . .

"That day, when you saw him at the Gare de Lyon and followed him here: that was itself a gamble. I think you came here to ask him for money. And I think he said no."

Charlie Levitt has listened to all this in a kind of malevolent silence. Now, a change comes over him. His boyish features sharpen into something hard and other. He looks like a demented pixie, almost diabolical: his eyes too bright behind his glasses, his teeth bared. There's something horribly fascinating about the transformation. I can absolutely imagine him, suddenly, committing a murder, though probably more in a fit of pique than premeditation.

A little spittle leaves his mouth as he leans forward and says, in a low hiss: "His own flesh and blood and he flat out refused to give me a penny. Worse than refused, I really think he was trying to get rid of me that day on the mountain, just as he tried to get rid of me twenty years ago. Well . . . I'm *glad* he's dead. Good riddance to bad rubbish."

SYLVIA SINCLAIR

The Star

"Down, Herbie!"

He has leapt up at the French detective, claws scrabbling at his lap. He's only doing what others would love to: the fella is quite something. As I sit down in the armchair opposite, I give him the full Silver Screen Movie Goddess Spectacular: chin tilted up, eyes nearly closed, lips set in a pillowy pout, the kind a man wants to rest his weary face on.

Funny thing is, the closer I get to losing "it," the more I feel the power of it, you know? Like an old half-lame soldier who's got to being the best shot in the whole damn army. But does it work *now*? Difficult to tell: he's got a good poker face, this one. And *what* a face! Those eyes. *Phewy!* Time was I'd have eaten him up with a spoon. But I don't go in for boyish types these days and he is all boy. I do love that accent though. French has to be the best, doesn't it? Though he probably speaks English better than I do.

I walk over to the cigar cabinet and find myself a nice big Cuban, slide it between my lips and light up. "You want one, honey? Or you two?" I ask the little old lady and the younger one with the typewriter who's been watching me with her eyes narrowed. She looks sharp as a Gillette blade. All of them shake their heads.

"Did you ever do any film work?" I ask the Frenchie. "You would be perfect. You know if you wanted me to, I could pull a couple of strings, I've heard they're looking for a more European sort now."

He smiles. "I happen to like my chosen profession, Madame. Do you know, I think I'm rather good at it. And I'm sure I would be a terrible actor."

"It's not that hard, darling," I tell him, waving the Cuban. "There's all this *mystique* made about it, just like there is with anything people want to keep to themselves. And I guess it justifies the pay. All this nonsense about The Method and all that. But really, anyone can do it. If little old me from nowheresville Montana with no schooling to *think* of can do it, so can anybody." It's true, I don't have ego about such things. "You learn on the job. Or you find someone to teach you." I do The Bit on him again. "I've taught others! I'd be very willing. Bet you'd make a *quick* study. To be honest, though, I'm not sure it's worth your while. Sometimes I've been thinking fame is not all it's cracked up to be. Not when one has the temerity to not look how one did at twenty-one. It's enough to make a girl want to run off to Illinois or . . . or Istanbul, or you know just anywhere a person can properly disappear and just grow old in peace . . ." I laugh. "Hark at me, coming over all Garbo!"

He coughs. "I'd like to start, Madame, by asking about your relationship to the deceased."

"The deceased?" I shiver. "Oh, I don't like that. I don't like that at all. Say, would you like one of these?" I ask, offering the box of chocolates I have on the side. "From Maxim's in Paris. Had them brought down from my room. One of my *very* favorite spots . . . maybe you know it?" He shakes his head, at both the chocolates or Maxim's or both. "And for you, ma'am?" This to the little old lady. I barely even noticed her at first. I have absolutely no idea what she's doing here, but I like the look of her: that fleecy white hair and that pretty pink and white face, like some faded English wildflower pressed in an old book. Wonder if she'll ask for my autograph, after this. Maybe that's why she's here. Watched a few of my flicks, maybe, or—more likely—

read about me in the magazines while getting her hair set. Some of these old dears turn out to be the most ravenous fame-hounds.

"Oh," she says, per the chocolates. "How kind of you, but no, I couldn't possibly. Such a charming box, though."

"You like to knit?" I ask. "You know, I was once part of a sewing circle myself."

The French detective clears his throat again. "If you don't mind," he says, "I'd like to get started."

"Oh, I'm so sorry, baby. I just couldn't help myself! Please. Do your thing. Where were we?"

He clears his throat again. Have I got under his skin? There's no more delicious feeling than getting under someone's skin. "Your relationship to Monsieur Narracott," he says. "There was a . . . scene, in the restaurant the other night," he says. "The martini. I wonder if you could . . . elaborate on what happened."

"Oh, baby, we don't need to make a mystery about it! No use in being coy, it's 1950 after all." I suddenly remember the old sweetheart—Miss Marvel? "Unless *you* mind?" I ask.

"Oh," she says, seeming a little flustered. "No, not at all."

"I sense there is little you could say that would shock my companion," the inspector says. "If you don't mind my saying so, Madame Marple?"

"No, indeed," she says, prim as you like but I'm sure I spot a gleam in her eye.

"Well, we're all adults then. He and I were lovers: there it is. Why should I deny it? It isn't shameful to me. Frankly, I'm bored of pretending to play by the so-called rules. Not my fault if he couldn't find what he needed at home. We had fun for a while. Life's too short not to have fun. Tony was my lover. I was his piece, however you like to put it. How do you say it in French? *Maîtresse*, yes, I like that. Almost regal!

"Anyway, that prissy little wife found out. Something about an earring. I'm so careless! And she didn't take too kindly to the idea of it. But she should have looked to her own house. Thing is, if a man's satisfied with his car he don't go shopping for another, you know? Actually," I chuckle, tap some ash, "scratch that. Some men want *lots* of cars. Some for everyday use, some for special occasions. Some they hardly ever use, just want them sitting pretty in the garage making them feel good about themselves. So perhaps that wasn't quite the right metaphor."

"We've spoken to his wife," says the pretty Frenchman. "And she claims that her husband told you it was over. That you might even have left that earring out of spite, to . . . well, to stir up trouble, just when things had finished between you."

"Oh, that's what she said, is it?" I laugh. "Ah, well, you know what, I'm impressed! Doesn't look like she'd have any fight in her, does she? And I suppose every woman must have her pride. But that's not how it was, baby. Not at all. Quite the other way around, in fact: he was going to leave *her*. Sure, he might have said what she wanted to hear, but of course he did. The man's a politician, have you ever known them to speak much truth?

"He was expecting to come into a bit of money; he'd be a free man. He could leave his little wife and politics too, if he chose to, and take up with me. I know I look like money but I look that way because I spend it and leave nothing to gather dust and he was the same. He married her because her daddy was rich, though maybe less rich than he thought. Anyway, he didn't need *her* money anymore . . . though in all honesty, I think he'd spent what was left of that." I take another drag on my cigar. "I can see it, actually. Her as a poisoner. Can't you? Walking past that—what was it—coffee flask? With a face like butter wouldn't melt. It's always the quiet ones."

"Madame Sinclair," the inspector says, sitting forward in his seat, rounding those beautiful broad shoulders just a little (he could give Rock Hudson a run for his money there). "Madame Narracott says that she was in the spa all morning. More than that, she gave your name as someone who had definitely seen her in there."

"Oh . . ." I frown. "Huh."

"You did see her?"

"She was in there, yes. Lordy, and she was such a little prude! Towel up to her chin in the hammam like this!" I mime with the neckline of my dress: not so easy to yank it about a mile up.

"The hammam?" the little old lady asks.

"That's the one."

"I do wonder if it might be a cure for my rheumatism," she says. "I do suffer, and especially here, with the cold, you know. Only . . . I'm not sure I'm brave enough to try. But, you know, perhaps you have just convinced me. Thank you."

"It'll fix any ache you've got," I tell her. "Heart, body or mind. And then a trip to the ice room afterward."

"Oh goodness," she twitters. "No, I couldn't do that. I really can't abide the cold. And it affects one so much more, as one ages."

"Did anyone see you in there?" the inspector asks.

"Oh, plenty of people. But mainly I saw the little wife in the spa itself and I saw the dame on the Reception when I went in. She was not a fan of poor old Herb here!"

"Thank you, Madame," the inspector says. "I think that's everything."

"If you're sure. But do let me know"—I smolder at him—"if I can be of any further help. I'm all yours." I uncross my legs. I'm not wearing underwear underneath this silk skirt. (Learned that one from my old drinking buddy Tallulah Bankhead. Hitch had forty fits on *Lifeboat*.)

I blow another smoke ring. "But what's the thing they say? It's always the husband . . . or the wife! I know I saw her in the spa but I wouldn't put it past her to have killed him some way or somehow. Ask her again about her trust fund! If I were her, I'd have been feeling *pretty* nose out of joint about the whole thing. Pretty *murderous*, you might say."

BRUNO CRANE

The Friend

"I don't have to talk to you," I say. "I can wait for the real police."

The Frenchman shrugs. He's too good-looking. He looks like the pretty-boy hero from some foreign film, not a proper plod. It's like Narracott: easy to charm if you look the part. I've had the cards stacked against me ever since I was born with this face. Then I remember that Narracott is dead, so in the end his cards were worse than mine and, what do you know, it makes me feel a little better!

"It might be . . . wise," the French chap says now. "Some of the other guests are keen on locking you up until the *real* (he puts an emphasis on the word) police arrive here. But I think perhaps if you can explain a few things, I can set their minds at ease."

What business does he have speaking such good English?

"Fine," I say. I suppose sitting here talking to this Frenchman beats being locked up in some hotel broom closet. "But I don't want her here," I say, per the madwoman who chased me onto the train earlier. "I'd never have crashed the blasted train if it weren't for her meddling. Try telling the others *she's* the reason we're all stuck in this place. And what in the blazes is *she* doing here?" I nod toward the old woman sitting next to him. "Do the French police employ ancient crones to do their work for them, too?"

"Madame Marple," says the Frenchman, "is helping me in my investigations. And with my English, should I need it."

The tweedy old cat smiles at me. She's probably senile anyway. I study her as she looks back at me with a half-smile on her face, head tilted to one side. No: definitely not *all there*. Maybe this is some assist-the-demented-elderly scheme. "Suit yourself," I say.

"Thank you, Mr. Crane," the Marple woman says, her smile widening. "I will be so interested to listen to your account of everything." She doesn't *sound* all that demented, but you never can tell. My old man went a few years back and toward the end he'd be talking sense one moment and trying to beat me with his walking stick like the good old days of my joyful childhood the next.

The Frenchman starts by asking me where I was, that morning, *blah blah blah*, just like they would in some half-baked detective book. I tell him: "Face down in my pillows, sleeping off the night before. Had a few too many cognacs after dinner."

"And can anyone vouch for this?"

"No, of course they can't, because why should anything in my life be easy?"

I don't like the way the old fossil is watching me. She's a little too beady for my liking, come to think of it. Wish I'd refused to have her in here but no point making a fuss now.

"Mr. Crane, I passed your room on my way to breakfast," she says, "and the housekeeping team were just coming out of it, carrying your linens. I do not think they would have been able to do that if you were asleep in bed all morning, as you have told us."

Fool. Dolt. Dunce. Christ, I can hear his voice as loud as if he were sitting here beside me. *Shut up,* I tell him, silently.

"Excuse me?" the French detective asks. Or perhaps not so silently. "Did you say something, Monsieur Crane?" God. What's happening to me?

"So maybe I wasn't there at nine o'clock on the dot," I say. "Well, for God's sake, I wasn't checking my watch every moment! I'm on holiday. Perhaps I got up earlier than I'd thought and . . ." I finish rather lamely: "went for a walk."

"Where?"

"Oh, I don't know. Just outside. It's all white and cold, isn't it? And like I said, I'm on holiday."

There's a long silence. They're waiting for me to fill it, I'm sure—incriminate myself. Well, I won't do it. I could do with one of those cigars. Just not sure I could trust myself to hold it without my hand jerking around all over the place.

"And the pill," the Frenchman says.

"What of it?" I say, and then realize that was a stupid thing to say. But when has that ever stopped me before? "I mean, what pill?" I correct, quickly, but it's too late.

The Frenchman smiles, very slightly, and I think of Narracott smirking at me that day up on the mountain. *Fool. Dolt. Dunce.*

"Oh dear," the old woman says. "Is that sweater causing you some discomfort? I do sympathize—the heating is positively barbaric. And wool: so effective yet so abrasive. I heard recently of a wonderful trick of using Brilliantine in one's washing . . . it softens the fibers, you know."

I force myself to stop tugging at the neck.

"The pill you kept in your room," the detective says. "Quite a few guests heard you discussing it the other night. What did you call it?" He turns to the old crone.

"An S pill, I believe," she supplies.

"Yes. That was it," the Frenchman says. "We had something similar. A little capsule, filled with cyanide. Kept on one's person always. Find oneself in a tricky spot, pop it between the back teeth and—*voila!*—oblivion. Anyway, I heard you were in possession of one of these. In fact, most of the guests heard that you had one of these because you had a particularly loud conversation about it with your dead friend. Tell me," he says. "Where is it now?"

"It's gone," I tell him. "I think Narracott probably destroyed it that very night. I swear to you . . ."

"You do see how this appears?" he asks. "Your friend is poisoned.

You have been heard to loudly discuss a poison pill in your possession, which now you cannot produce."

"Perhaps someone knew it was there and took it—"

"Ah," the old woman says. "I think quite a number of people knew it was there, Mr. Crane. I almost wondered," she says, earnestly, "if that was no accident."

"What do you mean?" For God's sake, does the woman ever blink?

"I mean only that a large number of us, hotel guests I mean, heard you discussing it last night. I think if twenty or so people heard you speak of it then twenty or so people might also have been minded to steal it from you. And therefore twenty or so people might have had the means to poison your friend, besides you, and could become suspects, if motives were found. Yes, it does certainly widen the field."

"Yes," I say, uncertainly. "Exactly! Or . . . are you trying to imply something, Madam?"

"Oh, not at all, not at all," she twitters. "I apologize—sometimes I like to do my thinking out loud."

"Anyway . . ." I say, still wondering if the old cat was just trying to spin some sort of trap, "I tell you. If it *was* the pill, then I've been framed. Someone has it in for me. I think someone here has it in for both of us. Narracott knew it, too. You should have heard him. 'Someone is out for blood,' he said."

The Frenchman frowns, very slightly. "But how odd! Two friends, here for a skiing holiday in a country foreign to both of you! Why should somebody here 'have it in for you' as you say? Is there some aspect of which I am unaware?"

I could almost swear. Walked into that trap too, didn't I?

"Look," I say, trying a different tack. "There are things that I cannot talk about here. Things that happened in the war. Perhaps you have heard of something called the Official Secrets Act?" Oh yes, I like that. It sounds bona fide, a whiff of heroism. And it feels right, too! After all, I *could* have been heroic, in different circumstances.

"Anyway. Suffice it to say there were things that both of us did—had to do—that made us some enemies. I think they came for him."

The French detective just looks at me. His eyes are a weird color. In this light they seem to have no pupils. I feel a sudden chill.

"And now," I say, "I think they're coming for me."

DIANA GLASS

The Help

By the time the interviews are concluded, dusk is falling and the snow beyond the windows is tinted indigo.

"I can't bear spending any more time in the hotel itself," Mrs. Bantry says. "Shall we go to the spa, to discuss? Half the guests don't seem to know it's there, so it should be nice and quiet. I want to hear everything! I'm very jealous that you can type, Diana—otherwise I think I'd have volunteered myself."

The spa is a twenty-minute walk along a fir-lined path and the snow is coming down heavily, so we ask the hotel for a horse-drawn sleigh instead. We are swept along through sweeping curtains of white. I look up and am dazzled by the vortex of falling snow against the darkening sky, the flakes smattering my face, melting upon the warmth of my cheeks. The music of the little bells on the horse's headdress is an ethereal accompaniment.

The woman on the desk welcomes us in; she seems delighted to have some company. "Hardly anyone comes in this weather. We had a few yesterday. I was here when that film star came in. That dreadful animal jumping up, claws on the desk, barking . . . *une vraie horreur*. She actually tried to drag it *into* the spa with her! Can you imagine? In the end I had to arrange for a member of staff to take it back to the hotel for her."

"She wasn't much better in the spa!" Mrs. Bantry says. "Keeping the hammam all to herself! One wonders if these people get so used to being fêted they actually think everyone else is beneath them. I'm not sure I'll read those magazines at the hairdressers anymore—Oh!" She suddenly looks rather thrilled at the entrance of five nuns, who move quickly into the depths of the spa.

"Some of the most demanding spa guests," the woman tells us, *sotto voce.* "They all want very much to know if the water we offer is really sacred."

Miss Marple eschews the hammam and indeed the Finnish sauna for the solarium, which has several comfortable seats arranged around a central open fire and large windows offering a stunning view of the glacier through a veil of steadily falling snow. It also has the advantage of requiring no removal of clothing and no sweat; somehow, I cannot imagine Miss Marple wanting to sit in the sauna in nothing more than a towel. The nuns must be using one of the other rooms.

Miss Marple gives Mrs. Bantry a quick précis of the interviews. I notice that she has not missed a single detail—and has remembered, in fact, a few that I had forgotten.

"So, what do you think?" Mrs. Bantry asks us. "Judging by the scene in the restaurant last night, I might have put my money on Mrs. Narracott, but it couldn't have been her unless she tampered with the flask in some way in the room before Narracott had it filled up, and that doesn't seem very likely if they washed it out. And relations between husband and wife can be very misleading. If you'd caught me on the wrong morning you might have been convinced I was only *minutes* away from murdering Arthur. But of course I loved him very much, even if he could be maddening at times." She stares for a moment out at the mountains, her eyes a little misty. "Where was I?"

"The interviews," I supply, gently.

"Oh yes . . ."

"Then there's the actress," I say, giving Mrs. Bantry some more time to collect herself. "She had a motive to kill Narracott, if she was really about to be thrown over by him as the wife claims."

"And the bruising about her neck," Miss Marple says.

I turn to her in surprise.

"Hidden fairly well by her scarf," Miss Marple continues, "but definitely there. A couple of days old, I would say, from the color. I noticed it last night at dinner, too: she'd used makeup to disguise it, I think, but bruising is so difficult to conceal. Any attempt only seems to make it stand out more."

"I wonder," Mrs. Bantry says, "could she have asked a member of staff to place the poison in the flask for her? Telling them, oh, I don't know, that it was medicine or something? That maid, for instance, who was seen with the bundle of laundry?"

Miss Marple shakes her head. "In my experience any domestic would have been extremely suspicious about the request in the first place and then, upon learning that it had caused a man's death, would I'm sure have had some crisis of conscience. I know they are Swiss, but I have spoken to a couple of the girls here and really, they are of the same type as the ones I have had under my roof. Fundamentally honest—or certainly when it comes to something as large and terrible as murder—and on the whole happy with their lot. They will be paid well enough in a place like the Grand Alpine; even a large bribe would not be worth such a risk. They also like to gossip. So, if one had been acting strangely, or guiltily, we would have heard of it already. No, I don't believe it."

"The young doctor?" Mrs. Bantry says. "I think you hit on something there, Jane! That he could have been blackmailing Narracott. I don't think it could have been anything to do with inheritance, because he was illegitimate."

"No," says Miss Marple. "If Anthony Narracott died intestate—young men in the prime of health often fail to leave wills—I believe that legitimate offspring are favored over a spouse but illegitimate children tend to be left out in the cold. Otherwise, a certain parishioner of St. Mary Mead would have left very little indeed to his young widow. Eight was it, Dolly?"

"Rumored to be nine, I think, Jane."

"I was thinking," I say, "that there's another possibility. I know there's a physical resemblance there, but could it even just be something he made up—being Narracott's son, I mean? To explain why he was following Narracott everywhere, accosting him? But actually it was for some other reason. It's the problem with being stuck here like this . . . there's no way of properly checking any background detail someone gives about themself."

Mrs. Bantry likes this. "It could be a cover! He could be an agent for the enemy. That sort of thing often happened in the books Arthur liked to read—Eric Ambler and such. His medical bag, full of lethal poisons—"

"It's certainly possible," Miss Marple says. "But I think there was real emotion there, real hurt, when he told us about his mother. I for one believe that he is Narracott's son. But I think you have touched on something important there, Diana. We are in a snowbound hotel in the middle of a foreign country. It isn't like an English village where everyone knows everyone else—an English village of the past, I should say, because even in our villages that aspect is being lost. So, I think it is worth remembering that not everyone here may be exactly what they seem."

She looks at me earnestly for a moment, before Mrs. Bantry says, "So who does that leave us? Within Narracott's circle?"

"Bruno Crane," Miss Marple says. "He certainly seemed to have no love for his so-called friend. Did you hear the coldness with which he spoke of him? Even after the man's death, he couldn't bring himself to pretend. I don't think it can have been friendship that bound those two together."

"So you think that he did it?"

"I think that there is a great deal he is keeping from us," Miss Marple says. "Whether or not he is a killer is another question. All that talk of enemies . . . he seemed genuinely fearful."

"*I* think he has it in him to kill," I say, "from what we saw in Catherine Narracott's room, and from what I saw today on the train, I mean."

"I think you're probably right, my dear," Miss Marple says. "But whether he could have pulled it off is another matter. This was something that took some planning and forethought."

"Do you have anyone else in mind, then?" I ask her.

But Miss Marple only smiles, enigmatically. "Oh, only a few wild ideas and vague suppositions that I'm sure would all seem very foolish, were I to say them aloud. Sometimes one has a premonition of something and it grows and grows—rather like a snowball rolling down a hill. There are things that don't quite *fit*. It is true that I am not a real detective, so I have to rely on a kind of intuition about these things, and sometimes that takes time. But I do think it likely that there is something or someone else we are not considering. Someone who is not what they seem . . . or something that seems almost beyond notice."

"Speaking of detectives, isn't Inspector Moreau divine?" says Mrs. Bantry, wistfully. "Wouldn't it be wonderful to have a son, or indeed a nephew, like him?"

"But I have dear Raymond, of course," Miss Marple says, with a note of gentle reproach. "And he has always been so kind to me."

"Ye-es," says Mrs. Bantry, "I suppose he has, in his way." She sends a look in my direction that lets me know, instantly, that she does not count herself among Raymond's foremost admirers.

"What about you, Diana?" Mrs. Bantry says. "Don't you think Inspector Moreau is divine?"

"Oh . . ." I say, feeling put on the spot. "He certainly seems very . . . capable."

"What are you looking at, Jane?" Mrs. Bantry asks, because Miss Marple is staring out of the window. "What have you seen?"

Almost dreamily, Miss Marple answers: "Oh, I was thinking of the glacier. All that ice. Hidden by a covering of snow, so that, at present, it seems like any other part of the mountain, unless you know it is there—hiding in plain sight, moving inexorably downward. A powerful, even dangerous force. Working away secretly, all the time."

BRUNO CRANE

The Friend

I sit on the end of the bed in my rabbit hutch–sized room and smoke one of the ersatz Camels I brought with me. God knows what's in them: radioactive waste and tea leaves probably, but it helps me think. I'm turning it over and over in my mind. Everything I've experienced in the last twenty-four hours. Something I saw. Something that didn't make sense. Something *wrong*. Someone who is doing a very good job of pretending. And suddenly I've got it! I know who has the stuff. The second I realize it, I know I'm right. It all makes a crazed kind of sense.

Look, I haven't always been the brightest spark. I'm certainly not the quickest either. But I'm not an idiot, for all that Narracott tried to make me out to be one. I know what is happening here—what has happened. And I think this might be my chance, to claw back what is rightfully mine.

I pull out the pad of hotel letter paper.

I know you have it, I write. *I know what you did.* Nice bit of threat there, but nothing too specific in case it falls into the wrong hands. *Half the gold for my silence.* Then I think, cross it out. Best not to get greedy. Narracott got greedy and look where that got him.

One third of the gold for my silence, I write instead. Yes, that feels reasonable. That should do.

Now I just need to hang about until the rest of this place is asleep and push it under the door in question. Then: await the reply.

DIANA GLASS

The Help

I sit for a time in the great hall after Miss Marple and Mrs. Bantry have gone upstairs to bed, nursing a small *digestif* of Génépi while the fire burns late in the grate.

Dinner was a subdued affair tonight: palpably less laughter and chatter among the guests, and it seems to me that most have retired earlier than usual.

I gaze into the dark beyond the windows. I'm on the valley side of the hotel and I think somewhere down there I can make out the faintest glimmer of the lights from the town at the very bottom.

"It's a strange feeling, isn't it?" says an English voice nearby. "The world feels . . . so far away, all of a sudden." I look up and see a young couple sitting there. "We're here for our honeymoon," the woman says. She runs a hand nervously through her brown bobbed hair. "It all sounded so magical in the brochure! Staying right up in the mountains, away from it all. But I have to say it isn't feeling very festive. Not with poor Anthony Narracott dying this morning—imagine, being a war hero and then perishing here . . . it seems such a waste, doesn't it? And then knowing that we're presumably stuck up here now . . ." Her voice breaks.

"Darling," her husband says, soothingly, reaching out a hand to rub her back.

"Sorry. You'd think I'd have more backbone after the war, after what we have all experienced. But this . . . oh, it's spooky. People have been saying he might have been *murdered*." She whispers this last word.

A little while later I manage to make my excuses and make my way up to my room. It's late—past midnight, the clock on the wall says—but the idea of lying down on the beautifully made bed with its plump pillows, shutting my eyes and expecting to fall asleep seems absurd. I am contemplating the cocktail cabinet in the corner and the sedative effects of a stiff drink when I hear a soft knock on the door. Could Mrs. Bantry need something? But hers would be a more imperious rat-a-tat-tat, no subtlety in it. I must have imagined it.

No . . . there it is again.

I make sure the chain is attached; then think of Bruno Crane crashing into Catherine Narracott's room and how much use it would have been then. As a precaution I take hold of the heavy paperweight on the desk and grip it in one hand as I open the door a crack with the other.

Inspector Moreau stands there, in the corridor.

"Oh," I say. "What are you doing here? It's past midnight."

"I'm sorry to disturb you," he says. "I thought I would see if you were still awake. I wanted to talk to you."

"It can't wait until the morning?"

He gives that small Gallic shrug of his. "Partly I wanted to check that you were feeling all right, after the train crash."

"I'm fine," I say.

"It's important to keep an eye on these things. A head injury can be worse than it seems. And I wanted to ask you a question . . . without your companions." The most subtle of glances over his shoulder and I know straightaway that he is referring to two elderly Englishwomen with surprisingly sensitive hearing. I'm suddenly filled with horror at the idea of either Miss Marple or Mrs. Bantry opening their door and discovering us standing in the corridor like this. I can't put my finger on exactly what feels improper about this situation—the lateness of the hour perhaps. I could refuse to let him in and answer his questions, of course. But would that seem in some way suspicious to him?

"Come in," I whisper, looking up and down the corridor to make sure we aren't being observed, before hurrying him into the room.

The door closes behind him. We seem to be standing rather close to one another. For a few moments I dare myself not to move, and then—like someone who has held her palm to the flame for as long as possible—I take a step backward.

"Would you like a drink?" I ask him. "I was just going to make myself one."

A short hesitation. "Yes," he says. "I would like that, thank you. A Ricard—if you have it. With a little water."

I go to the cocktail cabinet, surreptitiously replacing the paperweight on the desk as I pass it, and make up the drinks.

"So," he says, "you cannot sleep either?"

"I haven't tried," I say. "But I don't feel tired, yet."

"It was very impressive: what you did today, on the train. You were very brave."

"Funny," I say, carefully, "because I felt rather foolish, dashing off after Mr. Crane like that. I can't think what possessed me."

He frowns a little. "But you do not seem like a woman who does anything unintentionally."

"Well," I say, "I suppose I'm generally quite good at keeping a cool head in a crisis."

"Have you had many such crises?"

"Haven't all of us? The war, I mean."

I am unnerved by him. I can feel my heart rate increase as though I were stepping closer to danger: a snarling lion, a cliff edge. It seems impossible that he shouldn't be able to hear it, even from several yards away. I keep my back to him as I concentrate on pouring the gin.

"You said there was something you wanted to ask me," I say.

"Yes. You knew him, I think. Mr. Narracott?"

"No . . ." I say, my hand pausing in stirring the drink. "I think you must be mistaken. What gave you that impression?"

"I heard you in the Reception when you arrived," he says. "You said you worked at the War Office with him."

"Oh," I say, wondering where on earth he was in Reception to hear that on the first day. "No, we didn't work together. It's a very big place and I was just a secretary there. He wouldn't have had the first idea who I was!"

"But you knew who *he* was?"

"Everyone knew—Mr. Narracott was a big figure, a respected politician, a war hero."

"Ah," he says, apparently satisfied by this. Then he changes the subject: "Tell me, your Madame Marple. Do you think she is the real thing? You have spent some time with her, I think, and you strike me as a very intelligent person."

"I have only known her for the length of this trip," I say. "Definitely not long enough to call her 'mine.' But having spent a few days in her company I think I would not underestimate her."

I walk to him and hand him the drink. As he reaches for it our fingers brush. An electric moment. The rush of adrenaline I experience now is like the good twin of what I felt on the train.

This man represents a possible danger to me. And yet . . . there is a part of me that is rather fond of danger. A more reckless, impulsive part that I have spent the last few years keeping subdued.

"Well," he says. "I will be going now, Madame Glass." He checks his watch. "It's late." He sets his drink down, untouched.

BRUNO CRANE

The Friend

In the small hours of the morning, I hear a strange rustling sound. I'm not asleep, of course. I won't sleep again so long as I'm still here. I turn on the bedside lamp to see a piece of paper being pushed under my door. I go to pick it up, unfold the little twist of paper and read:

> *SILENCE IS INDEED GOLDEN*
> *AWAIT INSTRUCTIONS FOR WHERE TO MEET*

For the first time since I arrived here, I smile. I'm glad, now, that I didn't manage to hightail it out of this place. My gamble has paid off.

DIANA GLASS

The Help

At breakfast the scene beyond the windows is a blur of white; the snow coming down in thick skeins, the mountains lost to view. This weather has set in so emphatically it is hard to imagine it ever stopping, as though this white wilderness is a permanent state.

"What is it, Dolly?" Miss Marple asks. I had been so lost in my own thoughts I hadn't noticed—but now that I come to think of it, Mrs. Bantry does look very flustered.

"A bit of a bother," Mrs. Bantry says, "very foolish of me but I seemed to have mislaid my key. Of course I *will* keep leaving it around. You haven't seen it have you, Diana?"

"No, I'm afraid not," I say.

And then, in response to Miss Marple's curious expression: "Oh Jane, there's no great intrigue or mystery here! This *does* happen, you know, to some of us in this later stage of life. Not to you, my dear, your memory is as flawless as ever. But for us mere mortals. It is the machine wearing down. I'll have to ask Reception for another."

I don't mention to either of them that I have lost something, too: the roll of film from my camera. I do not want to draw attention to the fact and am trying not to worry about it.

Mrs. Bantry stops short at the sound of a glass being struck. The little hotel manager steps into the middle of the room, fingering his moustache.

"Ladies and gentlemen, Mesdames et Messieurs, meine Damen und Herren"—(I see the old colonel positively wince at the German address)—"we appreciate your patience over the last twenty-four hours. We know that the situation is . . ."—a delicate cough—"less than the perfect relaxation you might reasonably expect from the Grand Alpine. To provide a little amusement and some much-needed distraction and normality while we wait for the current situation to resolve itself, we have decided to go ahead with our open competition on our world-famous toboggan run, the Verglas, as scheduled. We are very proud of the Verglas . . . it is built anew every winter, always according to the same age-old design. But because it is built by hand and with the natural materials of packed snow and ice there are . . . slight variations in the course each year. Sometimes it is a little faster, a little slicker. Sometimes certain bends are a little more hair-raising. I hear that the bend at Red Folly is particularly something this year. It has claimed several riders already."

"Their *lives*?" one female guest asks, aghast.

"No indeed, Madame," he says, with a slightly obsequious chuckle, "only that they were thrown off the course and into the snow at the side. Although—" he seemed to be about to say something, but evidently thinks better of it. "Anyway. Those who wish to take part may register their interest at Reception. Unlike the Cresta, we allow women riders, and there is no upper limit"—I'm sure his eyes fall on Mrs. Bantry and Miss Marple as he says this—"on age."

A few hours later there is a festive air of nervous excitement outside, the guests pink-cheeked and huffing clouds of steam in the cold air, muffled up in sheepskin, wool and fur. Almost everyone seems to have come out, in spite of the still-falling snow and stiff breeze. There is a sense of relief just being out of the still, warm air of the hotel; the oppressive, endless sense of waiting.

"Seems a little odd, though, doesn't it?" a man says. "After a fellow's been killed and with our being trapped here."

"Well," his wife replies, "they expected us to keep calm and carry on while bombs were raining down on our heads and boys were dying in their thousands overseas. So I choose to enjoy our holiday."

The crowd is splitting now, into spectators and competitors: some of the guests claiming positions at the foot of the run, which winds up the mountainside as far as the eye can see and then disappears around the bend.

The course of the run is displayed on a metal map at the bottom and because the thing was devised by the early Victorian visitors to the area, the notable sections are annotated with English names: *Red Folly, Flying Fox, Howzat!* and *The Fourth Horseman*.

"Trust the English," I hear an American man say to his wife, "to turn some kids' playtime activity into a lethal sporting pastime."

Some of the spectators are hiking up the mountain on foot or on skins to view from a more elevated position, while others are traveling up the mountain with the would-be competitors via the button lift, skis on their feet. I see Charlie Levitt in his distinctive bobble hat making for the lift. He seems to be casting his gaze about the crowd as though looking for someone in particular.

"Doesn't it smell delicious out here!" Mrs. Bantry exclaims.

The rich sweet scent of cloves and cinnamon drifts from a large vat of Glühwein that has been set up at the bottom of the button lift, where smartly dressed staff ladle the stuff into cups for the competitors lining up to be yanked up the mountain.

"In the German-speaking areas," the little manager says, materializing suddenly at our side as if from nowhere (apparently we are in his favor, now that we have helped set the investigation in motion), "such a thing is known as *schnapsidee*—something that seems like a good idea *once* you have had a little drink!"

"I'm not sure that it would seem a good idea after three of those," Mrs. Bantry says. "It seems absolutely frightful. And that *contraption*"—she nods toward the button lift—"looks incredibly uncomfortable and really rather undignified. I'm not sure you could have tempted me even in my youth—Arthur would have loved it, however."

"I would like to do it," I say, as though I have just decided as much and hadn't already made up my mind to do so. The two elderly ladies look at me in surprise.

"Goodness, Diana," says Mrs. Bantry. "Are you sure you're up to it? That knock on the head . . ."

"I'm fine," I insist. "In fact, I think it will be good for me."

Mrs. Bantry looks unconvinced. "Well, rather you than me."

"But will you watch?"

"Oh *yes*," says Mrs. Bantry. "It sounds most thrilling. Jane and I will sit at the bottom, won't we, Jane? I heard there are more crashes than not—the last bend is apparently a real killer." She looks thrilled by the prospect.

In the registration area I am given a pair of metal shields to wear over my knuckles—made for a man's hands, they gape on either side and I can't fasten them as tightly as I would like. I have a leather helmet, goggles, knee and elbow protectors, and boots with spiked toecaps to help me slow my progress.

And finally, I am led to the start of the run, where for the first time I can look straight down the bluish-white chute of the Verglas. As I stare down at the near vertical channel, I am shot through with pure animal fear. I haven't been scared like this for a very long time. The worst that can happen now is that I might die. And, oddly enough, I haven't felt so alive for years. The snow has continued to fall all morning and there is a rime of fresh powder on top of the ice, the tracks of the previous rider running through it. It gives the run an almost deceptively soft look, as though it were lined in white ermine. But looking more closely at the tracks themselves you can make out the lethal sheen of the hardened ice underneath, in places glinting black as onyx.

CATHERINE NARRACOTT

The Wife

I am sitting with the two elderly women at the bottom of the run, where they have set up several rows of deck chairs for spectators beneath a kind of marquee canopy to protect us from the snow. Fur blankets have been provided. From here you can see the tobogganers on the final loop of the run before it ends in a straight chute and a run-off. I am wearing the best version of mourning I could assemble in the circumstances: my black mink coat with its matching hat, trousers made from the finest black wool, and black boots upon my feet.

"How are you, my dear?" Mrs. Bantry asks. "I know that it is not really the same, but I lost my own husband not so long ago, so I think I understand a little of what you must feel."

"It's just such a shock," I say. "I keep expecting to wake up and for it all to have been a bad dream. And . . . it's horrible being stuck here like this. Horrible, having people staring and whispering about one." I have always been a very private person, even with a politician for a husband. I was brought up to have a horror of scandal. Mummy always says a woman should appear in the paper only for her birth, marriage, the birth of her own children, and then for her death. She made allowances for Anthony's career, because she says it is my duty to support my spouse, though I think she always rather wished he were landed gentry, a general, or an ambassador in some grace and favor post where nothing really happens.

"I suppose this toboggan event may seem in rather bad taste," Mrs. Bantry says, "so soon after your husband's death."

"I imagine there is a fear of the guests being idle," Miss Marple says. "Idleness breeds iniquity, in my experience."

I say, "I do find it a little strange, but I have to keep telling myself that Anthony would have liked it, really. It is very much in his line. He would have been first to volunteer to compete. He was so courageous about such things . . . and something of a daredevil!"

"I'm sure I read somewhere that he won the Victoria Cross," Mrs. Bantry says.

I nod. "Yes, he did."

"May I ask how he won it?" Miss Marple says. "If you don't mind. Only, I know that sometimes it can be rather cathartic, to talk about a lost loved one's achievements."

"It's true," Mrs. Bantry says. "These days I rather enjoy talking about Arthur and his pigs. I found them a little . . . well, tiresome, when he was alive."

"Well," I say, smiling apologetically, "he didn't speak of it much. I'm not sure he *could*, you know. Such things are very hush-hush. But I know it was of course something very brave. And almost all the others had been killed."

"It was in the mountains?" Miss Marple asks.

I stare at her. "Why do you say that?"

"Oh, it's only a guess. Because Mr. Crane was his wartime friend, I suppose. And they talked of climbing together 'for old times' sake.'"

I am wondering if there is more to this old dear than I had first thought.

"Look!" Mrs. Bantry exclaims. The first rider has just shot out of the bottom of the run in a cloud of snow. He staggers to his feet.

"Oh!" I say. "How horrible!" Because as he stands you can see the blood pouring from his face, spattering onto the snow in crimson spots. But then he raises the hand not clamped over his mouth to give the spectators a thumbs-up. Finally, he removes the hand and grins . . . and I let out a little gasp: the smile reveals several missing teeth.

A whiskery old English type—I think at first glance it's Colonel Chapman but he's nowhere to be seen—turns to his wife and says: "There's normally at least one death every season. Could be today!" He sounds cheered by the prospect.

"Jane!" Mrs. Bantry says, turning to Miss Marple. "Should Diana really be doing this?"

"It's too late," says Miss Marple. "She's already gone up. Besides, I have the idea that once Diana has set her mind on something very little will dissuade her from her chosen course."

DIANA GLASS

The Help

As instructed, I lie down on my front on the small leather-padded platform of the sled. My face is a few centimeters from the ice. I can feel the cold breath of it on my cheeks. It is hard as stone beneath the rakes of my toecaps. I take a shaky breath. The nerves are getting to me now. Skiing, upright and with some degree of control, is one matter . . . I'm not sure I had quite appreciated what it would feel like, readying myself to hurtle down a mountain *headfirst.*

What am I doing?

I think of Mrs. Bantry's words at the bottom . . . I'm not sure I *am* up to it, actually. But then some rebel impulse moves me to push off, before I can change my mind.

The bone-shaking, terrifying descent begins. The ice is a deafening roar, even through the protective shell of my helmet. Flurries of loose snow fly up into the lenses of my goggles, temporarily blinding me at times, although I'm not sure it is helpful to see. Perhaps better to only feel—and pray. My knees judder against the ice and I scrabble for purchase with my splayed feet but the rakes don't seem to make any difference to the constant acceleration. A couple of times the sled rounds a bend and I find myself slung right up the wall of ice and sure I'm about to fly out of the side of the chute, but miraculously I stay the course. For the finale I'm tossed off a small ledge and for what seems like an age feel the air rushing about me and beneath the sled before it slams back onto the ice, rushing faster and faster and I'm gritting my teeth, actually closing my eyes in terror . . . until finally the track begins to flatten and then rise upward. The sled slows, slows and eventually comes to a halt on a bed of soft snow.

Afterward, I lie panting in the snow until two of the staff run to help me off the sled. I haven't felt pure terror like that for a very long time and yet there was something about the fear . . . something fortifying. It felt almost cauterizing, like a hot knife used to cut away rotten flesh. It feels as though it returned me to myself. A complete contrast to the numb gray fog I have existed in for the last few years in London.

I check the time on my watch. Just over a minute, from top to bottom. I want to go back up. I find my skis again, shuffle my way to the button lift. There is Bruno Crane, going up just in front of me. I take hold of the metal with one hand and am yanked up the slope. A couple of times I see Crane wobble and keel to the side as though about to fall, though it is difficult to tell if bad balance or alcohol is to blame.

At the top of the button, he does something strange. Rather than turning left toward the top of the toboggan run he turns right and begins to walk across the slope toward an isolated copse of pine trees, which cluster together some way above the main tree line. In the white expanse they look like a band of brave souls who have managed to make it farther up the mountain than their peers.

A few paces from the trees he turns around as though checking to see if he is being observed. I don't quite manage to look away in time, so he catches me watching him. Then he gives a horrible sort of leer and gestures toward his crotch. "Have to answer a call of nature, m'dear!"

Lucky I am so wrapped up that he likely can't see my expression, because it's difficult to conceal the powerful wave of dislike I feel for him in this moment.

BRUNO CRANE

The Friend

That should do the trick. Think I managed to put that nosy little spinster off pretty effectively too: the look of disgust on her face! She's already made enough trouble for me here, for God's sake. That's the problem with these spinsters, young and old. Too much interest in other people's business.

I can feel the point of the new note in my pocket, sharp against my thigh. My instructions:

> *MEET AT THE COPSE OF TREES TO THE EAST OF THE TOBOGGAN RUN, DURING THE COMPETITION, AND YOU WILL RECEIVE YOUR DUE. REMEMBER: SILENCE IS GOLDEN.*

Clever, suggesting the meeting take place during the event. Enough hubbub and distraction that no one should notice. And I will stay silent as the grave if I am required to. I will happily leave this place and never speak of it, or him, ever again.

I begin to plan my next move. Perhaps I do risk the pass over the mountains. It feels better than waiting here like a sitting duck, trying to keep my spoils hidden. Besides, I feel capable of anything now. A few ascents on skins, a few rather steep descents. How difficult can it really be?

I take a long pull of schnapps from the hip flask and hold the burn in my mouth for the Dutch courage. Booze and bullets: I've come prepared. The pistol nudges itself against my thigh.

This note writer clearly knew about the existence of the gold . . . but do they know what I had to do to get it? What I'm capable of? Well, if they get on the wrong side of me they'll find out—

Listen to me. Who am I trying to convince? Myself? No chance of that. I know I'm a coward, always have been. Now I don't even have Narracott here to force me to act. Suppose he was good for something.

Wish it wasn't such clumsy work going through this thick powder. I'm sinking to the knees and with each step I can feel the snow holding fast for a moment before I manage to pull my foot free. It's making me realize I couldn't get away all that quickly if I wanted to, which isn't a nice feeling. Was this their plan? I'm starting to feel a little foolish. But it wasn't as though I was given the chance to suggest an alternative meeting place.

I feel like I'm being watched. Like a mouse hunting for crumbs on the floorboards while knowing that the cat's about. The sensible mouse would go back to its hole. But I can't do that. Not if I want my share.

Was that . . . a movement? Up ahead, in the copse of trees? A shower of snow from one of the lower branches. They must be there, waiting for me. I push my hand into my pocket and grip the nice solid shape of the pistol. Slide my fingers around the cold shaft, find the trigger. Careful, Crane. It would be just like me to fire too quick, shoot myself in my own thigh or something equally stupid.

Idiot. You clumsy fool.

Well, you're dead, I tell him. *Who's the idiot now? Didn't see that one coming, did you?*

Another rustling from the trees. Still can't see anything there. Doesn't stop my heart going like the clappers and my stomach twisting in knots. Is that the figure of a person, crouched beside the trunk there? Or is it just the shadows? Damn hard to tell with the white glare of the snow in my eyes, that's the problem.

"Show yourself!" I shout. The sound echoes off the trees. Feel like an idiot, shouting alone in a snowy clearing. My voice sounds thinner than I'd like it to, scared.

A long silence. Nothing happens. But yes, there is definitely movement among the trees. And now I can see . . . yes, a face there, moving among the shadows.

"It's me," I say, "I've come to make a deal." A noise like a gunshot and I jump half out of my skin, only to realize it's a pine cone cracking beneath my foot, though I grip the cold metal in my pocket a little tighter. And there's something I don't like about the figure in the trees. Something that makes my skin crawl, though I can't work out why.

I pull the pistol from my pocket now, clear my throat. Want them to know I'm no fool. "Don't try anything funny. I'm armed! Come out of the trees where I can see you, and then we'll talk."

Closer still. A noise, too, different to the rustle of the pines. A creaking.

There's something wrong about the face in the trees. It's disfigured in some way. Ghoulish, monstrous even . . .

I don't like this at all. Every instinct is telling me to turn back. And then, stepping closer again, I see the face clearly. Not a person at all. One of those hideous troll masks from the dining room . . . hung in the branches and swinging back and forth in the wind—that creaking sound is the rope rubbing against the branch it hangs from. I feel my stomach clench with fear. What *is* this?

This is when I hear something behind me. Is that . . . the creak of the snow beneath footsteps? My bowels feel suddenly loose.

I grip the pistol, start to turn around, try to make sense of what—who—I'm seeing. "*You*?" I say. "But I don't understand . . ." And then—*crack*. My head. Something . . . hit me. My feet go out from under me as I lose my balance and tumble forward. I am scrambling to get up, scrabbling at the ground, but I cannot find purchase in the softness of the snow. My pistol has gone. And even as I am looking for it another *crack* that sounds very far away but I think might be the sound of my own skull, splitting.

A strange, quiet moment after the terror. I think I am alone now. Something warm in my mouth, taste of iron. I manage to roll over. Don't want to be face down for this.

I think of the youth now. Eight years ago . . . was it? Could have been yesterday, hard to keep track . . .

I felt worst about him. Lying there on the ground that night, he looked almost peaceful. An almost pretty face beneath the short fringe of his hair. His whole life ahead of him. And such bravery at such a young age . . .

Narracott pulling my arm. *Come on, Crane, you stupid lump of lard. We need to get away from this place . . .*

Crossing the border into Switzerland a few hours later . . .

Perhaps it was always meant to end like this . . .

I look up and glimpse the white sky through the tops of the pine trees. Hear the *shush shush shush* of the branches in the wind. Feel the cold clutching at me, entering me. The snowflakes falling upon my face as indifferently as they fall upon the earth and the rocks and all other dead things.

DIANA GLASS

The Help

"How was it, Diana?" asks Mrs. Bantry, over a late lunch of cold cuts and pungent mountain cheese, brought to us in the library where a few other guests are thawing from the cold.

The actress is here too, flicking disconsolately through a fashion magazine, several martinis in, judging by the collection of empty glasses around her, but looking the picture of glamour in a slightly-too-tight white silk shirt and charcoal wool slacks, her silver hair upswept.

"We couldn't really see very much, with the snow," Mrs. Bantry goes on, "but also with the way it is all laid out. All we could see from our seats at the bottom were the riders hurtling out at the very end of the run. It all looked like the purest form of madness, to me. Poor Catherine Narracott sat with us . . . I hope we gave her some succor, Jane. She seems rather a lost soul."

"It was terrifying," I say. "But also rather wonderful."

"Oh," says Mrs. Bantry. "You've hurt yourself."

I put a hand up to my lip, which is tender and slightly split. It has stopped bleeding, at least. "Yes, I think I must have bitten it on the run. I've definitely been in the wars . . ."

"We saw all sorts of people come down!" Mrs. Bantry says. "People you really wouldn't expect to be doing it—Colonel Chapman, that Prince Gustav, the young doctor . . . even a couple of nuns!"

"May I join you?"

I look up, see Inspector Moreau and, hating myself for it, feel heat rising to my face as I think of the late-night conference in my room. It is also because he is looking irritatingly attractive; his cheeks flushed from exertion and cold and his hair ruffled by the wind. It suits him; he looks as though he is in his natural state. There is a thick dusting of snowflakes on the jacket he is shrugging off and I find myself—ridiculous—admiring the breadth of shoulders revealed beneath. His eyes meet mine unexpectedly; I look quickly away.

The little manager passes by us on his way back to Reception, stopping briefly by Inspector Moreau to say: "Thank you, for suggesting that the toboggan competition should go ahead as planned. I would have thought it might be better to cancel, but it has improved spirits."

"Oh, it was your idea?" I ask Inspector Moreau.

"Yes," he says. "I thought it would be a way of suppressing the panic and claustrophobia of being trapped in one place—neither of which are helpful to me in my investigations. And you see how well it has worked out!" He checks his watch. "I think the competition should be coming to an end shortly."

"Diana took part!" Mrs. Bantry says.

He smiles at me; a generous smile revealing a deep dimple in one cheek. "Somehow," he says, "I am not at all surprised."

"And did you take part?" Miss Marple asks Inspector Moreau. "We didn't see you."

"No, Madame," he says. "Unfortunately not. I was investigating a couple of other leads back at the hotel while it was relatively empty of people. I was asking, for example, about the maid that some of the staff claimed not to have seen before on the morning Monsieur Narracott was poisoned. Unfortunately—for the investigation at least—she has been identified as a new employee, but a bona fide one."

"Oh, but you are dressed in outdoor clothes," Mrs. Bantry says.

"Yes, I went for a walk to think through the case," he says. "It does help the mind to do something physical, don't you think?"

"Oh indeed," says Miss Marple. "I do agree. I find gardening works very well for me. There was a—situation—in Dillmouth, a few years ago, where I found simply pulling out some bindweed in someone else's garden most edifying. Of course, it isn't possible here. I suppose a walk would be the next best thing." She glances up as the door flies open. A member of staff bursts into the room in a state of great agitation. He wears the fur hat and fur-lined uniform jacket that mark him out as one of those who was attending the Verglas competition. He makes straight for the manager; an urgent conference takes place. Finally the manager comes over to our group and whispers urgently to the inspector. I distinctly hear the words "*un autre mort.*"

Inspector Moreau turns to us, his expression now very grim. "Unfortunately there has been another death," he says. "Bruno Crane. Up the mountain. Some of the staff noticed the unusual activities of the birds. Apparently fifty to a hundred ravens, circling above the patch of trees some little way up the mountain from the top of the toboggan run, making a great racket and commotion. They appear very quickly at this time of year because there is so little food"—a quick grimace of distaste at the implication here—"in the winter, so high up. And they usually only gather in such numbers when there is a big carcass: a cow, in the summer, for example. The staff went to investigate and found Bruno Crane, lying in the copse of trees." He lowers his voice. "And it would seem he met a violent end."

DIANA GLASS

The Help

Apparently Moreau didn't lower his voice enough. There are gasps and exclamations from the nearby tables and I hear the word repeated over and over in several different languages, the whispers dancing strangely about the room: *dead . . . mort . . . morto . . . tot.* And then: silence. All are apparently waiting to hear what comes next. I suggest it might be more practical to move into the privacy of the *fumoir.*

"I would like to look at the body," Miss Marple says, once the door is closed. "But I fear it would not be wise."

"It is quite a grisly sight, Madame," Inspector Moreau says. "Not for the fainthearted. So I think you made the right decision."

"But that isn't my concern at all," Miss Marple says. "People do like to try and protect the old, as though we really *were* in a second childhood, with the innocence of infants who have just been born. It really is very odd, because what they forget is that in having lived the longest—and those of my generation have survived two world wars—we have experienced far more than the young. Unless one has lived the most sheltered life, and in an English village that is simply not possible, one has borne witness to most of the depravities and horrors to which human beings may lower themselves. And nothing, really, can be worse than finding the body of a child, can it, Dolly?"

Mrs. Bantry shakes her head, sorrowfully.

"Dolly and I experienced that horror together. So no, it isn't that. It is just that I will not make it all the way up there without being a very great hindrance to you. I am not as fit as I was even a few years ago, and with the altitude—But perhaps Diana can go with you and look at the body?" Miss Marple asks Inspector Moreau. "And report back to me here."

He turns to look at me. "If you feel up to it, Diana, I am happy to take you."

"Yes," I say. "I too have a strong stomach, these days." Is there anyone who lived through the last ten years who hasn't?

We make our way up on the button lift together and then, once we reach the top, leave our skis and hike up toward the trees to the east of the toboggan run. The same direction that I spotted Crane walking in just a short while ago. The mountainside is deserted. The emptiness echoes around us as we approach the site of Bruno Crane's death, the wind howling down over the peaks and flinging eddies of snow into our faces.

"I am impressed by your stamina," Inspector Moreau says, as we tramp ever upward through the thick powder. "I suspect if you were alone you would be moving even more quickly. I think perhaps I am holding you back?"

"Oh," I say, "I do a lot of hill walking, at home. And I got quite fit when training in Scotland with the FANY—though nothing on this scale." I had actually been thinking how unfit I feel.

"There!" he says, as we arrive at the copse of pines. We push through the laden branches of the firs, snow scattering down about us in thick clots. They open into a small space, within which the temperature seems to drop several degrees further. I find myself thinking of fairy rings and the strange things that are meant to happen in their enclosures. There is a strange hush; we are sheltered from the wind. The only sounds are our breathing and our steps: the sigh and squeak of the snow, the occasional crack of a pine cone breaking underfoot.

And there it is: the long dark shape among all the white. As we get closer, I can see more detail: the body, lying on its—his—back. In the fading light the stained snow beneath the head appears a blackish red. "Oh." The sound's involuntary. He's really dead. The knowledge goes through my body like a charge.

Finally I manage to drag my gaze away, to look about us. There are a few dull impressions in the snow that might once have been footprints.

"There appears to be one other set of footprints in this area—besides Crane's, I mean," Inspector Moreau says. "But of course it does not mean that they walked up at the same time as all of the other guests were about for the competition. Our murderer could have come up before, and waited."

"Can these marks tell you anything specific?" I ask Inspector Moreau, pointing. "The tread of the boot, anything like that?"

"Very little. Footprints when the snow is still falling this heavily are like . . ." He tries to think. "Oh, trying to decipher who it was that licked an ice cream cone. The impression is vague at first, anyway, and then quickly fades away into nothing."

A few feet away we stop and stand, just looking, in silence. I'm glad Inspector Moreau doesn't seem to require me to say anything, I don't think I would be able to find the words. I'd never really understood the expression blue with cold before, but now it is adequately illustrated by the corpse of Bruno Crane. He is such a strange color that it is a struggle to remember the figure before us was ever a living man. He looks like a wax effigy. But the blood that has seeped into the snow, in contrast to the dark clotted mass at the back of his head, is a vital living red, staining the snow all about the brightest crimson.

Inspector Moreau turns to me. "Are you all right, Diana?" The use of my first name is a surprise. He steps a little closer and in contrast to the freezing air I can feel the warmth of his breath upon my cheeks. "Here," he takes a silver hip flask from his pocket. "Brandy. This will help."

As he passes me the flask our gloved fingers brush, but I feel the contact as though it were skin upon skin.

I take a sip and feel the liquid scorch its way down my throat, lighting a warm fire in my insides.

"Thank you."

"You are welcome," he says. Then, "This note was found on his person." He shows it to me.

> *MEET AT THE COPSE OF TREES TO THE EAST OF THE TOBOGGAN RUN, DURING THE COMPETITION, AND YOU WILL RECEIVE YOUR DUE. REMEMBER: SILENCE IS GOLDEN.*

Inspector Moreau points, "It looks as though he was hit on the back of the head with something very heavy. Possibly a sled or even a ski. A sled, it is easy to see how that would be fatal, but a wooden ski could also do a lot of damage. I think he must have been surprised from behind by somebody.

"The question is how did he—such a powerfully built man—come to be taken by surprise like this? It looks as though there was something of a struggle. Look here—" He shows me the larger disturbance in the snow around the body. "I think perhaps he did not die straightaway. Perhaps he even lashed out at his attacker after he was struck.

"And how did the killer get away? The snow has been falling all day, definitely thickly enough to cover any tracks, so that helped them. But we will ask around: it is possible someone noticed them returning to the competition from this direction."

"It might not have been a tobogganer," I say. "Look at the *couloir.* It goes almost all the way down to the hotel itself. Because of the steep sides they'd be almost completely hidden from view and they could be back to the grounds of the hotel in minutes. Isn't that a ski track—look, there?"

"Possibly." He seems dubious. I think I sense some resistance to the idea. "But whoever skied it would have to be a true expert. It was practically a whiteout up here and that *couloir* is very steep and full of rocks." He shrugs. "Though it is true that there are plenty of excellent skiers here. Yourself included." He frowns at me.

"What is it?"

"You're bleeding—here." In one sudden movement he reaches up with one gloved hand and smudges his thumb against my lower lip. I close my eyes against the intensity of the sensation: a smart of pain mingled with a strange pleasure.

Over dinner, I relay everything to Miss Marple and Mrs. Bantry.

Finally, Miss Marple speaks and when she does her voice rings with an unfamiliar sternness: "There is real wickedness at work here." Any softness has vanished from her countenance, too; she suddenly seems quite formidable. I watch her, struck by the change.

"It seems a rather clever way to do it," Mrs. Bantry says. "Oh, I don't mean the murder itself—that I agree sounds utterly barbaric. I mean, in the midst of the toboggan competition, all of the chaos and excitement and busyness of that. People coming and going up on the button lift, coming down the run . . . so hard to remember who was actually where," Mrs. Bantry says. "Who was watching, who was up there, or ranged along the run—or indeed back at the hotel. Certainly it seems that *everyone* was everywhere, for a time. Did you see anything up there, Diana, during the competition?"

"You took the button lift up after Bruno Crane, I think," Miss Marple says, and as I am beginning to realize with Miss Marple, the "I think" usually seems to stand in for: *I am absolutely certain and recall with complete clarity.*

"I did," I say. And I might as well tell them: "I saw Crane make his way toward the trees. He—there is no way to put this delicately . . . he told me he was, well, going to relieve himself in the snow."

"But really he had a rendezvous!" Mrs. Bantry says.

"Or something that was presented to him as one," says Miss Marple.

"A rendezvous with death!" Mrs. Bantry says, in macabre tones. Miss Marple gives her a very mild *look* and Mrs. Bantry looks slightly abashed.

"He was such a big strong-looking sort of a man," Miss Marple says, "that it's rather hard to imagine anyone getting the better of him."

"Not if he were worse for wear," I say. "He looked as though he could barely hang on to the button going up. He might well have been drinking. Or it's very likely he hit his head on the train yesterday, and had a mild concussion."

"Well, it is all a great shame," says Mrs. Bantry. "Another man's life . . . of course, even if he was quite evidently what Arthur would have termed *Not a Gentleman*. In addition, I don't know about the two of you, but he was *my* chief suspect for the first murder."

CATHERINE NARRACOTT

The Wife

I sit with a Lillet Blanc listening to this evening's musical entertainment. It's hard not to think they're trying to enliven the atmosphere with a bombastic rendition of Cole Porter's songs. The vampish singer—spangled wiggle dress, peroxide hair and lacquered red lips—could be a double for the hotel's most famous (infamous) resident.

"Would you like some company, my dear?"

I look up to see Miss Marple, toting a generous knitting bag.

"Oh," I say, "yes, please. If your companions can spare you." In this lonely, fraught time she is a comfort, in spite of everything. She reminds me a little of Great-Aunt Elizabeth, on Daddy's side: very discreet and proper.

"All of us being trapped here," I say, over the clicking of Miss Marple's needles and the strains of "Night and Day," "it's like a nightmare! Everyone is frightened . . ." I gesture toward the other guests. They hunch over their *digestifs* talking in low tones and darting suspicious looks at the strangers about them.

"It's just awful," I say. "My husband, and now his friend . . . Mr. Crane was not particularly . . . pleasant, of course. I was very frightened when he burst into my room and threatened me. But all the same. And I can't help thinking that now *I* might be in danger," I say. "What if they come for me next?"

She nods. "Inspector Moreau is working hard to find the culprit. But, my dear, if you notice anything or anyone behaving in a way that seems odd will you promise to let *me* know, too?"

"Yes of course," I say, though wonder how on earth she, a frail old woman, can think she might be of any help. Both of us observe the crowded room for a few moments in silence as though someone might in this very moment be about to reveal themselves as a murderous madman.

Then Miss Marple sits forward a little in her chair. "And I have been thinking, Catherine. I couldn't help noticing that there seemed to be some confusion from Bruno Crane about your being here too . . . I wondered if that meant there was some other *business* element to his and your husband's trip here. Did Mr. Narracott mention any other motive in coming to the mountains?"

"Not to me," I say. "But I am beginning to wonder about it myself."

Back up in my room I go to the bathroom and brush my teeth and then my hair one hundred times, like Nanny used to, until my dark hair shines like jet. I find grooming soothing at times of high tension; it feels like a way of keeping body and soul together. I go to pluck my eyebrows too, but realize I have forgotten to bring my tweezers. Overlooking a little qualm of *wrongness*, I look through my husband's washbag for a pair. I do not find any tweezers, but I happen upon something else tucked deep into the inner pocket of the bag. I pull it out. It is a photograph. The shock of it is as sharp and unexpected as a wasp sting. I *know* this person, though only in the sense that they are currently staying at this hotel. But what possible business does their picture have being in my husband's washbag?

I pace up and down as the clock ticks cacophonously in the silent room, looking at the photograph and feeling Anthony's absence as I wonder about his possible connection to this person.

DIANA GLASS

The Help

Late night, but a fire still crackles in the grate in the near-empty bar, throwing strange shadows across the silk-lined walls. Smoky jazz seeps from the gramophone. The few guests sitting at tables talk in low murmurs. The staff move about silently, grim-faced: no longer chatting and joking with guests and one another. I realize I haven't heard the sound of laughter in some time.

I use the not-so-secret painting entrance to step into the deeper privacy of the rustic Stübli, order a whisky from the bartender and take a seat at one of the stools. *"Pas de glace, merci."*

"For a moment there you sounded like one of my countrywomen!"

I turn. "Inspector Moreau."

"Call me Christophe, please," he says. "I am off-duty. May I?" He indicates the seat next to me.

"Of course," I say, take a sip of my drink and wince as the alcohol stings my injured lip.

"It hurts?" he says.

I shrug. "Only a little."

"But then you seem like someone who is very brave. I imagine it would take a great deal for you to complain."

There is a long pause. In this darkened room, empty save for the two of us and the man behind the bar, the air suddenly feels as though it has a weight to it—a charge. I am conscious of the physical presence of the person beside me, the warmth of his body, the movement of his hands as he picks up his glass, even the rise and fall of his flat stomach as he breathes.

For goodness' sake, Diana. This is what being cooped up like this does to you. This is what being alone for too long does, too.

"I wish the circumstances were different," he says, in a sudden rush, "in which the two of us were sitting in a bar together."

I can't think of anything to reply. I feel suddenly stupid, tongue-tied. But there is also a kind of triumph. *So he feels it too.*

A new record on the gramophone. Charles Trenet's "*Que Reste-T-il De Nos Amours.*"

We listen for a moment in silence. "You know this one, I think?" Moreau asks, looking at me closely.

"Yes." I clear my throat. "I haven't heard it for a few years. Perhaps . . . '43?"

The part where it unexpectedly picks up in tempo—a sudden memory . . . capering like children, cackling with laughter . . . then the song becomes wistful again.

"Did you know," he says, casually, lifting his glass, "I've just realized your eyes are the same color as this cognac? No," he lifts it up to the fire so that the light shines through. "This is it."

"Oh," I wave a hand, embarrassed.

"I'm sorry," he says, with a sudden grin, "am I being too French? I apologize . . . but you know, ever since I lost my wife I decided that I would never pass up an opportunity to pay a compliment. I wish I had told her every day how beautiful, how special she was, how rare. Beauty, youth, even life—they are so fleeting, no? And those fascinating elderly ladies you spend your time with . . . they know it better than any, I would think. And you, did you lose someone too?"

"What makes you ask that?"

"Nothing in particular. Or everything, I suppose. You carry it with you."

I actually laugh out loud at this. "Well, that's just wonderful! You make me sound deformed . . ."

He smiles, but says, earnestly: "No, I didn't mean it like that. Only that I know it because I recognize the burden myself."

We order another drink and all too quickly, it seems, these are finished too. I feel a little too buoyant, as though a few of the strings that tether me to a particular code of behavior have been cut. It feels precarious—and exciting. Then the barman tells us that he is closing up the Stübli for the evening.

"That is a sign that I should go to bed," says Inspector Moreau.

"So should I." But I have a dread of returning to the solitude of my room and my thoughts. I walk with him out of the bar and into the elevator. We seem to be standing very close to one another. I can feel the warm draught of his breath against my cheek. My skin prickles. I am suddenly aware of the nerve endings in my fingertips, on my scalp, between my shoulder blades; the sensation of my clothing against my skin. Each of us could give the other more room if we chose to, but neither of us makes any immediate attempt to move away. There is something about space, or lack of it, that is so eloquent. Our proximity to each other makes a mockery of any pretense we have made up until this point that there is no attraction between us. The elevator seems to rattle agonizingly slowly up through the floors. If I stand here with his gaze on me for a moment longer I feel that I will say or do something humiliating.

His room is on the same floor as mine; the third. Finally the doors open and I find myself taking a deep breath, as though the space inside the elevator was short on air.

We walk along the corridor. We reach my door. His gaze slides across to meet mine.

"I suppose I could come to your room," I say. "For a nightcap."

He blinks quickly a couple of times. Those thick-lashed dark blue eyes. In spite of the dim light I think I see a faint blush surface on his cheeks. He is flustered, on the backfoot—and I rather like it. This beautiful man; this man who perhaps represents a danger to me . . . I have a brief power over him. It is like rediscovering a muscle I thought had atrophied. Coming so close to death on the train yesterday reminded me of this, but also the war taught us too. If you want something, take it while you can.

We pass my door and keep walking.

Inside his room, I find that I suddenly have to think about how to breathe. My heart is going double time—whether with excitement or nerves I cannot tell. I excuse myself to go to the bathroom. I splash water on my face, dab scent on my wrists, stare at myself hard in the mirror. I do not look quite like myself. I have the slightly glassy eyes and flushed cheeks of a woman with a fever. But I am also reminded of someone. It takes me a moment to understand who. It is myself, but my younger self—who feels these days like a stranger, divorced as I am from her. I hadn't realized she was still in there. I pinch my cheeks and then feel silly for doing so . . . will he notice the effort I've made? Hopefully not, in the low lighting.

This sort of thing was easier in the war. There was an unspoken code. Niceties could be forgotten when death was so near. To cling to another warm body, even a stranger's, was a way of clinging to life.

It has been so long. At first it would have felt like some terrible infidelity—and besides I was simply too sad. And then I worried that I might forget the smell of his skin, as though it might be eclipsed by another's. Recently, I realized I had forgotten it anyway.

I step out of the bathroom. I step toward him.

Afterward, I stand and begin to dress. I forgot myself for a while: a blessed relief. But now I am aware of a knot of feeling in my neck, like unshed tears. I'm not sure if it is more from guilt or grief. But there is definitely both.

"Are you all right?" he asks.

"Yes," I say, with effort, through the knot. I reach for my necklace, clumsily, and as I lift it the ring slides down and off the chain; it clinks to the ground and rolls away underneath the bed. "Oh!" The whole thing feels freighted with meaning, somehow—an ill omen. I drop to my knees and reach a hand under the bed just as Christophe Moreau shouts: "No!"

But I am already reaching with my hand. I encounter drifting pieces of lint and dimly register that even in this grand hotel they do not clean that well under the bed. Then I finally touch the ring and then . . . my fingertips nudge up against something else.

"What—" I draw the thing out. Things . . . photographs. I am aware of him standing there in an attitude of great tension, as though he wants to snatch them from me but knows he can't. Instead he lets me spread them across the coverlet of the bed. "What are these?" I ask, dread mounting before I even fully understand what I am looking at.

The photographs show two men, on the mountain, at night. They are familiar—*very* familiar—and yet they don't make any sense here, like this. I look across at him and see his expression of dismay. "These . . . are from my camera?"

A long pause.

"I had them developed," he says, finally.

"You *took* the film?" I feel winded. "The other night, when you came to my room?"

It must have been in that brief few minutes when I turned my back to make the drinks. I'm ashamed at myself too, at my own stupidity. I have been so careful, for so long. All my planning, all my hard work . . . all of it thrown away over a man, who, it appears, has simply been using me for his own ends.

He at least has the good grace to look apologetic. "I'm sorry. I have an investigation to conduct here. I sensed that you were very reluctant to hand the film over. So reluctant, in fact, that I thought it would probably *disappear* or even . . . suffer some accident if I didn't act quickly. So yes, I confess it: I took the roll of film from your room when I visited you there. It was easy to create a darkroom downstairs—there are many small, lightless spaces in a hotel. The staff were very accommodating. They understood it was important for the investigation. No, it was not orthodox. But nothing about this has been. I have to . . . to do things I wouldn't normally do."

I stare down at the photographs, unable to look at him. My face burns. Could the latter be a reference to what just happened between us?

"Can you explain why you took them?" he asks. "They are nearly all of Anthony Narracott and Bruno Crane." He moves a new photograph to the top of the pile to illustrate this point, then another, pointing with his finger as though I can't see it all myself with my own two eyes—as though, for goodness' sake, I wasn't there that very night on the other side of the lens. I simply follow the movements of his hands stupidly, obediently, still unable to speak. "Here they are, talking together. Here—it is difficult to make out, because I think it is taken using the light of the full moon as your only source, but it shows them going into some sort of mountain hut. You followed them up the mountain, at night . . . why?"

I don't answer. I try to pick up one of the photographs but it vibrates in my hand so much I have to set it back down. I am shaking with shame, fear and perhaps, most of all the sense of betrayal.

When he speaks again, he is on the offensive, the police detective once more: "All of your photographs, Madame Glass"—Madame Glass, no *Diana* now—"are of two men who have recently been murdered in this place. Other than this one and this, which shows some of the nuns, and this mountain scene . . . You do see how this looks, don't you?"

"I—"

"It looks as though you were very preoccupied with the activities of these two men."

He points at the photograph taken by moonlight. It is blurry, but it has come out better than I might have expected in the conditions. In very different circumstances I might almost find some pride in my work.

He points to the one with the men entering the mountain hut. "What are they doing here? Can you tell me?"

I don't think I could get my mouth to form words even if I wanted to.

He tries again with the next one. "Did they take anything out of the hut?"

I shake my head again, dumbly.

"And here," he says, putting the next in front of me, "do you see this? There is another figure in this photograph. Do you see?"

"What?" It is more a sound than a word—a shocked yelp. I look properly at the image in question and as I do a chill washes over me, like an echo of the cold felt on that freezing night. No, I had not realized there was another person caught in the frame. I had not been aware that there was anyone else there that night.

I stare at the figure. They are almost completely in silhouette and a blurry one at that, because they were clearly moving during the long exposure. Someone else was up there on the glacier. But who on earth could it have been? I wasn't aware of anyone other than the two men at the time . . . but then I was so focused on them and their activities that I perhaps wasn't paying as much attention to the surroundings as I should have been. I squint at the figure, my heart racing. Did they see me? The idea that someone else might have been watching me while I watched the others is truly frightening.

"Who is it?" I ask.

"Impossible to tell," he says. "But if I can develop it again and blow it up this time . . . I believe there are ways you can make an enlarger from scratch."

"Whoever that is," I say, "might be the murderer."

I look at him and realize he is watching me with an inscrutable expression. Understanding dawns. "You can't think . . ."

He shrugs. "I'm not sure *what* to think, Madame Glass." Again, the formality of my surname stings. Then he sighs, softens. "The truth is, I wanted to show you first," he says, "even though it is—

yes—unorthodox. I am not the official investigator of this case. I—I like you, Diana. I want to give you a chance to explain yourself. *Can* you explain yourself?"

Again, he is watching me closely. He waits for an answer, but again I find that I cannot speak.

Then, all of a sudden, there is the faintest sound: it comes from outside, from the corridor. His head snaps up. He is thinking the same thing I am, that someone is listening at the door.

How much have they heard?

"Who's there?" Inspector Moreau calls.

No answer, of course. He stands and walks in quick strides to the door, throws it open.

"No one," he says, showing the empty corridor beyond. He shakes his head, stepping back into the room. "Whoever it was, they were too quick."

I have the strange and slightly outrageous idea that it could have been Miss Marple, listening hard with those keen ears of hers. I'm sure that she is nimbler than she appears. The idea of it fills me with dread.

SYLVIA SINCLAIR

The Star

Three a.m. Closing time for any self-respecting nightclub on the Sunset Strip. I tramp along the snowy path toward the trees, Herb trotting alongside me. I suck in nice big lungfuls of air. The little black moths came for me in my room. This is so much better than sitting there, ruminating, hoping for sleep that even Nembutal won't bring.

"This is blowing them away, huh, Herb?"

Herb is having a great time, snuffling through the fresh powder like a furry snowplow. Guess they'll have to use one of those special brushes on him when we get back before he can shake wet snow all over the place.

It's so quiet out. But a better quiet than inside the hotel where the silence is *loud* and my room too warm and close. I look back at the Grand Alpine. I like the place a damn sight better from here. Right now it looks like a fairy-tale palace, light streaming gold from some of the windows. All aglitter. But then I guess Hollywood glitters from a distance, and behind the scenes it can be one of the dirtiest, most demeaning places you've ever been. The things they make you do. Well. Just have to keep putting one foot in front of the other, like now. *Tramp tramp tramp.*

I'm at the trees now. Each one is wearing her white fur coat: very much my style. The lights of the hotel have nearly disappeared. It's a little spooky. I'm kind of wishing I had a flashlight to hand. I clutch Herb's lead and stop awhile, waiting. Because I think I heard . . .

I listen hard. Is that . . . footsteps? The soft pad and squeak of boots on snow? Hard to make out what's just the shush of the wind in the trees or the occasional *whoomp* of powder falling from a branch.

"Hello?" I call softly. My voice casual as old Frankie Sinatra's attitude to fidelity, but my heart going fit to burst. "Anyone there . . . ?"

DIANA GLASS

The Help

"I have been thinking, Jane," Mrs. Bantry says at breakfast. "I must get out of this place, if only for a couple of hours. Don't you feel it too . . . the *oppression* of it? It's rather like being . . . oh, inside a snow globe held in the grip of an angry giant."

Miss Marple's fine eyebrows rise at this unusually poetic description from her friend. "Yes, but Dolly—"

"Oh, I know, I *know*. We're stuck here until the snow stops, until they can clear the tunnel . . . but I thought that we could still have a little outing. I've arranged with the concierge that we go on a little excursion in the horse-drawn sleigh. Apparently there is a charming route into the trees. It's funny . . . there was a little confusion over the arrangement of it, but it is all ironed out now."

"What do you mean, Dolly?" Miss Marple asks.

"Oh, it's silly really." For a moment Mrs. Bantry looks oddly upset, and I see Miss Marple watching her in concern. "Let's not dwell on it—it's all too boring to bother explaining. Only . . . only that I am becoming so forgetful these days. But no matter . . . it seems a very good idea. Don't you agree, Jane? Let us just enjoy a charming outing in the snow! It is exactly the sort of thing I imagined us doing before all of this awfulness happened. If it sets your mind at ease, I will ask for our sleigh driver to be the burliest man of the mountains they have available. And the snow has grown a little lighter so we won't be absolutely covered. Look!" She gestures through the window. It's true: the falling snow now appears like lightly sieved icing sugar, rather than shaken goose-down. "And I have been assured we will be well wrapped up in furs and sheepskins."

"All right," Miss Marple says, "if that's what you would like to do, Dolly."

"Diana," Mrs. Bantry turns to me, "will you come with us? It isn't a three-line whip, however."

"If you would like me to come, of course . . ." I say. "But I suppose it would make things more comfortable for the two of you," I say, "more room in the sleigh, you know . . ."

"I don't *need* you there," Mrs. Bantry says, benevolently, "if you would rather not."

"Then I shall stay here," I say. "Take a nap perhaps. I'm feeling rather tired."

I did not sleep well last night.

CATHERINE NARRACOTT

The Wife

The waiter brings my breakfast: scrambled eggs with wafer-thin shavings of black truffle. Miss Marple turns to give me an approving nod. She told me to keep my strength up, though I have little appetite. I decided to risk coming down to breakfast this morning. To ready myself for the occasional stare I still seem to attract, I have had my hair freshly set at the hotel's coiffeuse and a manicure. I am wearing a gray silk shirt and jet earrings. Mummy was right: when times are hard, one's wardrobe should work even harder.

I smile back at Miss Marple. There seemed to be some small confusion or upset among the three ladies, but now all is calm again. I watch the companion as she turns away from them. As she does, her face changes. The smile slips to a grimace. It reminds me of something. Then it comes to me. It's what my husband used to do, when he was speaking to constituents. He'd put on what I thought of as his politician's mask, his elderly-lady charming smile. Then, as soon as he was out of sight, he would let it drop—usually with some muttered remark about the low intelligence and breeding of the average person.

She stands and leaves the table. I watch her, thinking that she seems somehow very different to the woman who arrived here. As though—how to put it?—some camouflage or pretense has fallen away. It isn't the clothes. They are just as dreadful as before, quite frankly. It is the woman *inside* them. She seemed rather meek and mousey that first day in Reception, but now I have the sense of someone steely . . . strong. She passes by my table, her gaze fixed on the door that leads out of the room. The phrase *wolf in sheep's clothing* floats through my mind.

DIANA GLASS

The Help

I accompany Mrs. Bantry and Miss Marple outside to get ready for their sleigh ride expedition, then head back to my room. Walking to the elevators, I nearly collide with Inspector Moreau. The last person I would have wanted to see in this moment.

"Diana," he says. "I'm sorry. Last night. . . " He dips his head and I can feel him trying to meet my gaze. But I won't allow it. It is painful to look at him now.

"It's no matter," I say.

"I know you must think me duplicitous. It . . ." His tone is regretful. "If the circumstances were different. You see, don't you? I am bound by the role I must perform. I came here for a reason—"

"What? I thought you said you came here for a holiday."

"Oh," he says, "I mean that it is—ah—almost like Fate has *provided* me with a reason for being here. An inspector, snowed up in a hotel with two murders! So now that I am here, I find I must perform my duty. Do you see?"

"I think so," I say. "Now, if you don't mind, I'm going to my room now. Perhaps I will see you later." And then, dully: "In the meantime, I'm sure you will want to show Miss Marple the photographs. I know she would be interested to see them."

Miss Marple and Mrs. Bantry will already be embarking on

their sleigh ride by now; I don't bother to tell him this. What can it matter now?

As I pass him, he reaches for my hand. In a moment of weakness, I let him hold my fingers for a second in his warm grip, feeling the ache in my rib cage grow.

SYLVIA SINCLAIR

The Star

I sit in a sleigh wrapped in my furs and a generous cloud of Shalimar, with Herbie beside me, rushing down a track through the fir trees with the snow landing frozen kisses on my cheeks. No, I didn't get murdered in the woods last night . . . and I just had to get out of the hotel this morning!

The horse pulling the sleigh is white as the snow itself, very picturesque, with a lovely silvery mane (about the same color I ask my hairstylist Bobby for) and steam huffing in big clouds from his pink nostrils. I guess for the full movie version I just need Jimmy Stewart sitting beside me, not Herb.

We've been out for a good hour, so it's a good job I chose my thickest mink. It's a little addictive: the speed, the cold on my cheeks. The thrill of it reminds me of the bottom of the second martini, when everything seems to sharpen just before it all starts to blur. Sitting here in my fur-lined chariot I feel like an ancient queen. Or perhaps Garbo in *Anna Karenina* (Vivien Leigh just didn't do it for me, poor doll). Either way it's a nice change after sitting in my room—and especially after the phone call I had with my agent before I set out.

"So, this guy?" I asked, picturing him sitting there in sunny Palm Springs on the other end of the phone, "this . . . *Brando* you said his name was? How old is he?"

My agent coughed. "Twenty-six."

"And they want me to play his mother? They do realize I'd have been ten years old when I had him? That don't seem a little wrong to you?"

"I'm afraid that's Tinsel Town for you. Don't sweat it a bit. You'll do a number on them. Besides, I've got them to agree to a great fee!"

He named it, like it was something to be celebrated. Less than half what I used to go for.

I wanted to say to him: *Screw you and the horse you rode in on. Oh yeah, and you're fired.* But of course I couldn't. So I said, "Fine. I'll do it, so long as they don't age me up like some frumped-up old matron. I want to be the kind of mama that really fires up the old Oedipal complex, you hear me?"

Speaking of old matrons, I pass those two old English dears in a sleigh and give them a little wave, while holding tight to Herbie's collar with the other hand so he can't leap out and terrorize them. They look rather sweet all cozied up together in the back of the sleigh and chattering away together the way gossipy old broads do.

We round a bend and the hotel comes into view. We're nearly back there, in fact, when all the birds take flight from their branches and the horse rears up, hooves flailing at the air, as the most god-awful scream comes tearing out of the place.

DIANA GLASS

The Help

Even before I open my door, I know that the scream must have come from Mrs. Bantry's room. I hurry into the corridor from my room, just as a maid stumbles from my employer's. All the color has leached from her face; her cheeks are streaked with tears.

"*Que s'est-il passé?*" I ask. "What happened?"

It is several minutes before I can get any sense out of her. She is so upset that she is hyperventilating. Finally, she is able to find her voice. In French she says: "Something"—she covers her mouth with her hand—"something very terrible has happened, Madame. I went to do the room service, you know and . . ." She trails off, then continues in another language, one that I don't recognize—Romansch, I think—as though she can't express the horror in anything but her native tongue.

"Please," I say. "I don't understand."

"*Un mort*," says the maid, finally, her face ghastly. "*Un autre mort.*"

"*Dans cette chambre?*" I ask. "This is my employer's room—please, I need to go inside."

She moves aside to let me pass. I have a moment of hesitation on the threshold as the anticipation of what awaits me inside surges in my chest. And then I step, alone, into the room. I look about me, making sure not to miss a single detail.

There is the faint sound of voices, English voices, chattering quite merrily, but the room is apparently empty, seeming to look back at me with a blank, innocent face. Neat as a pin due to the maid's efforts: the bed immaculately dressed in its white linen, the chair tucked in at the little dressing table, a light scent of the pine resin they must use in the cleaning products upon the air.

It is very cold in the room; my breath mists as it would outside. The balcony doors are open.

"They were *not* open when I went into the room," the maid says, entering behind me. "I went out onto the balcony to let in some fresh air." I notice the slight nicotine staining of her teeth and wonder if this provides the explanation. "And because I heard the voices . . ."

We move out onto the balcony and it becomes apparent that this is where the voices are coming from. A wireless radio, propped just out of sight of the room itself, has been set up on the little ironwork table, the volume turned up to full. Two patrician English voices squawk animatedly from it: unmistakably the BBC Light Program. I learned during the war that it was possible, albeit dangerous, to tune in from France.

There is only one last place to look. And so we peer downward, through the vortex of falling snow and mist. Because the hotel is built on a promontory on this side, the drop is even bigger than expected. At first it is very difficult to make anything out. Then the freezing mist ebbs a little, and a large shape comes into view. A sprawled figure, arms and legs splayed at angles they could never have found in life.

He has fallen three stories onto the snow below. It seems somehow impossible that the apparent pillowy softness all around should not have totally cushioned the fall and prevented the death; that instead—it is clear from the angle of the limbs it has broken his body as surely as if he had fallen onto rock.

I find that I can't stop looking. Which is odd, as I know that the image will already be burned into memory, as clearly as if I had taken a photograph.

"Diana!"

I drag my eyes away and look back into the room.

"What's going on here?" This spoken by Mrs. Bantry, followed swiftly by Miss Marple.

"Something's happened," I say. My voice sounds oddly distant, as though I am hearing it from the end of a long tunnel. "Another death." *Un autre mort.*

Mrs. Bantry and Miss Marple step carefully onto the balcony. They too are now able to make out the long shape of the body, the distinctive blue Alpine sweater.

"Oh, but it can't be . . ." Mrs. Bantry says. "Inspector Moreau . . . dead! I don't believe it."

I watch Miss Marple. In spite of everything that has happened here I think this is the first time I have seen her appear truly shocked. I might even have believed her unshockable. She frowns. "But I had thought . . ." She trails off, apparently lost to this unspoken reverie.

"Who would dare kill a detective?" Mrs. Bantry asks.

"Someone very desperate," Miss Marple says. "And very wicked."

An unnerving change has come over Miss Marple's countenance. The softness of her elderly features seems to dissolve and the planes of her face become harder, unforgiving. Those faded blue eyes are suddenly as cool as steel. I would not have believed it possible if I had not seen it myself, but an elderly lady who at times dithers and twinkles and is prone to rambling and flights of fancy, suddenly looks like the personification of some dreaded winged creature from an ancient myth. She even seems to grow in stature. It sends a chill through me.

"I suppose," she says, "he must have seen or learned something that meant the killer was prepared to take the very great risk of murdering him, too."

"But why was he in *my* room?" Mrs. Bantry asks, once we have stepped back inside and closed the doors to the balcony, as if by doing so the horror of the scene outside can be kept somewhat at bay. "There is so much that cannot be explained, of course, but that is the thing I keep coming back to."

"Well," Miss Marple says, frowning, "that at least I think is rather easy to guess. I imagine he received a message, from 'me,' ostensibly. Saying I had some detail that I just *had* to tell him, must urgently discuss with him. A phone call, perhaps . . . or even a simple note. And whoever it was must have known that I would be out for some time, that the coast would be clear for them to stage their horrible plan. The problem is that so many might have known, or indeed seen us getting into the sleigh, that it really doesn't narrow things down in any useful way . . ." She trails off, apparently lost to her thoughts.

"Jane," says Mrs. Bantry. "Oh, but it's too awful . . . I think it might have been worse than all that. This might be partly my fault."

"What do you mean, Dolly?"

"When I told you, before, that there had been some confusion about the sleigh ride, what I really meant was that I forgot that I had booked it. I could not for the life of me remember having done so. But I was too embarrassed to say. After the incident—losing my room key. In all honesty I suppose I was a little frightened. One hears of this happening in later life . . . forgetting things. Small things at first and then increasingly larger things until in the end one loses oneself entirely. I did not want to make an *issue* of it. I did not want to acknowledge the possibility that it might be happening to me. But now I wonder—"

"If you never booked it in the first place," Miss Marple finishes. "Dolly, I think it highly likely that you did not. Moreover . . . I do not think you ever lost your key. It seemed odd at the time and it is now perfectly clear to me that it was stolen. That of course explains why Inspector Moreau was called to a meeting in your room, rather than mine.

"Somebody wanted to ensure you would not be in this room, not even in this hotel. And then I have no doubt that a message was somehow conveyed to Inspector Moreau that we needed to talk to him as a matter of greatest urgency. He came in here and heard the voices on the balcony. The voices on the radio, that is. With the balcony doors closed they would have been harder to recognize for what they were."

Mrs. Bantry nods. "Oh how devious, and how horrible." She frowns. "And I suppose any of the guests or anyone working at the hotel could be a suspect in this . . ."

"Yes," says Miss Marple. "We saw the actress out on our sleigh ride but apart from her, I think, most others would have been here. It *was* devious, as you say, Dolly. And yet," she says, "there are also aspects of this that feel more hazardous than the other two crimes. Still a certain degree of planning, but with more risks taken. He was killed in this very hotel, thrown off a balcony where the whole thing might have been witnessed from outside by a guest. Unlikely, but possible. Why, you and I could have become too cold and decided to come back from our sleigh ride earlier!"

"We nearly did just that," says Mrs. Bantry.

"So I think," says Miss Marple, "that this shows an element of desperation. They, like the rest of us, are trapped here, unable to escape. Diana," she says, suddenly, turning to me. "Where were you, when this occurred? You didn't see, or hear anything odd?"

"I was in my room," I say. "And no, I was . . . well, I was having a rest. I haven't been sleeping well. I woke only a little while ago. I heard the maid's scream and I ran here."

"This must be stopped," Miss Marple says now, "before it can go any further. Before they kill again. Because this is what happens—" Now the transformation reverses, like the spell in a fairy tale wearing off, and a frail old woman stands before us once again. In fact, she looks almost slightly frailer, as though the change cost her something. And I see the sadness now, too, that this has hurt her, personally. "I have seen it before. The first killing is planned in advance. They have been clever; it is planned out. It is the only one they think will be necessary. But then they need to kill again, and again, to prevent detection . . . and the poison spreads. They need to be rescued from themselves."

"And you can do that," Mrs. Bantry says. "Can't you, Jane?"

Miss Marple nods once, grimly. "Yes. And they will have their just deserts." I feel a whisper of that same chill I felt before.

A short while later we are let into Inspector Moreau's room on the floor above, the hotel manager putting up no fight when we request the key. Perhaps he has decided this elderly Englishwoman is now his best hope. Or perhaps, more likely, he has given up entirely in the wake of this third killing.

The air inside has a particular stillness about it. It is not like me to be fanciful about such things, but the clothes—the jacket hanging from the back of the chair, the tough-soled boots tucked away beside the wardrobe—they somehow *look* like the clothes of a dead man. Forlorn relics, never to be worn again. I swallow, my throat dry.

The photographs will be in here somewhere: I know it. There . . . on the little desk. I can see them laid out. Pulse quickening, I try to move around the bed toward them without looking like I am rushing, trying to block the view with my body.

"There!" Mrs. Bantry says. "On the desk—look. Are those . . . photographs?"

My heart sinks. I can't very well seize them and hide them now.

The three of us move toward the desk. They are spread out, a magnifying glass beside them.

Miss Marple turns to me. "These are your photographs, I think, Diana?"

"Yes," I say, trying to keep the dismay from my voice.

"And here," Mrs. Bantry says. "Look: a note."

Something to discuss with you as a matter of great urgency. Will you come to see me in Mrs. Bantry's room? JM.

"So this is how the killer tricked him," Mrs. Bantry says. "You were right, Jane."

"It is all very wicked," says Miss Marple. "And a great tragedy, that another young man has been cut off in the prime of life." Then her tone changes, becomes more purposeful. "Now I suppose we will find out who he really was."

"What do you mean, Jane?" Mrs. Bantry looks at her.

"Only that he was no policeman," Miss Marple says. "Of that, at least, I am quite certain."

DIANA GLASS

The Help

"What can you mean, Jane," Mrs. Bantry asks, "that he was not a policeman?"

I am glad that she has asked the question because it is the one I too want to ask, only I don't seem to be able to form the words.

"Just that, Dolly. Perhaps he was really called Moreau. But he was not an inspector with the Paris Judiciaire as he told us, I am quite positive of that. What I do not know—and perhaps we will never know—is whether his killer knew that, or whether it was the disguise that cost him his life."

"But how have you decided all of this?" Mrs. Bantry asks.

"I have suspected it for a while," Miss Marple says. "Probably even since the moment he introduced himself. It was too convenient, too much of a neat coincidence, him simply appearing like that. But more than that, I thought it strange that he didn't want to prove his identity to us from the outset. Policemen I have known seem to have such a fetish for badges and other pieces of official regalia.

"And now there is this note, which certainly proves he is no detective, because even though this is written in lower case and the one Bruno Crane received was in upper, it is clear to me that it is the same hand. Even the same pen. And finally, there are these photographs," she says, looking at me now. "He took the film from you without asking."

"How did you know?" I ask her.

"He asked you for the film in that first meeting and you seemed to me extremely reluctant to share it with him. I thought then, watching you, that there was no way you would part with it unless forced to do so. I've seen how you carry that camera bag around with you as though it is something very precious. So I assume he took the film against your will. That is what has really decided me."

"Why?" I manage to ask, finally finding my voice.

"Because it was duplicitous. It was an underhand trick—ungentlemanly, too. A policeman should not stoop to such measures, even in the pursuit of truth. It was, really, theft. In my experience even those police officers who sometimes use rather wrong-headed methodology and jump to wild conclusions—Inspector Slack comes to mind, Dolly—follow basic laws of decency in their investigations and certainly do not break the law. The French are different from us in many ways, but I am certain their morals on such a matter would be the same. Stealing a piece of property from your room seemed beyond the pale."

"But you didn't say anything, Jane!" Mrs. Bantry exclaims. "You didn't ask to see any badge or anything like that."

"No, Dolly, I didn't," Miss Marple says. "I'm afraid to say that I myself was a little duplicitous in that respect. Though I assure you I did so with the best of intentions and my conscience is somewhat salved by knowing that. I realized, you see, that by staying close with Inspector Moreau I myself could try and stay close to the investigation, could hear the interviews, and perhaps bring my own—of course very amateurish—experience to bear. If I had revealed that I knew he was a fraud none of that would have been possible."

"Jane!" Mrs. Bantry sounds partly admiring, partly scandalized.

Miss Marple opens the drawer of the desk and draws out a large leather portfolio. "Ah!" she says, pulling something out. "His passport." She opens it. "Not even French. He was Swiss. And the name, look . . ."

I do. Kristoph Mauer. Inspector Christophe Moreau was a phantom, a cipher.

Miss Marple gives me a quick glance, then continues. "And as you'll see here, in the '*profession*' section it says '*banquier*.'"

"A banker?" Mrs. Bantry asks.

"Yes. Whereas if he were really a detective for the Paris or indeed any Judiciaire, as he claimed, it would of course tell us as much. Diana, perhaps you can continue to look through this." She hands me the portfolio. "My rheumatic fingers—you will be quicker."

I continue to rifle through the rest of the wallet. I pull out scraps of paper and documents and spread them on top of the desk: an edition of the Swiss daily *Die Tat*, a train timetable for the Zürich–Bern line, even—it falls onto the desk with a metallic clank—a small pistol.

"What dupes he made of us all!" Mrs. Bantry says. "Well, not you, Jane. But I wonder what he can have been up to, pretending to be a policeman? And talking to everyone in such detail . . . he must have wanted to get something out of it. If he were still alive and we'd learned all of this I might have thought we'd found our murderer, but as it is . . ."

"I think," Miss Marple says, "he was pretending to be a policeman in order to seek information."

"But why? He had some kind of . . . what, hero complex? Wanted to help?"

"It is natural to want to help in some way," Miss Marple says. "When something dreadful occurs. I know the instinct very well myself. But no . . . I think his reasons were perhaps more mercenary. 'Banker' is the clue, I think." Her eyes go to the pistol on the desk. "I wonder what sort of banker he really was—"

"Here," I say. "I've found something."

A telegram. I show the others:

> **Arrived Switzerland. Await instructions for meeting at Grand Alpine to make transfer. Swiss Bonds preferred. AN**

"AN must be Anthony Narracott, of course," Mrs. Bantry says. "But what does all this mean?"

"This, I think, is our answer," Miss Marple says. "Inspector M—sorry, this Kristoph Mauer—was trying to find the treasure."

A stunned silence.

"The *treasure*?" Mrs. Bantry asks. "What can you mean?"

"Treasure," Miss Marple nods. "The same thing that Anthony Narracott came here for. Oh, I think it very clear that Mr. Narracott did not just come here for a skiing holiday with his wife. From that first meeting, Bruno Crane seemed confused as to why Catherine Narracott was here too—even rather put out, as though the men had some other prearrangement between themselves. I think he had come for the same thing Narracott had. There was the time he barged into Catherine Narracott's room, searching frantically for something. And finally the note he received, 'silence is golden . . .' Of course it is a turn of phrase, but there was something about how the 'golden' was underlined, don't you think? And we know he was a desperate and frightened man, so whatever drew him up the mountain that day was something that had a powerful hold over him."

"And the 'inspector'?"

"This telegram suggests Mauer was supposed to make some sort of transfer, no doubt in exchange for the treasure. After the other men's deaths, of course, he was probably even more interested in finding it. Once they had been killed he wouldn't have had to give anything in return. Posing as a detective was a clever way to try and gain information as to its whereabouts: through his 'investigations' of the hotel, through his lines of questioning."

"But he seemed so nice!" Mrs. Bantry says.

"He was very attractive and very charming, I suppose," Miss Marple says. "But that is not necessarily the same thing, unfortunately. In fact: often quite the opposite."

"But treasure?" says Mrs. Bantry faintly. "It—it seems like something from a book by Hammond Innes! Don't you think it's all a little far-fetched?"

Miss Marple shakes her head. "One only has to pick up a paper these days to learn of gold hidden inside salt mines, or on trains hidden deep inside mountain tunnels, or sunk in Austrian lakes. I have learned all of this from an armchair in St. Mary Mead. I think perhaps whoever is now in possession of the treasure—I have no doubt that someone *is* in possession of it—decided Mauer had become a danger in some way. That he had to be stopped." She turns and looks at me. "Do you agree?"

I'm suddenly finding it hard to swallow. "I suppose . . ." I clear my throat. "I suppose that all makes sense."

Miss Marple nods and then says, almost kindly: "And now, Diana, I think we need to have a little talk."

DIANA GLASS

The Help

"Firstly, there are aspects of yourself that I think you have been concealing, my dear. Your fluency in French for a start. When you speak it in our company, it is with a marked English accent, and full of errors. But every so often you forget, or perhaps you think you are not overheard, and it sounds quite different."

"I don't know what you mean," I say.

"At those times you speak it like a Frenchwoman; or as close to as my ear can detect. I suppose if one is fluent, it is a challenge to pretend *not* to be. It would be like me trying to pretend not to speak English properly. It must be very trying. It would be easy to forget and make mistakes. But what a curious thing, for someone to conceal their proficiency in a language. It must mean that you are concealing some aspect of yourself."

She is right. It *has* been difficult, to remember not to slip back into a language that comes almost as easily—though a little less easily these days—as my mother tongue.

"And of course that wasn't all. There was your laundry."

"My *laundry*?"

Miss Marple looks a little flustered. "This is not the sort of thing one should really talk of in polite company. But there was that laundry bag of your underthings that was delivered to me in error. For a woman of your position and salary one would expect good, serviceable cotton. Not silk of the finest *momme*, trimmed in leavers lace. Each of those pieces, and again I apologize for my indiscretion, would cost more than your monthly wages. If they had been several years old, that would have suggested a falling on more straightened times. But I like to go up to London for the sales, to refresh my linens. And I saw at least two of those pieces in the "new" collection last year in Harrods. It was the lilac silk that stood out particularly in my memory. They belonged in the wardrobe of a wealthy young woman.

"It is a little like pretending to be *worse* at French. Someone wanting to make themselves look better off—well, that is understandable. But the opposite . . . well, that is something one sees much less often. It made me think that you hadn't taken this job for the money. You had taken it for some other reason."

I try my best to brush this off. "I don't know what to say, Miss Marple. Perhaps I am just silly with money."

"No, Diana. There is nothing silly about you whatsoever. You are the sort of person who always has a plan, I think. Speaking of which, I think it was no coincidence that we came here at the same time as Anthony Narracott, was it? On the train journey up here, Dolly was trying to recall what it was that prompted her to choose this hotel and you were so quick to remind her that it was the advertisements. I remember thinking at the time that you seemed anxious to deflect any credit from yourself."

"It was *you*, wasn't it?" Mrs. Bantry says, suddenly. "I hadn't really any idea of coming to the mountains before you came to work for me. When we first met I told you that I was looking for some help at home and with booking some travel . . . but *you* were the one who suggested I come here. *I* had wanted to go to the Caribbean, originally, as I had heard the warmth was very good for one's joints. But you said that the cold air and the waters of the spa here would be better.

"I think that you did it subtly, over a little while, so I didn't notice what you were doing at the time. It is only when I think back on it now . . . like at the end of a game of bridge, when it becomes clear that one's opponent has been playing a truly fiendish strategy all along." Mrs. Bantry frowns. "But the dates," she says, thoughtfully. "That at *least* must have been a coincidence: that we were here at the same time as Narracott."

"Ah," says Miss Marple. "Yes, it could only be this weekend, because the hotel was full on *all other dates*. At least, according to Diana, who booked the whole trip herself." She turns to me. "*Was* it really full, in all other weeks? It seems unlikely—such a huge place, so newly reopened." Almost kindly, she adds, "You don't have to tell me but it will be easy enough to check."

I shake my head, which seems to be about the most I can manage. "No."

"It is as I thought then," Miss Marple says.

I can feel my hands shaking, so I fold my arms to hide them.

Miss Marple continues, "Now we have the photographs, of course, of the two dead men, which I believe you were trying to conceal from us when we entered the room. You wanted to remove them, I think, before we spotted them."

"I—"

But then Miss Marple changes the subject. "Your fiancé," she says. "I am sorry to bring up something painful for you, my dear, but he was French, wasn't he?" And then, before I can answer: "You know, I think it's only the second time I've ever seen such a ring. We had a French Mam'zelle at school and I used to admire hers. The two silver hearts and the seven garnets *a la Duchesse Anne*: It's a wonderful example of the type: a beautiful French antique. Not a style one really sees in Britain. I do pride myself on a certain attention to detail in such matters."

I shouldn't have worn it. Except I have to wear it, close to me always. It is the only thing I have left of him.

"There is something else I have noticed about you. You run toward danger. The train, for example. It made me realize that you are someone who is very brave . . . and possibly also somewhat reckless. It led me to wondering whether your work for the FANYs in the war might have had something more to it than sitting in an office in England. Would that be correct?"

The eyes are so very blue in her pale, heavily lined face. Suddenly I feel a great weariness. What is the point in pretending any longer? I've kept all this inside for such a long time. I have more to lose now, I realize, by staying silent.

I take a deep breath. "They stole something. Narracott and Crane. I knew they would come back to try and take hold of it. I wanted to make sure they couldn't. Make sure I got hold of it instead. Not for myself, but in honor of some very brave people who died in vain. But it wasn't me who killed them. I promise."

I turn to Mrs. Bantry. "I admit it. It was me who suggested this place to you, not the brochures. I had been keeping an eye on Anthony Narracott for a while. That's why I took the job on the switchboard at his offices. I was here, during the war. Well, not quite here. On the other side of the mountains, in France."

"The FANYs?" asks Miss Marple.

"Well . . . at first." I will not—cannot—name the organization I became a part of. Instead I say, "My mother was French. People like me . . . we were useful, during the war." I have a sudden vivid memory of how it actually felt to get the call-up. The thrill of it. When you are as young as I was only seven years ago—and I mean this more as a state of mind than of age—you believe you are immortal.

"Very brave work," Miss Marple says.

"Yes. I suppose so," I say. "Though a lot of people were very brave."

"But many were not," Miss Marple says. "Very easy, for people to claim, in hindsight, that they were. Who is there to check?"

"Especially if everyone else is dead," I say. The words are out in a rush, before I can stop them. "I know this for fact: Anthony Narracott was not brave. Neither was Bruno Crane. There—there is ordinary cowardice and then there is something far, far worse . . ."

I find that I am shaking. I am incriminating myself, I'm sure. And yet I can't stop. It might as well all come out now.

"There was a German caravan," I tell them, "full of gold, coming through France to Switzerland, because that is how the Nazis funded their war machine—with gold that the Swiss magicked into banknotes." Gold stolen from the central banks of occupied states . . . but also from people's homes, from their fingers . . . from their very teeth. "It was our job to intercept it . . . like a hold-up, I suppose you could say. I was seconded to help an Alpine chapter of the Resistance, as a pianist."

"A . . . pianist?" Mrs. Bantry asks incredulously.

"Sorry—a radio operator. It was how I met my fiancé. The chapter . . . they called themselves 'the wolves of the mountain.'"

Somehow dusk has already fallen. When did that happen? I stare out into the growing darkness beyond the window and for a moment I am somewhere else entirely. That night. The soft rain. The scent of the wet earth after a spring day of surprising heat. The headlamps, rising over the curve of the hill and then coming closer and closer through the pitch black, wobbling and blurring a little in the light drizzle. The single lights of the two motorbike outriders, the twin lights of the truck.

Crouching behind boulders among the damp gorse, legs scratched through my thin trousers by its barbs. My heart in my chest like a hunted rabbit's; though we were supposed to be the hunters that night. Fabien beside me; his hand over mine, warm and dry. *Only when I make the call.*

"What about the others?" We were supposed to be receiving support from another Special Operations group.

"They haven't shown. We'll have to make do. It has to be now."

Closer, closer, until they were nearly upon us; until they were nearly past. And then the howl—the howl of the "mountain wolf," our signal—and all of us springing from the shadows.

The driver: shot dead almost instantly; the two outriders too. A couple of others with their hands up. But then, horrible surprise, a second set of headlights. A second truck, unexpected reinforcements—members of our group falling now.

I was punched back by something. I didn't feel the pain at first. Just a strange wetness, a tight pressure. And then agony all at once: livid, incredible—my whole shoulder on fire. My legs gave out and I fell forward into the gorse. I could only watch, helpless, from my prone position, my head on one side, as they were all killed. People I had slept and eaten beside, exchanged childhood stories with. People whose parents had given me shelter, whose children I had looked at picture books with. People who had become family in a matter of weeks, because what we shared was more binding than blood. All now lying dead or dying in the road.

"Your fiancé, too?" Mrs. Bantry asks.

"What?" I had forgotten I had an audience—I had forgotten where I was. I was there, that damp spring night in 1943, on the other side of the mountains.

"No," I say. By some miracle, he was unhurt. "And then they arrived."

Just when it seemed it was all over, two men appeared as if from nowhere. Our help, at last. We had expected more of them, but they would make all the difference. In a matter of bloody minutes the rest of the Germans were dead. Most of our group were dead, too. Only four survivors. Fabien and I (barely), and the two British officers.

"Fabien—my fiancé—got up, went to meet them in the road, to thank them. And then he turned to start checking on some of the others in our group . . . I thought at first he had tripped. Even though I heard the sound."

One of the newcomers had raised his gun and shot him at point-blank range, in the back of the head.

A terrible silence. Then a few more shots, which I suppose was them making sure of the others.

The teenager. Look. Is he still alive?

Who could they mean: the teenager? There wasn't any teenager. Then I realized that it must be *me*, with my short hair, clean jaw and bulky men's clothes.

"Go and check, Crane. Shoot if you're not sure."

He stood over me. I could hear him panting, felt the toe of his boot nudge me in the ribs.

Oh God, oh God, he was whispering, over and over. He sounded terrified. I could only play dead and pray. It wasn't difficult—I *felt* near death. Could hear the sigh he made; the sigh of someone deciding upon a course of action. I knew then that he was about to shoot. Maybe I even longed for it, because what did I have to live for, now?

Then the sound of his steps, retreating. The two of them talking at a distance once more.

Are you sure?

Yes, dead as a doornail.

Before I slipped into blissful oblivion again the last thing I heard them say was: ". . . *over into Switzerland. Neutral territory. Hide the stuff there and come back for it if we ever win this war.*"

"The next thing I knew, I was being transported to a prisoner of war camp in the Vosges. I stayed there until Liberation. I had no idea who those men were—they had had *noms de guerre*—but I knew from the accents that they had been British."

The next time I saw one of them was in the *Evening Standard*, at an Underground station. There on the third page: one of our most promising new politicians. *Wartime hero; Victoria Cross.* I didn't even consciously make the connection at first, but my body knew: I had to run and vomit onto the tracks.

I feel now a little as though I have just vomited—or when one does after a storm of crying. Shaky, weak, every nerve ending exposed . . . and yet purged of something.

"I took a job at the War Offices," I say. "And then I began to tail him, using everything I learned in my training."

It wasn't even difficult, to listen in on his drinks with Bruno Crane in the grimier drinking holes of the capital, stand in line behind him as he made his bookings at the travel office for a few months' time. He thought he was so clever, so wily—but he was arrogant and arrogance made him stupid.

"My dear child," says Miss Marple, with true sympathy. "Such terrible things. I am so sorry, for all that they did to you, for all that you lost. You do see, though, that all of this . . . this *awfulness* provides you with a rather strong motive for having wanted both these men dead? And then, with Inspector Moreau finding the photographs—"

"Yes," I say, and even I am surprised by the fierceness of my tone. "But what I had planned for Anthony Narracott was worse than death. A man like Narracott lives on his reputation. I wanted to see him eviscerated, publicly, by exposing what he did. Hence the photographs. I wanted to find the gold and hand it to our government. And I wanted to make sure that our country could never be led by a man like him. Ultimately, I hoped that with a little evidence he might be tried for treason. He would be hung for that, I suppose. So, in a roundabout way I *did* want him dead. But not by my own hand. That would have meant stooping to their level." I take a deep breath. When I speak again my voice is so harsh I don't even recognize it as my own. "I didn't want to kill him. I wanted to *destroy* him."

CATHERINE NARRACOTT

The Wife

The hotel is gripped by fear now. Many of the guests have retreated to hide in their rooms. The ones that haven't are louder than ever, frantically demanding they be allowed to leave, which we all know is impossible. Since Bruno Crane's intrusion my room is no sanctuary. So I've spent most of the afternoon sitting quietly in the library, hiding from the frenetic atmosphere elsewhere in the hotel, watching the snowfall beyond the windows begin to lighten. As I gaze about the room I catch the eye of the young doctor: Charlie Levitt. A shock: He must have come in here without my noticing. His look seems particularly malevolent. I reach for a book as a distraction and also to hide behind. I think of all my unpleasant interactions with him so far in this place. I shiver. He is still an unknown quantity.

Just before dinner, those guests that can be tempted from their rooms are called into the great hall for an announcement.

"The weather is improving," the hotel manager says. "I want to reassure all of our valued guests that the Swiss police should be here tomorrow morning—at the latest. They have sent a climbing team up the mountain. And a team of engineers is already at work on the derailed train in the tunnel."

A couple of people send up weak cheers, but then: "How many more people will be dead by then?" a woman cries.

This encourages a man to shout: "There's a maniac on the loose! You expect us just to wait here?"

"*Armons-nous!*" from another man.

"He's right," the first woman calls. "If you aren't going to protect us, we should arm ourselves."

Perhaps more disturbing, though, are the few guests who now choose to behave as though all that has happened has been a mere inconvenience in the middle of their holiday.

"Will we be able to go skiing?" asks one man, standing up. "The gondola will be open again, surely? All this fresh powder going to waste . . ."

"I'm afraid not, sir," says the manager. "With the conditions—the heavy snowfall in such a short space of time, and the wind, there is a very great risk of avalanches. We must make sure that it is entirely safe before we allow you to go out."

The man tuts crossly and sits back in his seat.

All this violence, all this death: and they can talk as though it didn't really happen. I suppose it is because it didn't really happen to *them*.

"How are you feeling, my dear?" I start a little; I hadn't seen Miss Marple standing so near to me.

"Odd," I say. "Very odd. Frightened, of course. I agree with those guests . . . who knows what might still happen before the police get here? But also . . . I don't know who I *am* now. I came here as one thing—a wife—and I will leave as another. I'm not sure who I am without all of that. I wasn't always happy with my husband, he could be rather cruel—I'm sorry if that's a dreadful thing to say—but it is all I was ever brought up to be. That," I say, with real feeling, "might be the most frightening thing of all. I feel like a climbing plant that has had its support removed. But thank you," I say. "For everything. You have been such a comfort to me, here."

She nods solemnly. "You're welcome, my dear. And I can understand all of that well. But, you know, I think you are stronger than you realize."

Back in my room once more, I step out onto the balcony and realize it is no longer snowing. Up above me the sky is huge and luminous with stars.

Several hours later, the small hours of the morning, I wake to the sound of someone entering my room. Footsteps crossing the boards, coming closer and closer.

My breath is caught in my throat, my heart pounding so hard I think I might be sick, or faint. I close my eyes and try to summon all my courage. I am going to need it. Little sheltered Catherine Narracott, forced to prove her mettle at last. I think of Miss Marple's words to me earlier: "I think you are stronger than you realize." The moment has come, just as I knew it would. Fate has caught up with me at last. This, then, is how all of this ends.

DIANA GLASS

The Help

A thundering on my door. I open my eyes to a dim blue gloom. I know from the light that it must be very early in the morning. I sit up in bed, heart thumping and suddenly very alert. Before I answer the door I call out "Who's there?" and am relieved to hear the unmistakable patrician tones of Mrs. Bantry. "It's me, Diana! Quickly, open up."

"Do you hear that?" she says, as I join her in the corridor, pulling a robe hastily about me. "The most inhuman and awful howling—coming from somewhere above. Please don't say there has been yet another death. I have never been the sort of woman to talk about my nerves, but I am beginning to feel that mine will not take much more of this."

I can hear it now and understand why it has so upset Mrs. Bantry. The sound is truly hair-raising, an agonized wail. It seems to be coming from the floor above us. We wake Miss Marple and the three of us climb the stairs to the next floor, following the noises which seem to grow ever more tortured, more animal. My sense of dread mounts. What are we about to find?

"I can't bear it," says Mrs. Bantry, as though echoing my thoughts. "Is this safe? It sounds as though someone else is being murdered at this very moment."

DIANA GLASS

The Help

As we near the door from which the noises seem to be coming, something odd in the tone of the sounds becomes apparent. And as we move closer still, I hear something else: a scrabbling at the wood.

"It sounded animal," Miss Marple says—wearing a very simple, sensible high-necked dressing gown that somehow makes her appear just as proper as the wool and tweed suits, "because it actually *was* an animal. If I am not much mistaken, this is Sylvia Sinclair's room, and that is her Irish wolfhound, howling and scratching at the door."

"So she's . . ." Mrs. Bantry grimaces, "in there, dead?"

"No," says Miss Marple, "I think not. Not if my intuition has been correct."

Members of the hotel staff are summoned. As Sylvia Sinclair's door is opened the animal leaps into the hallway with a volley of barks, knocking the poor manager flat on his back and terrifying one porter into a dead faint.

Of Sylvia herself, there is no sign. Inside, the room bears the sign of a hasty departure: the plush carpet has dirty marks from what appears to have been a pair of heavy-soled boots, the bulky packaging of several food items has been discarded, clothes have been pulled onto the bed and most of them, it seems, rejected, including the priceless furs, the velvet evening gown. There is a feeling of absence, of abandonment.

In the bathroom, the sink is thoroughly stained with black dye: a packet of which has been crammed into the bin.

"So where is she?" Mrs. Bantry asks.

"Gone," says Miss Marple, sounding almost satisfied and as though all of this is absolutely as expected. "And I think—unless I have got this all very wrong indeed—we will find that Catherine Narracott has gone, too."

CATHERINE NARRACOTT

The Wife

The snow is a pristine, glittering mantle over everything. We are at the top of the world. Or so it seems. Switzerland is behind and beneath us, on the other side of the pass. We made the climb in the small hours by the light of the moon, seal skins strapped to the bottom of our skis, the packs on our backs full of gold.

The dawn is a pale pink haze on the horizon to the east . . . the very same pink as the washed-silk of my wedding dress. It's not very *proper* of me to say that, is it? But I have finished with proper. Proper found me in a marriage with a man who was an oppressor and a phony, a man who spent all of *my* money, my inheritance, and then planned to leave me like a dried-up husk once I had expended my usefulness. Even though I did everything that was expected of me, everything I was trained to do. A man who made me smaller and smaller, who seemed to bite little pieces from me every time he snapped or scorned or belittled or bullied. But fear and anger are not so far from one another, it turns out. Like a much-kicked dog who suddenly remembers she has teeth.

I said that phone call in the London apartment changed everything. Imagine, if I had hung up the receiver as I had wanted to, had gone back to my life of pretending not to see, not to hear, not to know or care . . . how differently things would have turned out. But after I had taken that message and number "for Tony" I couldn't stop thinking about that voice on the other end of the line. The loneliness in it that seemed to speak to something inside me. And so I slipped that piece of paper into my own pocketbook. I called the number back, a few days later. We talked.

Down there, somewhere below us, is Italy. And then . . . onward. Even Sylvia will be able to disappear, if it all goes to plan. Especially with her new raven hair. You might think: but how will *she*, a Hollywood bombshell, go unnoticed? The key is the "shell" of bombshell. Sylvia's hallmark is her hair. You'd be amazed how much of a difference it makes. Think of those icons of the silver screen—Marilyn Monroe, Jean Harlow—and try to imagine how different they might look like without the platinum blonde, without the makeup. You can't really, can you? Sylvia's face, without all of *that*, is really surprisingly, wonderfully, ordinary. She has been *creating* herself, as Sylvia Sinclair the movie star that is, with more and more effort over the passing years.

Of course, we may not be safe in one place forever. But I have been still for too long. Still and good. I have spent so much of my life already trying not to take up too much space. Behaving. All things nice and sugar and spice. I don't have to pretend at all, don't have to hide any element of who I am. No longer do I have to tamp down the unsightly parts of myself. The unacceptable yearnings. And I'd take constant movement with her—a lifetime of running, if needs be—over stillness anywhere else.

DIANA GLASS

The Help

"It really all comes down," Miss Marple says, "to hair and dogs."

"Hair and . . . dogs?" Mrs. Bantry repeats, faintly.

"Oh, and nuns!" says Miss Marple, quite cheerfully. "Hair, dogs and nuns. Some clever—and very wicked—planning. And several rather foolish mistakes."

"But Catherine Narracott and Sylvia Sinclair hated one another!"

Miss Marple nods again. "Yes. We have all seen that. Haven't we? The martini thrown in the restaurant, the disdain. In fact, I wonder if we have seen it a little *too* clearly. If the performance was not a little too convincing, a little too perfect.

"The scene we all witnessed in the restaurant . . . it seemed to me not to fit. Particularly for someone of Catherine Narracott's sort of upbringing. The English upper classes, in my experience, employ similar tactics to the breeding of young women as to horses. I am not saying that they are one and the same thing. But there are certain aspects of one's upbringing—and as a late-Victorian I do not say this lightly—that are very difficult to overcome, even with a great effort of will.

"Think of Catherine Narracott, a young woman educated and bred at Cheltenham Ladies' College and finishing school. 'I would never normally make such a scene,' she said. And that is precisely the point . . . she *never* would. Her breeding and education would absolutely prevent it, even under the strongest of provocations. For an Englishwoman from a certain level of society, brought up in a certain way, the breeding would always be the stronger: just as certain show jumpers are so well bred that they will injure themselves fatally attempting a jump that is too big, rather than shying away from it. It wouldn't even matter how much wine she had drunk which, by the way, was probably not nearly so much as she made out, because she was too coherent for that. Certainly not enough, anyway, to cause her to take leave of her senses. No . . . only enough to give her the courage to do the thing she *knew* she had to do: the thing that was essential in establishing an animus between the two women for all to see.

"Then there was the little conversation you overheard in the women's bathroom, Diana, afterward. Sylvia Sinclair congratulating Catherine Narracott on her 'little performance.' Of course, one might assume that all of this was laced with sarcasm but actually it sounds as though there was no display of hostility until after—oh, excuse me for saying this"—Miss Marple looks suddenly overcome by Victorian modesty—"until you flushed the lavatory and they knew they were not alone together."

Mrs. Bantry's eyes widen. "But Jane. My goodness. Do you mean . . ."

"I mean that the whole display in the dining room was to demonstrate ill will between the women and in doing so conceal something other than hate. Perhaps the opposite of hate. But at the very least a connection between them. It is so simple and rather clever, in a way. Because of course no one would question the validity of an alibi that had been given by a near-stranger, but especially not a stranger with an enmity toward the other."

"The alibis are one thing," I say. "But for the first murder neither of the two women *were* there. I didn't see them in Reception and by all accounts they were both in the spa when Narracott's flask was tampered with. They were seen by others!"

"Yes," Mrs. Bantry says. "Sylvia was seen on her way to the spa—and I saw both of them inside the spa with my own eyes!"

Miss Marple nods, agreeably. "You saw *Catherine Narracott*, Dolly, I have no doubt of that."

"*And* Sylvia Sinclair!"

"But did you *really*, my dear?"

"Well, I saw her in the hammam . . ."

"Through the steam?" Miss Marple asks.

"Yes. I suppose not very clearly. Mainly the hair."

Miss Marple says nothing, her expression quite serene, letting Mrs. Bantry's comment sit for a moment.

"Oh, I see," Mrs. Bantry says. "You mean that the hair might have been a wig . . ."

Miss Marple nods. "The power of simple suggestion and the steam, obscuring everything else. That was something else that didn't fit for me. The hair. I kept thinking of Mr. Geffin and the barber. Do you remember, Dolly? The business with the Turkish barber?" Mrs. Bantry looks rather put out to admit that she does not. "Well," Miss Marple says, "you remember my little maid, Gladys? Her cousin was the daily for the Geffins. George Geffin claimed one day that he had spent the afternoon at the barber, in London. He was indeed clean shaven, when Mrs. Geffin got home, so she didn't think anything of it until she saw his ears."

"His ears?" Mrs. Bantry asks.

"Yes! At the Turkish barber's they always use a match to burn the . . ." Miss Marple's mouth pinches a little in distaste, "the hairs inside. So Mr. Geffin had remembered that he needed to give himself a wet shave, for the story to hold. But it is very difficult and I imagine extremely unpleasant to burn one's own ear hair. Men are so silly in thinking that we women are going to be blind to such details. I think it was indeed one of the things Mrs. Geffin most enjoyed about her husband's trips to the barber's, even more than his smooth jaw. So she saw through the whole thing straightaway. At first there was some accusation of an . . . indiscretion. In fact he had been at the horses, which may have been worse: the household budget, you know. So there you have it," she says, rather triumphantly, as though this explains everything.

"But Jane," Mrs. Bantry says, with the faintest note of exasperation to her tone. "I know you do like your . . . comparisons. But *really*, what on earth can all this have to do with Mr. Geffin's *ears*?"

"Well," says Miss Marple pleasantly, "Sylvia Sinclair claimed that she was in the hammam the whole morning. And yet she appeared at her interview with that beautifully set style; the same style precisely that she had had before the murder. If she really *had* entered the hammam the steam would have done for it completely. I feel very silly for not seeing that sooner, because it should have told me that she simply could not have been there, just as clearly as Mrs. Geffin knew her husband had not been to the Turkish barber's."

I say: "But what about all the others who saw her leaving the hotel for the spa, with her dog in tow?"

"Ah," Miss Marple says, "there was something you said on the first day, I think, Dolly: 'she is like an icon.' About her hair, her dark glasses, her coat . . . all of them marking her out as clearly as a king might be marked out by his crown. It made me think how one might be able to manipulate impressions, using those simple elements, the signifiers that made up the icon. If one saw them, one might not look too hard to see *beyond* them . . . would simply accept the icon for what it seemed. I do not think anyone saw the actress that morning at close quarters.

"The hair, the sunglasses, the coat, the dog: they would all make a very effective disguise. No one would look more closely—why should they? Incidentally, I thought it odd, when Bruno Crane charged into Catherine Narracott's bedroom, that instead of standing in front of the chest of drawers, with her underwear exposed for all to see, she chose to stand in front of the wardrobe. A girl of her upbringing, not rushing to conceal her unmentionables! Did you, too, glimpse the white fur, the winter ermine, among the others in the wardrobe? When did you see Catherine Narracott wear white on any other occasion? This was a woman with a faultless knowledge of what suited her and she did *not* wear white, knowing it would wash out one with her coloring." For a moment she goes very still; as though she has just thought of something else. "Perhaps, now I come to think of it, Bruno Crane saw the white fur too, and was led to try and blackmail her . . .

"But back to that morning in the spa. We come to the one truly face-to-face interaction Sylvia Sinclair had to have: with the spa's receptionist. The only person who presented a real challenge—by which I mean the only person who would see the actress at a shorter distance before she entered the changing room and became, I am sure, Catherine Narracott once more—was that woman. But then the dog jumped up and frightened her to death! How much would *any* of us notice if we had a huge animal leaping up at us and barking? Which brings me on to the dog . . ."

"The dog!" Mrs. Bantry explodes. "Jane, you aren't going to tell us the poor animal had anything to do with it?"

"Only in the sense of what it *didn't* do, dear. Another rather silly mistake. The evening when Catherine Narracott threw the glass of martini in Sylvia Sinclair's face. The creature was on a leash but to judge by the rest of its behavior it should have leapt up at her . . . especially in such circumstances. A dog would view something like that as an attack on its mistress. It certainly behaved far more aggressively with everyone else—even members of staff who were simply asking Sylvia Sinclair a question. You saw how it was in the hallway just now! I hope that poor man recovers. But with Catherine Narracott . . . *nothing*. I did not think much of it at the time because I don't have all that much experience with dogs. But later, talking to that woman in the spa and then observing how it was to others, it occurred to me that there was something odd. That night in the restaurant the dog's reaction—or lack thereof—showed most clearly that it knew Catherine Narracott. A great mistake, really, though again they got away with it at the time because the scene itself caused such a commotion."

"But then how did Sylvia kill him?" I ask. "If you're saying it was Catherine Narracott in the spa the entire time?"

"Ah," Miss Marple says. "Well. There was a lot of fuss made about the maid who no one recognized, poor thing, and the fact that she was carrying laundry at that time of the morning. Well of course that has all been put to bed. But what about a nun? A *much* better costume than a maid, really. With her famous platinum hair covered, a face free of all makeup and her figure swamped in fabric, who would recognize her? What a clever way of hiding in plain sight! Nuns are like the elderly: their individuality disappears to the outside world. I would bet many of the guests here would be hard-pressed to distinguish Dolly and I, though I am a little taller."

"And I a good deal broader!" Mrs. Bantry says.

"With nuns, no one really sees the person," Miss Marple says. "They see another kind of icon, if you like. Actually, I say *a* nun, but I wonder if at other times there weren't *two* of them. The pair we saw on that first day, with their sunglasses on, on the terrace, chatting away when Anthony Narracott was up on the mountain . . . I think that was no coincidence."

"You don't really mean that they were sitting there in plain sight?" Mrs. Bantry exclaims.

"I can't be sure," says Miss Marple. "But really, what an ingenious way to meet up and discuss any plans that might need to be gone through. But luckily, for us at least, they made another mistake here. On the morning of Anthony Narracott's murder they forgot—or more likely didn't *know*—about Terce. We learned on the second day here that the nuns are up the mountain for the third prayer of the day, around nine o'clock, worshipping at the statue of the Virgin. The nun in Reception was seen a little *after* nine o'clock meaning they were in the wrong place. Whoever was impersonating her had planned carefully, but not carefully enough."

"Bruno Crane's murder," Mrs. Bantry says, "we know that can't have been Catherine Narracott, because she was sitting with us for the whole tobogganing competition, when it must have taken place."

"And Sylvia Sinclair was one of the few people who was not in the crowd or the competition at the event," I say, "she was sitting drinking martinis in the hotel when we got back there as though she'd been there all day."

Miss Marple nods. "Didn't you say, Diana, that there was a *couloir* that would have made a good getaway? I think it was no coincidence that such a show was made of Sylvia Sinclair being an absolutely terrible skier the day before. I have no doubt that she is a very talented actress, for all that people seem to talk of her as though her talents equate mainly to her bust-waist-hip ratio. She grew up in Montana, didn't she? I suspect they have mountains there! I did wonder, Diana, when you said you saw her falling over at the hot chocolate spot the day before, how she could possibly have *got* there, alone, if she was so awful at it. And if she didn't want to reveal she was a good skier she wouldn't have been able to risk coming down via the piste."

"She would have had to come cross-country, through the trees," I say. "Which means she's even better than most. So she *could* have come down via the *couloir* after killing Bruno Crane. And if she had, she could have been most of the way back in minutes, disguised in some shapeless clothing, with very few guests or even staff around to see her because most were watching the tobogganing."

"Then for the *third* murder," Miss Marple says, thoughtfully, "the discovery of Moreau's true identity helps us to understand why he had to be killed. The women must have discovered that he too was here for the gold and felt he posed a danger to them. I wonder *when* they learned it. The apparent hastiness of his murder compared to the others suggests it was more recently.

"Sylvia Sinclair, having committed the other two murders, made well and sure she was out on a long sleigh ride while it took place, so there was no chance that suspicion could fall on her. It must all have been Catherine Narracott's work instead, using the key they stole from you, Dolly—" She stops, because the hotel manager has just burst into the room, still looking very wan and now apparently in a state of panic.

"They have gone," he says. "I have had staff search the hotel from top to bottom, Mesdames," he pants. "But they are nowhere to be seen."

"How can they have escaped?" Mrs. Bantry asks. "The mountain tunnel is still blocked. There's no way down!"

"Up," says Miss Marple lightly. "Over the mountain, I expect."

SYLVIA SINCLAIR

The Star

We're in Italy now, even if the mountains all look the same. Far off in the distance, though, I can see a beautiful powder-pink church and I don't think they have so many of those in Switzerland. Crazy, that you can hop over a mountain here and find yourself in a different country, whereas I didn't leave the state of Montana 'til I was sixteen, then ran like hell and never looked back. I feel like I've just clicked my ruby slippers together. Except I'm not going home—unless I count her as home now, which maybe I do.

The snow rushes around my skis. I don't have to pretend to ski like a baby deer on skates now. Oh, and it's so nice to wear trousers that actually fit, you know, rather than cutting off circulation to a girl's . . .

Catherine looks across at me and grins. I wink back.

The voice on the other end of the line that day. She sounded so . . . lost. Course I knew she wasn't his secretary: I'd already spoken to his secretary.

"Do you want to meet, honey?" I asked her. "I think there are a few home truths you might want to hear. Call me if you want to talk."

And you know what? She did. She came to my dressing room at the Almeida. I thought at first she was exactly like she had sounded on the phone: a stuck-up, dull, none-too-bright little princess. Later I came to realize that was just the mask she had created to hide her true self from the world. That she was smart and cute and droll and even secretly a little rebel. Some gardener that she nearly ran off with at school. After that, we called each other several times a week, when her husband was away. Sometimes she had to travel to London to "visit a women's clinic." Funny how the length of her treatment coincided almost perfectly with the entire run of *The Cherry Orchard*!

We realized that both of us were being lied to by the same man. I'd already done my homework. Knew he had other women besides me. Knew I was the latest plaything, that he'd throw me over soon as I hit forty.

I make a nice wide turn, snow sparkling up like powder from a puff and feel the lovely, lovely weight of the gold shift on my back. You know what this weight feels like? It feels like power. It feels like freedom.

Look, maybe I wish we could have done it without the killing. But we couldn't. I've known some takers and some users in my time and Narracott was one of the worst. He'd taken from Catherine until he used up all she had. He had it in him to destroy a woman. Maybe even to kill. Her: that day on the mountain. Me: that night in the bath if he could have got away with it. I could *feel* it, that he half wanted to. I can make myself feel better about the Bruno fella, too. He was half ready to go as it was. You know, he looked almost peaceful, after I'd done it.

We played our parts beautifully. Her invisibility like a magic cloak. My razzle-dazzle a bright painted mask. Together . . . lethal (and delicious) as absinthe and rye in a Sazerac. It took a few slips on his part. A map of the Swiss Alps left out at home. Both of us began to pay attention. Yours truly getting him drunk (said Sazeracs and martinis and the rest with a nice little finishing dash of benzos which I find *highly* effective in loosening any lover's tongue), him telling me tales of derring-do, of the fortune he was going to find in the mountains that would more than replace the one he'd already gobbled up (his wife's). Even telling me the name of the hotel, even half-inviting me, before he realized that was a terrible idea. It's astonishing, really. The number of powerful, supposedly smart, men who have followed their peckers to their doom.

Catherine knew her husband was a phony. When he told his tales about his wartime heroics they'd change every time. She knew the limp was a hoax. Stuff he shouted in his sleep. Stuff he'd say to me when he was deep into his third drink: "I'm never going to heaven, my sweet, so we might as well have a good time down here." We'll never know the whole story but anyone with a cache of Nazi gold hidden in the mountains is probably not someone who deserves a medal for heroics.

When I think of my little brother, brave boy, gone to his end in the South Pacific. No grave, no medal, no nothing. Just a sense of duty. And Tony, pretending to be a hero . . . the thought of it makes me sick even now. Looked at that way, it might even have been a righteous execution.

Together we put together most of a pretty little puzzle. And then we made a plan. The doc that called Narracott and told him he should take his wife away for a trip? That was me. Didn't take all those voice classes at The Actors Studio in New York for nothing! What a schmuck! For her part, Catherine was a beautiful little schemer. She threw away her sleeping pills and replaced them with paracetamol so she could play dead to the world and sneak out after her husband on his nighttime adventuring. She threw away the low blood pressure stuff too, so she could stand up and faint straightaway on "finding out" he was dead. And she was the one who came up with the whole bit about the earring, blocking it all out like a piece of stagecraft! I slipped it into her hand when she helped me to my feet that day on the slopes. Oh, I did love seeing Tony's face . . . he knew there was no way the thing could have been found in their hotel bed, as we'd never had a rendezvous there, but he couldn't argue the point without exposing our other sordid little trysts.

You could say Catherine played director, the finest I've had. And you know what? I think my performance here has been my best to date. The meatiest role I've had in years. When would they ever have let me play a nun, without having to bring sex into it? That was a clever touch of Catherine's. She's the sort of girl who has always been good at doing her homework. And boy did she do her homework on that place. She learned that it was a holy site, visited by many different orders of nuns. Much better than trying to disguise ourselves as, for example, hotel staff: where there'd be one particular uniform. That was *bold*. Even for me. But then I was taught the fear of God by a foster mother who I see now had nothing of God in her. Once you learn that, it's difficult to shake off.

She made a great little acting student, too. Thing is, she'd been acting for most of her adult life anyway. Fact is she'd gone so method on the role of Good Little Wife it took a while even for her to rediscover the real woman underneath it all.

That woman was more my type than the husband, really. I've always been an equal opportunities kind of girl. All the very best ones are: Marlene, Garbo, Tallulah B, Kathy Hepburn and the rest. But that ain't box office, baby, so we created our little "sewing circle." Now I'm done with Hollywood before it's done with me. I don't need its patronage—and patronization; the measly slim pickings handed out for women over a certain age. I'm ready to leave behind the loneliness, the pretense. In Tinsel Town I'm pretty well dried up. In the rest of the world, I have half my life ahead of me.

Still. Don't think we won't suffer for it. We will. But we're only five years on from the biggest mass slaughter this world has ever known, when far, far better men were killed for far less. Gives a girl a little perspective.

DIANA GLASS

The Help

"But Jane," Mrs. Bantry says, "you always get your man—or, so to speak. And they have got away."

"They had to be allowed to go," says Miss Marple. "We are talking of two desperate, and therefore very dangerous, murderers. The more desperate someone becomes, the more dangerous, like a cornered rat that jumps straight for the throat. Did I ever tell you about poor Gladys finding one in the pantry—"

"Jane!"

"Sorry, dear. Well . . . you see, to let them leave was really my only option. The police are not yet here. They have, I am sure, a weapon. They have already killed three times—they would not hesitate for a moment to kill again. They have little to lose and everything to gain. I have not found myself in such a situation before: being confined to one place without any help from the authorities. I had to consider what was best in the circumstances. I could not put anyone else's life in danger."

"So you let them go?"

"I suppose it does appear that way," says Miss Marple. "If they ever manage to leave the mountains, that is."

Mrs. Bantry widens her eyes. "What do you mean, Jane?"

Miss Marple does not answer. She tilts her head to one side as though she is listening to something, beyond the hearing of the rest of us. There is something knowing in her expression . . . and a little sorrowful, too.

"Jane," says Mrs. Bantry. "You've gone a little spooky. You're scaring me a little."

Miss Marple seems to give herself another little mental shake. "Sorry, dear," she says. "What was I saying? Anyway, I must just go and do something—will you excuse me?" She moves off in the direction of the lobby.

Twenty minutes later and I am sitting in the gondola, on the very seat where Anthony Narracott took his last breath. I fasten my ski boots with clumsy fingers. I persuaded them to start up the mechanism: the two murderers have a significant head start, but they have had to scale the mountainside on skins and this will help me to close the distance.

The gondola is a marvel of engineering, yet seems painfully slow as it ascends the bleached slopes of the mountain. For the first time in days the visibility is excellent: not a cloud in the sky and the sun rising over there in the east sets the whole mountainside aglow. I press my face against the window and stare and stare but there is no sign of them, down below. They must be up and over already. I am aware of my heart beating powerfully in my chest, the blood rushing through my veins, my every nerve ending alive. Terrified—alive. Diana the Hunter. A clunk as the mechanism locks into place and I realize I have arrived at the top of the mountain.

I walk along the ridge, carrying my skis. The views, now that the sun is risen, are dazzling. Over there in one direction is Italy, the other, France. In the direction of the pass over into Italy are two pairs of ski tracks, leading into what appears from this perspective to be a great void of nothingness.

I put on my skis and push off. There is so much new powder—in places it is up to my thighs—but because of the intense cold it has stayed light as icing sugar and the turns are easy enough, as long as I concentrate on keeping the skis as close together as possible. It is such smooth going that my body registers a moment of pure pleasure before I am reminded of the task at hand.

I spot them, halfway down the slope. Two figures, looping down through the powder. They look so graceful, free and harmonious. For a moment, it gives me pause. Could I just let them go? Pretend I had never seen them? But I know that I can't. That gold, stained by so much death and suffering: no one should benefit from it.

I compress my turns, increase my speed. And then I make a turn that dislodges a small fall of snow. I regain my balance, but it has sent several larger pieces of the top layer rolling and skittering down toward the two women. There is a shout. I pause for a moment and realize they have turned to look up the mountain. One of them is pointing with an arm—no, something else . . . In the same moment that I understand I feel a white-hot bolt of heat entering my body. A short, animal bleat escapes me and I fall like a felled deer into the soft eiderdown of white.

I lie encased in the freezing softness of the snow as the sensation that I now dimly recognize as a bullet begins to make itself known as pain, pain that I understand has the power to swallow me whole. The external world seems to recede as it takes over. So it is through dim eyes that I watch as the snow twenty yards or so beneath me begins to move. It is like watching the stirring of some huge creature woken from its slumber. I am just above the fracture line. The women beneath will be directly in its path. *They have to ski to the side.* I had some brief training at Arisaig House in Scotland before I was deployed with the SOE—day trips to Aviemore—and this is one of the things I remember. But do the women below know this? In spite of everything, there is an impulse to call out to them. But they're too far away and I couldn't make a sound if I tried. The pain is astonishing now. And then a realization: I could stop resisting. I could allow it to overwhelm me. A strange sense of calm descends. Perhaps this is how my brothers- and sisters-in-arms felt at the end, on that long-ago night. The thought is a balm as I close my eyes and release myself to the void.

CATHERINE NARRACOTT

The Wife

I tuck the pistol away. I'm a good shot; I was always excellent at biathlon at the Swiss school. There was a strange sound afterward: a small pop or snap. The echo of the bullet, perhaps. For some reason, I think of the string breaking in *The Cherry Orchard*: everything different on the other side of it. A little like the change inside of me.

We resume our descent. We're like two swallows, soaring in wide and graceful arcs down the broad white slopes, matching our flight, wingtips touching. Then I think of everything we have done to get here. Eagles, might be better: beautiful, merciless. Taking what we need from the world. It's a strange feeling, imagining myself as a powerful creature. Before this I would have thought of myself as some fluffy ornamental pet—pretty enough but a little foolish, like a pink-headed cockatoo twittering away in its cage.

Who knew I had a dark power inside me? It turns out the line between good little wife and killer is cobweb thin. It started in the plotting of the killing. The moment, of suggesting, of deciding . . . from then on we have been tied together in a way few humans ever are. And once you have been responsible for one death you can never go back. It becomes—ghastly as it is to say—easier after that. There was a moment, however, when I thought we might not have to kill Bruno Crane after all. That he'd be a useful scapegoat, a distraction. Then he slipped his blackmail note under my door. I suppose he must have seen the white winter ermine in the wardrobe when he crashed into my room and realized I had worn it for my disguise. So he wasn't quite as stupid as he seemed. But stupid enough to try and threaten us.

The third killing, the so-called inspector, was perhaps the riskiest. But when I found that photograph in my husband's washbag I knew it had to be done. Sylvia and I met in the woods in the small hours the night before to plan it. We couldn't leave anything to chance. His questioning might have led him to us—and to the gold. Just as I had to do something about that woman following us. I glance back up the mountain to check: she is a crumpled dark shape now, lying completely still. As I do I see what looks like billowing gray smoke, unfurling from somewhere a little way beneath her, like someone shaking out the train of a long silk gown. I think I know what it is . . . but it is like trying to remember a word I've forgotten. I think it might be something bad, but really, it's hard to believe that because it looks so pretty . . .

And now there is a murmuring. Quite quiet and polite at first—the chatter of a ballroom heard from outside—but then swelling to something one can't ignore. And how strange . . . I seem to feel it, too, beneath my feet. And now the sound is no longer a polite murmur; it is a frightful roar and the mountain itself seems to be crumbling—

I look to Sylvia. She knows mountains . . . and now I am afraid because she isn't scared of anything, but she is scared now. And she is mouthing, or shrieking, something that seems important. But it is difficult to hear over the terrible rumbling roaring clamor that is now filling the air, shaking the ground beneath my skis, thundering toward us . . .

If this is the end—and I think it must be—then perhaps it doesn't matter. Because in the last few hours, perhaps for the first time in my life, I have known true freedom, true happiness. If I had gone on as I was, I would never have known these. Perhaps that is enough.

I look toward her so that if this is the end, hers is the last face I ever see.

Venice Santa Lucia station
Two days later

The Simplon-Orient Express idles beside the platform, grumbling and snorting like some great beast. It is perhaps not quite as immaculate, not quite as glamorous, as in its pre-war heyday, but there is a storied, blue-blooded majesty to it all the same.

The last calls for remaining passengers echo through the loudspeakers:

"The Simplon-Orient Express with stops in Trieste, Zagreb, Bucharest, Brod, Vincovci, Belgrade, Nis, Sophia and Stamboul leaves in . . . fifteen minutes' time!"

Train porters wheel luggage carts with kamikaze haste through the milling crowds, passengers consult tickets and board carriages marked COMPAGNIE INTERNATIONALE DES WAGONS-LITS. Lovers bid farewell. Well-heeled honeymooners stroll arm in arm, but with a quickening step as another whistle sounds. Gray men carrying nondescript briefcases move through the throngs with the sinuous ease of sharks through shoals of sardines. Their very featurelessness marks them out as agents of espionage, traversing the newly fraught barrier between West and East.

The loudspeakers blare again: "*The Simplon-Orient Express with stops in Trieste, Zagreb, Bucharest, Brod, Vincovci, Belgrade, Nis, Sophia and Stamboul leaves in . . . ten minutes' time!*"

People are running now—the last few stragglers. A faint note of panic. A man trips and curses, dropping a tin of cigarettes, which bursts open. He seems to contemplate scrabbling about for them before thinking better of it, hurrying on.

The platform is emptying out now. Just a few well-wishers, waving their goodbyes to travelers now inside the train. And then: two nuns appear from the depths of the station, small packs upon their backs, hurrying a little, which seems odd . . . when does one ever see nuns hurry? Perhaps the answer is: when they are this late to catch a train. They climb into the nearest carriage and disappear inside, just as the final whistle blows.

SYLVIA SINCLAIR

The Star

The whistle goes. The doors slam shut all along the train. And then . . . nothing. Catherine shoots a glance at her wristwatch. "It's two minutes past the hour. It should have left by now. Why aren't we leaving?" We're both trying to look back down the platform from the windows of our compartment. First class, which I guess might seem a little fancy for a couple of nuns but we need the privacy. To talk, to celebrate, to hide away.

"It's OK," I tell her, all calm on the surface. "We've come this far. I just know it's all going to be OK. We survived an avalanche, for God's sake!"

"Thanks to you," she says, allowing herself a small, nervy smile. "If you hadn't half dragged me to the side . . . I was like a deer in headlights."

Another eternity of waiting, or so it seems.

Then finally, goddamn *finally*, there's a clanking—the brakes releasing, I guess—and the train begins to move. Thank holy hell. "There we go," I say. Catherine sits back in her seat in relief.

One minute we're leaving the station and the next the train seems to be floating over water, water that slides by in a misty green-blue blur . . . partly because of the speed of the train, partly because of the tears in my eyes. Sylvia Sinclair never cries . . . but I think I left the shell of her somewhere in the mountains, along with the platinum blonde. See, all my braggadocio aside, I didn't truly believe we'd pull it off. Not 'til now.

"We're free," Catherine says. "I can't believe it. We're free." See, that's what the gold is to us: freedom. Even if we have to spend the rest of our lives looking over our shoulders.

"I don't feel too great about that woman," I say, after a while. "That's the one thing that's on my conscience."

"No," Catherine says, her jaw set. "It was her fault—her choice to come after us. She should have left well enough alone." I look at her, all English rose and then that ferociousness beneath the surface. Sometimes she almost scares me a little. All the planning: that was her work. I wasn't even sure we really had to kill the French detective, but after Catherine found the photo of him in Tony's stuff, she insisted we had to take him out.

She smiles and the fierceness all melts away. "Besides. It's all behind us now. I'm finally ready to believe it. A new life!"

I allow myself a smile, too. We sit for a little while, watching the Italian landscape rush by—I love the campy colors they paint their houses and churches here. Just sitting in silence together, I think of all the cafés in which we can do this, over coffee, watching the world go by. That'll keep the little black moths at bay. Someone to be silent with.

"Shall we hit the dining cabin?" I say, after a while, looking down at the nun's habit. "I could do with a martini and got up like this I don't think anyone'll—"

The next words die on my lips. A shadow, moving through the compartment. It's surely just someone headed to the next carriage . . .

But no . . . now the handle to our compartment door begins to turn. The door swings open.

I look to Catherine and see that her eyes have filled with tears.

EPILOGUE

DIANA

St. Mary Mead
A month later

"So how *did* you do it, Jane?" Mrs. Bantry asks, brandishing a copy of the paper. I've read the headline already: *WIFE CHIEF SUSPECT IN NARRACOTT DEATH! Hearing at Old Bailey today following dramatic arrest by Italian police.* "Explain it all to us properly, won't you? You were so mysterious at the time, but I just know it was your doing . . . somehow."

Miss Marple looks to the window, to where some rose canes tap against the pane as though politely requesting entrance. "I must prune before the spring growth starts," she says. "But this weather! And my rheumatism was not improved by the mountains." Then, as though this last word reminds her of Mrs. Bantry's question: "Well. You know, Dolly, that in the past I have made a habit of springing . . . I suppose for want of a better word one might say *traps*—upon culprits. I did so in this case, too. Simply not within the confines of the hotel."

"What can you mean? How?"

"I telephoned to Sir Henry Clithering. I asked him to use his old connections at the International Criminal Police Commission to have police waiting in Venice. It was a gamble, but all my little traps are gambles, really."

"But Miss Marple," I say, "I'm sorry but I don't quite follow. *Why* Venice? Why the Orient Express?"

"There are only so many places you can go if you are Sylvia Sinclair," Miss Marple says. "Even if you are in disguise . . . even if you remove the parts that make up the 'icon,' as it were. Sooner or later, you *will* be recognized. In the Western world, that is, where people watch your films.

"Sometimes people reveal more than they mean to," she continues. "Sylvia made that odd reference to a 'girl wanting to run off and hide in Illinois or Istanbul.' Illinois would not really be possible. But Raymond, who is so reliable about anything culturally *au courant*, tells me that Istanbul is something of a haven for creative types wanting to 'fall off the map' as it were. Rather like Marrakech—except *that* I think would be out of the question for our murderers because it is a French protectorate and therefore extradition might be possible.

"So I thought about what I might do if I were in her—in their situation. They couldn't go anywhere likely to have an agreement with the British government. They had to disappear—to go somewhere where Sylvia Sinclair is less known. Just as she talked of wishing to do. They had the gold, so they would be able to buy a nice kind of life somewhere . . . and I'm sure Istanbul would do as well as most places. Apparently there is some wonderful history there, and some very beautiful houses. My great-aunt, who had a great deal of trouble with her philandering diplomat husband, told me on her deathbed that she had at one time thought seriously about running off with an Effendi who had a beautiful *yali* on the shores of the Bosphorus . . ." She stops and gives a small, modest cough. "Anyway. That is how I did it. It was a guess. But not a *very* wild one, I shouldn't think. And the thing about being elderly is one learns that one gets rather good—by hard-learned necessity—at asking for help, at calling in favors. In youth, one feels one must rush off and do everything oneself." I feel gently implicated by her words. "Of course, that is very noble and brave." She smiles at me with genuine kindness. "But just sometimes the other can be even more effective."

"Jane," Mrs. Bantry says. "I hope you won't mind my saying this, but it is almost uncanny, your ability to think yourself into the mind of a murderer."

Miss Marple makes a prim little pinch of her mouth, apparently nothing more can tastefully be said on the matter. Then: "Would you like any more cherry brandy, Dolly? And you, Diana, my dear?"

We both accept a little more.

Mrs. Bantry says, "Anthony Narracott and Bruno Crane were clearly very unpleasant characters and Inspector Moreau—sorry, I know that wasn't his real rank or name but I still can't quite think of him any other way—was evidently not at all the Good Samaritan he seemed . . . so didn't you have a tiny modicum of sympathy with those women?"

"No," says Miss Marple, sharply. "There can be no excuse for taking the life of another human being. And you are forgetting that they shot Diana! If the gondola attendant hadn't come for her she would have been left for dead on the mountain. They were desperate, yes, but evil thrives in desperation.

"The men they killed *were* wicked men. But one cannot extinguish wickedness with more of the same. It is like a stain, an infection. It only grows . . ." Her voice has changed. It is somewhat lower, harsher. She seems to sit a little straighter in her chair and her look is at once distant and severe. Then the moment seems to pass and it is as though we have the ordinary, frailer Miss Marple returned to us once more.

"Would you like to stay for supper, Diana?" she asks. "I'm sure there is enough to go around, perhaps with a couple of potatoes. I can see . . ."

"No, thank you, Miss Marple," I say. "I should be going soon. My taxi to Milchester station will be here soon."

"Back to Paddington?"

"Yes."

"It *is* good to see you looking well, Diana," Mrs. Bantry says, from her armchair. "I only wish you hadn't had to leave me. I'm already in such a muddle since your departure. And I have great friends here—Jane, please do not be in the least offended by this—but it has been nice to have someone young around one. Everyone I know seems so very *old* now. I suppose I do have a new companion," she smiles indulgently at the scraggly wolfhound, lying beside the fire, who seems to have mellowed in the quiet of the English countryside. "But he's not much use at bridge."

"What do you think you will do, Diana?" Miss Marple asks.

"Oh," I say, "I don't know. I've got a new job at the Foreign Office. Secretarial, because they don't let us women do a great deal more than that—but, you know, I was thinking I'd like to try and get away and see the world. After I make sure the world knows what Narracott really was. I have the photographs. It isn't enough that he died. I have to make sure that people learn there are men like him in the world. Plenty more, I have no doubt, who will get away with even worse."

Miss Marple nods, as though this makes sense to her.

"And you?" I say. "Will you go abroad again?"

"Not in a hurry, I think," Miss Marple says. "I often find quite enough to interest me and keep me busy at home. If I do travel overseas, it will not be to the mountains again—or indeed any cold climate. My rheumatism, you know. Yesterday I pulled out some bindweed—only a very little and one always knows it is so hopeless anyway because the roots go so far underground—and I have had to spend the whole of today sitting just to recover. The cold was not good for my joints."

"Perhaps somewhere warm, dear?" Mrs. Bantry suggests.

"Perhaps," Miss Marple nods. "Raymond keeps suggesting the Caribbean but I'm not sure the heat would suit me—and the expense! I don't think it likely I shall ever go. But I do know I am finished with mountains."

"I thought we would never escape them," Mrs. Bantry says. "Amazing, really, how quickly they managed to mend the tunnel. One has to admire the efficiency of the Swiss. The greatest miracle, of course, was your recovery, Diana. Thank goodness for the quick thinking of that gondola attendant."

My hand goes instinctively to my side, where they stitched me back together. It is the funny thing about physical pain—one can't really remember it. All I can remember is that sense of surrender. How terrifyingly easy it felt.

"It wasn't . . . pleasant," I say. "Everything that happened there. But at the same time," I pause, think of how to put this, "I felt as if I'd discovered some part of myself I'd forgotten was there. There was a kind of . . . of thrill in it, in spite of the darkness. And I had a purpose. A *raison d'être*." I look carefully at Miss Marple to check that she isn't appalled. "If that doesn't sound too dreadful. I think perhaps what I mean is that I don't want a safe life." I look for another way to express it. "I want a useful life."

Miss Marple looks at me and I am sure I see a knowing brightness kindle there in the faded blue gaze. "My dear," she says, "I quite understand. In fact, I know exactly what you mean."

ACKNOWLEDGMENTS

I'm so glad I get the chance here to thank and acknowledge all the people without whose hard work this book would not exist. I'm not sure I've ever had such a long list: this one has been a true multi-team effort!

First of all, thank you to my family. To Al, first reader, cheerleader, research buddy, enabler, wise counsel and so much more besides: I'm so lucky. To my parents and parents-in-law for your support. To my little boys for being so understanding when Mum's locked away writing in her office and for your creative feedback on the cover! To my sister, Kate, for helping me look presentable at events (alongside the brilliant Chloe Kerins!) and to my brother, Robbie, for helping me with all things social media . . . truly a family affair. To Lisa Chennell, miracle worker and all-round superstar, for making so much possible.

To James Prichard, thank you for the very great honor of this commission. Thank you for trusting me and for (very flatteringly!) giving me the creative freedom to write *my* take on a Miss Marple mystery. It has been such a joy to work together.

To my agent dream team. Cathryn Summerhayes, thank you for everything you do—I am so lucky to have you by my side in all things, always going above and beyond (including joining me on the research trip for this one!). To Alexandra, thank you for being such fun, so fabulous and for having my back in everything. To Jess Molloy, for being such a cheerful delight to work with and also so efficient. To Georgie Mellor and Sam Downs, thank you for all your hard work, brilliance and patience on contracts signing and cover approvals . . .

To my dream team of editors: Charlotte Brabbin, Emily Krump and Frankie Gray—thank you for helping to make this book the very best version of itself that it could be. Not sure that sentence is the most elegant, and you'd probably suggest a tweak, but hopefully it gets the sentiment across! To David Brawn, thank you for providing such wonderful, wise and witty counsel on all things Christie.

To Georgina Moore, publicist extraordinaire—thank you for always going above and beyond and also being such fun to work with. What a joy to laugh so much every time we meet up and yet simultaneously achieve so much together!

To the wonderful Jamie Groves, who did such a magnificent job on the copyedit (LOVE the levels of cog railway geekery!) and sent me the wittiest copyedit notes I've had (who knew they could be so funny?!). And thank you too for putting up with my stealing your wife away so regularly!

To the HarperCollins transatlantic publicity and marketing dream team: Emilie Chambeyron, Felicity Denham, Abbie Salter, Lipfon Tang, Danielle Bartlett, Kaitlin Harri and Kelsey Manning . . . thank you for putting such joy, creativity and vision into everything you do and designing such a killer campaign!

To Sean Garrehy, for designing such a fantastic cover that (for the first time in my publishing!) is being used all around the world. Thanks for being so patient and collaborative . . . and so, so talented.

To the wider team at Harper UK:

Kate Elton
David Brawn
Kate Fogg

Kathryn Cheshire
Millie Kiel
Halema Begum
Leah Woods
Vanessa Coubrough
Melissa Okunsanya

. . . thank you for all your hard work, vision and attention to detail!

To the wider team at William Morrow:

Brian Murray
Liate Stehlik
Jennifer Hart
Chris Connolly

. . . thank you all so much and hope to thank some of you in person on the stateside tour!

Thank you to the brilliant Julia Wilde for your patience and support and to the wider team at Agatha Christie Limited:

Lydia Stone
Sarah Thrift
Ruby Hines
Christina Macphail
Nikki White
Annabelle Mannix
Helen James
Cristina Isoli

To all of my overseas publishers, ongoing and new, thank you for your belief in this book . . . I can't wait to watch the Grand Alpine wing its way around the world and I hope to visit many of you soon!

To Amanda Ross and Pollyanne Conway at Cactus, thank you so much for your incredible support of this book!

To Kemper Donovan, thank you for such an early, insightful and enthusiastic expert read, and for the wonderful Q&A questions. Agatha Christie fans: Kemper's podcast, *All About Agatha*, is a *must* listen. I went through every episode at least twice while writing this book.

THE AGATHA CHRISTIE COLLECTION

MYSTERIES

The Man in the Brown Suit
The Secret of Chimneys
The Seven Dials Mystery
The Mysterious Mr. Quin
The Sittaford Mystery
The Hound of Death
The Listerdale Mystery
Why Didn't They Ask Evans?
Parker Pyne Investigates
Murder is Easy
And Then There Were None
Towards Zero
Death Comes as the End
Sparkling Cyanide
Crooked House
They Came to Baghdad
Destination Unknown
*Spider's Web**
*The Unexpected Guest**
Ordeal by Innocence
The Pale Horse
Endless Night
Passenger to Frankfurt
Problem at Pollensa Bay
While the Light Lasts

POIROT

The Mysterious Affair at Styles
The Murder on the Links
Poirot Investigates
The Murder of Roger Ackroyd
The Big Four
The Mystery of the Blue Train
*Black Coffee**
Peril at End House
Lord Edgware Dies
Murder on the Orient Express
Three Act Tragedy
Death in the Clouds

The ABC Murders
Murder in Mesopotamia
Cards on the Table
Murder in the Mews
Dumb Witness
Death on the Nile
Appointment with Death
Hercule Poirot's Christmas
Sad Cypress
One, Two, Buckle My Shoe
Evil Under the Sun
Five Little Pigs
The Hollow
The Labours of Hercules
Taken at the Flood
Mrs. McGinty's Dead
After the Funeral
Hickory Dickory Dock
Dead Man's Folly
Cat Among the Pigeons
The Adventure of the Christmas Pudding
The Clocks
Third Girl
Hallowe'en Party
Elephants Can Remember
Poirot's Early Cases
Curtain: Poirot's Last Case

MARPLE

The Murder at the Vicarage
The Thirteen Problems
The Body in the Library
The Moving Finger
A Murder is Announced
They Do It with Mirrors
A Pocket Full of Rye
4.50 from Paddington
The Mirror Crack'd from Side to Side
A Caribbean Mystery
At Bertram's Hotel
Nemesis
Sleeping Murder
Miss Marple's Final Cases

TOMMY & TUPPENCE

The Secret Adversary
Partners in Crime
N or M?
By the Pricking of My Thumbs
Postern of Fate

PUBLISHED AS MARY WESTMACOTT

Giant's Bread
Unfinished Portrait
Absent in the Spring
The Rose and the Yew Tree
A Daughter's a Daughter
The Burden

MEMOIRS

An Autobiography
Come, Tell Me How You Live
The Grand Tour

PLAYS AND STORIES

Akhnaton

Little Grey Cells

Murder, She Said

The Floating Admiral †

Star Over Bethlehem

Hercule Poirot and the Greenshore Folly

* novelized by Charles Osborne

† contributor